LAST GOD STANDING

LAST GOD STANDING

A NOVEL

CHRISTIE W. KIEFER

LAST GOD STANDING
A NOVEL

iUniverse books may be ordered through booksellers or by contacting:

iUniverse
1663 Liberty Drive
Bloomington, IN 47403
www.iuniverse.com
1-800-Authors (1-800-288-4677)

Because of the dynamic nature of the Internet, any web addresses or links contained in this book may have changed since publication and may no longer be valid. The views expressed in this work are solely those of the author and do not necessarily reflect the views of the publisher, and the publisher hereby disclaims any responsibility for them.

Any people depicted in stock imagery provided by Getty Images are models, and such images are being used for illustrative purposes only. Certain stock imagery © Getty Images.

ISBN: 978-1-5320-7679-4 (sc)
ISBN: 978-1-5320-7678-7 (e)

Library of Congress Control Number: 2019907045

Print information available on the last page.

iUniverse rev. date: 06/25/2019

PROLOGUE

I, Professor Ashton Caldo, am a lecher. You need to know this in order to understand the strange story you're about to read.

In everyday parlance and mass entertainment, a lecher is a man who "can't keep it in his pants," or who "will chase anything in skirts," or "has the instincts of a goat." Think of Bill Clinton, Hugh Hefner. Being unable to perform a basic civilized virtue —that is, to conceal his animal side — the lecher reduces himself to an object of disgust and scorn in the eyes of those who feel injured or offended by him (his women, their men, his family, or self-appointed guardians of morality); or he becomes a comic figure in the eyes of those with less personal interest. How many jokes about Clinton and cigars have you heard?

Properly used, the word refers to a particular way of acting out male sexual addiction. It doesn't refer to all men with gargantuan sex drives, or even to those who seem obsessed with chasing women. A lecher is a man whose addiction to sexual conquest breaks social norms, often to the point of endangering himself and others. A guy with a big sexual appetite is likely to be admired by many — even by some women — if he leaves it at home with his wife or at least doesn't flout the rules about other men's wives and other taboo categories like those who are too young or whose trust he violates via seduction.

In the popular view, then, lechery is a serious character flaw. We want to distance ourselves from people with such flaws, and we tend to overlook whatever positive qualities they might have. It's commonly assumed, for example, that lechers are manipulative and dishonest in all sorts of relationships, or that they don't have the capacity to feel genuine love — one feature of which is of course loyalty.

This is what we might call the popular view of lechery. As with most off-the-shelf moral judgments, the reality is often much more complicated.

There undoubtedly exist men who fit the stereotype pretty well. But I believe that for most of us lechers, our addiction is a source of painful inner conflict. After all, we are human beings, and what we want most is to be loved. It's too facile to say we "don't know how to *get* love." Often we do know how and even have some success at it. But our sexual promiscuity is an addiction that often conflicts with our desire for intimacy. We're in that terrible position that endlessly punishes anybody who's addicted to anything: We know that by satisfying our craving, we're injuring ourselves and others, but we can't stop. The thrill of a sexual conquest without love is always followed by the deep sadness of self-betrayal. We're the most abject of people, those divided against themselves.

And this brings me to my central point. Far from having an overabundance of self-regard, we lechers have a hell of a time accepting ourselves — believing in our basic decency. You see, it's a vicious circle: Sexual conquest is, among other things, a way to convince ourselves of our own value and at the same time a source of shame and self-doubt, the knowledge that we are at best clowns, at worst repulsive villains. We have to continuously fool ourselves about our actions and our motives. We make up endless stories — that we are really in love with each new paramour; or that our successes simply prove the unique power of our person; or that we're somehow gifted with a special intelligence, with which we unlock the secrets of ordinary mortals' hearts.

Rejection by a woman, then, threatens to destroy our self-esteem altogether.

I've been through this cycle myself dozens of times — more than the number of successes I've enjoyed. As a psychologist, I should have long ago diagnosed it and found a cure, but addiction is driven by powerful brain chemicals whose effect is to beguile intelligence. I couldn't name my malady until I had passed through an odyssey of self-discovery, an odyssey filled with delusion, humiliation, and intense danger — my encounter with The Woman on Randy's Trail, and with the dark and terrible magic of the Raapa Uu. It began two years ago.

CHAPTER ONE

Today in Personality Theory we're discussing Socrates's speech from Plato's Symposium — the four levels of love. There's this woman in the seminar, Michelle, who's a painful reminder of my life's greatest and most tragic love, Delfin. Looking at Michelle, I can well remember why my passion for Delfin broke up my marriage. Eyes the color of a scuba dive. Skin like dulce de leche ice cream. In the nine years I've been teaching this seminar, I've only been this distracted maybe three or four times. Can't get used to it. Today she's holding a pencil in her teeth as she sweeps back her auburn hair and clips it in a barrette. She's wearing a sleeveless top, so I can see the creamy skin of her inner arms all the way down to the place where I can imagine her smell. Everything is colliding: Michelle's status as my student, the near-lethal history of my loving, and the fact that lately the eyes of Michelle and women like her pass me over without turning up the wattage.

And then there's Plato. You can tell a lot about the way a person relates to Plato. Jaqui has the twitchy stare that betrays nightmarish memories of missed quiz questions. Carlos looks bored. He remembers one thing about Plato: That the man disrespected poets, and that's enough to consign philosophy in general to the landfill of wrong thinking. Laura sits on the edge of her chair, thinking, "Plato must have been amazing — he was gay!"

Michelle takes the pencil from her mouth and is about to say something, but when she looks at me she seems to read my thoughts, and her eyes draw away, self-conscious. I ask her casually, "What were you going to say, Michelle?"

"I was thinking Socrates's four stages sound totally masculine. Where's the female perspective?"

I throw that to the class. Relief and anxiety wrestle for my heart. Relief that I'm able to speak, anxiety over her response to my eyes. But it was only a look. I think of Chekhov's *The Kiss*. There's one woman who could, who even might, restore the blighted kingdom of my bliss — Lisa — but she lives on Randy's Trail.

It's hot in the room, so I call a break. In the courtyard the breeze is delicious. Michelle catches up with me. She says, "You know the answer, don't you? What are the stages of feminine development, I mean."

"I think *you* know. You're a mature woman, after all."

"If you know that about me, then you must know the answer yourself."

"One can recognize a Ferrari without knowing how it's built. Think about how you got to be who you are, and you'll know better than Plato. And incidentally, who taught Socrates about the levels of love?" She knits her delicate brow. "The courtesan, Diotima. Maybe you can consult her on Wikipedia."

For the rest of the class I'm thinking: Michelle probably sees me as the professor persona I've spent years cobbling up. I used to think I could construct a personality for myself by imagining who I was. How could I have ever believed that? That makes no more sense than to believe that *they* construct me with *their* fantasies.

When class is over, I walk past a gaggle of Hare Krishnas, blissed out on whatever blisses them out, abasing themselves before that unseen power that they want me to share, imagining I might see what it was. If I could, their idiotic dancing might suddenly become something beautiful, like Michelle's face.

My phone pings me a text. It's my sister, Ysabel. "Somebody here wants 2 talk 2 u." This is suspicious. I haven't seen her since last Christmas, even though she lives a half hour away. We know better than to talk to each other if we want to keep the peace. Okay, she could be reaching out. I phone her.

"See if you can recognize this voice," she says.

The voice bellows, "Calderini! Surf's up, Prof!"

How could I not recognize Blake Orkowski? Yes, the guy who was still watching Captain Kangaroo in high school. The guy we nicknamed

Blank. The guy who once found three bags of green tea in my backpack and smoked two of them before he realized they weren't weed.

It appears I'm cornered. We chat. He's been driving a mail truck down in San Diego and happened to deliver a package to our mother. He used to be one of the few people who actually liked Mom's cooking, and of course she wasn't going to forget that, so she gave him Ysabel's address. She also gave him a huge tip, which made him realize what a shitty job he had, so he decides to quit and come up here. Now he wants to stay with me until he gets a job.

"Put Ysabel back on, okay, Blake." Then to her, "Shit, Ysabel, I thought maybe you wanted to bury the hatchet, not swing it at me."

"Remember how he used to patch your surfboards back in the day?" Then whispering, "Maybe you wouldn't be such a snob if you still surfed."

So Blake unloads his worldly goods at my house — a guitar, a stereo and a milk crate full of CDs, two battered cardboard boxes of clothes, a poster of Jane Fonda as Barbarella, two surfboards and two wet suits, a set of dumbbells and a Krupps cappuccino machine. He's going to sleep on my couch. To my surprise, he's scrounged up some money somewhere and wants to pay for his food, but I tell him he can pay me back when he gets a job. To my greater surprise, he cleans up after himself in the kitchen, but the bathroom is another story. Maybe he never had a home with indoor plumbing.

It's interesting. Mild stupidity can be infuriating, but Blake's level actually has a kind of grandeur to it, almost an art form. Last night he was out somewhere, which was fine because I was tired and went to bed early. I wake up to the sound of someone weeping in the living room. This startles me at first, but I listen for a minute and realize it must be female pleasure sounds. Pretty annoying. Ursula the Hun never once made noises like that. It goes on for maybe twenty minutes, and finally I say, I'm trying to sleep, Blake. Then I hear his voice, but can't make out what he's saying. It doesn't sound like he's speaking English, and this makes me really curious. What else would he speak?

Get up at daybreak after a crappy night. I'm trying to be quiet, but they wake up. He speaks to her affectionately, "You quiero food? Eat?" Makes spoon-to-mouth gestures. She giggles. "No tacos?" he says, but she just smiles. He sits up and points to himself. "Me hungry." He rubs his stomach. "Hombre!" he says. I offer that the word is *hambre*. "Hambre, hambre," he says. Then she says it, smiling.

"Ahmbrayy."

"Sí, sí," he says, then points at me. "Amigo! Boss this house, amigo!"

She seems fascinated by this and repeats it. Then she turns to me and says, "Do you speak English?" She has a Southeast Asian accent.

I point at Blake and say, "He speaks English when he's sober."

I haven't been surfing in several years, but reminiscing about Del Mar with Blake works its will on me. We take our boards down to Malibu. The waves are small but well formed, and there's cheerful sunlight on the water. I'm out of shape, but after a few rides my timing starts to come back. The taste and smell of saltwater, sound of gulls, watching for the swells and seeing the kelp heave far out, I had forgotten the feeling, the mixture of alertness and serenity, the sharpening of senses. Blake reads the break perfectly, and he's there where the best sets peak. His takeoffs are fast. When he makes his cuts, he doesn't flail his arms and bob up and down like the young yahoos; he moves easily, like a hunter stalking the best spots on the wave.

For lunch we buy milk, peanut butter, and cheap white bread, the surfer's soul food. The Safeway parking lot burns my feet, but I don't let on. At sundown the wind drops to nothing; the waves are backlit, emerald glass. My arms and shoulders ache and my teeth chatter as I carry my old longboard up to the car. I hardly notice that the skin on my right knee is torn. The fragrant brine and fine sand is in our nostrils and hair and towels.

We stop for drinks on the way home, but first he has to buy a bottle of Crema de Rompope, the sickly sweet banana liquor which he sips between swigs of bitter beer. We end up at the Zipper, talking about women. I want to tell him about the woman on Randy's Trail, my one hope of salvation, but decide he won't get it, so I tell him about Michelle instead. He wonders why I don't fuck my students. I lie and say I had my fill when I was young, but I can see he's onto my horniness.

A week later, Blake has moved out. He has a job managing an apartment close to campus. I go over there and find him contemplating the parts of a clothes dryer spread all over the washroom floor while eating gourmet chocolate ice cream from the carton by dipping wheat thins in it. Pieces of this confection are stuck to the week's worth of stubble on his face.

"I can fix anything with enough duck tape and coat hangers," he says. I try to tell him it's "duct tape," for fixing heater ducts, but he just laughs. "What the hell is a heater duck, dude?"

He says this job is just a stopgap until something better comes along, and anyway, he likes it. What's his plan? He doesn't have one.

He doesn't have a plan. The rest of the week the thought keeps coming back to me that maybe that's my problem.

It's Friday. I sit down at my computer feeling the usual pride and interest in my work, but in a few minutes I'm suddenly, nauseatingly, aware that this is exactly what I do every day of the week during school season. I try to brush this off and conjure a plan for today's class, but everything that comes up seems too predictable, musty, and lifeless. I close my laptop. I'll think of something on the way to class.

But my brain will not come back to it. I'm used to living in the future, but what the hell is the future, anyway? A steer grazing on the range has a future of sorts. A trolley rattling along its tracks has a future. On the way to class the nausea I felt sitting at my computer comes back. I sit on a bench and look around. A student sobbing into her cell phone. A squirrel, searching furiously for something among the leaves. There is a world here. My future is something I wield to fend off anxiety, not seeing that every day I'm also fending off a vibrant cosmos of life. Fuck the future! Fuck my job! On an impulse, I take my shoes and socks off and throw them in the nearest trash bin. As I go into Frikker Hall, I'm freshly aware of the rough concrete steps, the cold steel threshold, the smooth linoleum floor.

CHAPTER TWO

Today's class will focus on the topic of higher consciousness. As students settle into their seats, I'm thinking I'd like to talk about what's happening in my life — this strange new way the world seems to be presenting itself to me. Usually, I like what they say — they're grad students, after all — but today their ideas strike me as really limited, conventional. They're too are afraid of being wrong. They need to beat a path forward. Of course they'd be insulted if I said so. Here I am with bare feet, throwing a pair of glaring question marks into our circle.

Not knowing why, I stretch out my arms and say, "Everybody hold hands." . . . I can feel the shock, but they do it. I say, "Now sit like this for a couple of minutes and imagine that we have pooled our individual awareness, our knowledge, our emotions, our senses. Imagine that we aren't eleven separate states of consciousness, but one. What's it like?"

I can feel and see discomfort, adrenalin, anticipation. What's going to happen?

Marcos: "Our collective consciousness is an idiot!" They laugh.

Me: "Okay, why did you laugh? Is Marcos right?"

Laura (scowling): "Why are we doing this?"

Me: "Let's hear what everybody thinks."

Michelle (palms pressed against her eyes): "We can't experience ourselves as any way but separate. We can talk about consciousness, but it's as if we're talking to ourselves. If the experience isn't *in here,* we can't imagine it."

Jaqui (timidly): "I don't think that's true. I think . . . (Pause. We all wait.) something about feeling."

Me: "What about feeling?"

Silence.

I'm high as a weather balloon. Scott, who rarely talks, wonders if the highest state is one of pure imagination, unfettered by ideas of reality. Jaqui goes back to emotion, that without emotion there is no consciousness, and to be fully conscious means to be fully aware of what we feel. Their faces are flushed. They've discovered the fence and they're trying to get through it. It goes on like this until the hour is up.

"I had no idea what would happen when I started this," I say. "I just had this feeling that nothing really excellent would happen in this class unless we confronted what kept us separate. Was I right?" They look at each other, searching for a safe answer.

Jaqui: "We can't know that yet. This might be the beginning."

On the way home I reflect. One person at least — Jaqui — seems to have shed some kind of shell. It's magic. When and how did we lose our knowledge of magic? Why do I suddenly mourn that loss, and wonder why I never mourned it before?

I decide to stop for coffee on the way home, and I walk toward downtown. As I round the corner of Baskin and Third, I'm suddenly surrounded by the Hare Krishnas. Seeing my bare feet, a saffron-robed woman with a shaved head motions me to dance with them. I dance. People are laughing, I'm laughing. One of them approaches, bows deeply, touches the mark on his forehead, then touches me. My eyes fill with tears.

That was over two months ago. I bless my shoes. If I'd never worn them in the first place, I'd never have known the feel of the world without them. I have a pair of slaps in the house, but I don't wear those, either. I can walk on gravel, hot asphalt, cobblestones. I don't want to upset people by going to faculty meetings like this, so the last few weeks I've just stopped going. Nobody bugs me about it. I spend my lunch hours at the gym.

Blake has become a kind of bridge back to Ysabel. We go over to her house to watch a Netflick. It's *Face of Another*, by Teshigahara, the story of a guy who's in an auto accident that destroys his face, and a plastic surgeon gives him a face stolen from somebody else. He murdered the guy to get the face.

With a new identity, the guy with the new face ends up seducing his own wife. Then he starts to reveal to her who he really is, and she stops him, saying, "I knew it was you." Blake and I think she's lying, but Ysabel says, A man would think that, because men can't see past appearances. But she does. Women relate to character, to the inner person. I ask her if a woman would know if a man's character changed. Instantly, she says. Then she looks at me suspiciously and says I've been acting weird lately.

I hate the way Blake eats. He sits there rolling up baked beans in his pizza and eating it taco style. He grabs my foot and tries to show Ysabel my calluses, but I belt him and he lets go.

It's the last day of class. By the time I get there, the students have decided we're going to break early and go for beer. The Zipper is almost empty. While we're waiting for our beers, Jaqui says, "People say a smart child is like an adult, and a stupid adult is like a child. Maybe intellectually there's no difference in intelligence between adults and children, it's all just experience. Some experiences make us look smarter, some make us look dumber."

The beers arrive. We talk about their experience, of college and of life. Scott used to play drums in a rock band. Every morning he sits down at his drum set and plays until he's exhausted; otherwise, he can't force himself to go to class. Laura starts telling us what she knows about the sexual habits of various faculty members, and, yes, the variety is stunning. To my own surprise, for the first time I tell them the story of the Woman on Randy's Trail but I leave out one important detail. I don't tell them why I *know* the Zogon was me.

A couple of the students drink their beer and leave. People start to drift in. A clean-cut frat sort of guy Michelle knows joins us. His name is Nick. She gives me a conspiratorial look when he starts to talk to her. I put my feet up on the chair next to me, so Nick can see them. He pretends not to notice, but then he mutters something and excuses himself. A minute later Michelle and I walk out together.

Our arms touch. My head is spinning. As we walk, she says, "What you told us about the woman on the trail; that was totally fascinating. How did you feel?"

I turn and face her, so she can see what's in my eyes. "I'd like to tell you more about it. Look, class is over. You're not my student anymore. Everybody in the class gets an A anyway. I want to take you out."

"I'm flattered."

"No, no. Let's start over. I'm not your teacher. I'm me. Would you like to go out with me?"

"Okay, let's start over. I'm flattered. You're . . . Jesus, you're the most . . . You're a totally amazing person. I'd like to but I can't."

"You're in a relationship?" She nods. Then she takes my face in her two hands and kisses me on the corner of the mouth. Then she turns her back so I can't see her chestnut eyes and she runs. I start to walk, and notice pain in the toes of my right foot, and I see a little blood there. I guess she stepped on them, and my first reaction is to wish that they would bleed forever.

The good news is that she might have gone out with me. If I hadn't asked her, I wouldn't have known. The bad news is, of course, this doesn't do me a goddamn bit of good, does it?

At home I get the tequila bottle from the bookcase and sit on the couch in the dark, a Noah's Ark of savage questions jostling in my head. Is her "no" final, or is it meant to draw me on? What is "amazing" about me — my intellect, my professorial warmth, my rebel goofiness, my lust? Or is it something about my new primitiveness, something subtle but unmistakable, like a pheromone? Am I the Zogon of Randy's Trail, or the mild and erudite Professor Ashton Caldo? What would the Zogon do now? Pursue her? Get relief by turning his newfound power on other women? Is it possible that Professor Caldo is now Dr. Frankenstein, and the Zogon is but a tool of his exquisite stratagems?

The pain in my toes is worse, so I pour a little tequila on them. A bad idea — I hobble to the bathroom to wash it off. There I glance at the Zogon in the mirror and am shocked but not dismayed. To the pale bespectacled face I say, "You are *amazing!*" There is a hint of evil in his smile. I go back and slide a Bob Marley CD in the deck, and before it's over the three of us — Professor Caldo, the Zogon, and the pale man with the glasses — are asleep.

I feel very alone. Blake would advise me to go out and get laid. Ysabel would give me a lecture about responsible mutuality. I just sit down and start furiously typing my thoughts. If I then erase them, they don't exist anymore, but I can't stand their ugliness on the page even as I write them. Maybe I can turn them into poetry.

For the next hour, wrestling with poetic forms gives me a kind of pallid relief, like taking one aspirin for a severed limb. Here is what I get:

> See how Venus centering
> one's eye subordinates
> the moon, or how
> by laying stones
> precise as these
> the waves have shown
> their hands? How casually
> your words compound me
> out of nothing
> but my willingness —
> a stressed cosmology
> from that collision sprung;
> your impact on the dumb
> procession of normality.
>
> Oracular and far,
> stop puncturing
> my eastern sky
> to stamp your light
> on every drop across
> my thousand fields of dew,
> blown into wounded memory
> that every dawn makes new.

I open my email. Amid the spam and other flotsam there are two messages of interest — one from my daughter, Thelma, in Denver, and one from Michelle. I open the Michelle message first.

Dear Professor Caldo, I'm really sorry about yesterday. I didn't know what to do. I know it's corny to say I want to be friends, but the truth is, I don't want to lose contact with you. Can we have lunch sometime? A hug. Michelle. P.S. By the way, the course was tremendous. It changed my thinking about so many things.

Can we have lunch. Sometime. Why? So she can bask in my desire for her? Wait. Maybe *This Is It!?* No. She didn't give me her phone number. Of course not; she's in a relationship, remember? The simple truth is, she's ambivalent, undecided. She wants excitement, but doesn't want to forfeit anything to get it. Her attraction for me breaks her rules, confusing her, but she doesn't want to let go of it. Professor Caldo would show fatherly understanding, disguise his lust as platonic interest, to get close to her. Go piss up a rope, Professor Caldo! I am the Zogon. If she wants to play with me, she'll have to pay. If she won't pay, I'll find someone with different rules.

I hit REPLY. I type,

Dear Michelle, No need to apologize, I shouldn't have spoken to you like that . . .

No, no. Delete that.

Dear Michelle, You're confusing me. I'd like to see you but now I don't know what to expect from you. If you knew me at all, you'd know very well that my feelings . . .

No, no. Delete that too.

Dear Michelle, Neither of us knows what to do now, and I think the best thing for us to do is nothing. Don't worry about it, anyway. My assumptions about you were wrong. I hope this poem I wrote for you says some of it. Ashton.

Now I paste the poem into the message and hit SEND.

I go back to the message from Thelly. She hasn't written to me in months.

> *dear daddy. sorry it's been soooo loooong since I wrote! I hope you're doing well! i don't know if you heard, but hey, i got a job! now i'm working in the mail room at macfrugals. i told them i was sixteen, hah! i want you to know I feel better about life than i have in years and years. the thing is, i don't know if i can stay with mom any more, her negativism is driving me crazy, and i'm thinking of moving out. my boss at macfrugal's says he'll let me work full time but of course i'd have to quit school, but my grades suck anyway. the only other way is if you could help me so i can pay rent and just work part time — a couple hundred a month? how does that sound? love, thelly*

I've had a feeling that something like this was coming. She's smart as hell, but I know she's miserable in school, and I know what she means about Ursula's "negativism." Thelly is like I was, a free spirit, but she's growing up in different times. Now kids think life is a giant Visa account. She might be fishing for an invitation to come live with me. I know better than to try that. And I don't trust her judgment enough to send her money — she's smarter than her fourteen years, but has a long way to go. Eventually she'll be okay, but she'll have to figure it out for herself. It's a punishing situation for me, not to be there, not ever to be consulted unless she wants something, an adolescent quick fix for the crisis of the moment. There's no way she's going to listen to me, however close or far away. I hit REPLY. I type,

> *Dear Thelly, It's so nice to hear from you, and I'm so glad you're well. DON'T QUIT SCHOOL! That's a short-term strategy with really negative long-term implications. There must be a better solution. Tell me more about the situation with your mother. Where would you live, anyway? I need to be clear about what's going on. If you want, you can phone me. Dad. Love*

It's not as easy as I thought to make meeting somebody seem accidental. If I go into Frikker Hall, it'll look suspicious, but there's more than one exit, so if I wait outside . . . and so on. I go to the hallway outside the room Michelle is in. There's hardly anyone around, so I can't be part of a crowd. I'd better go downstairs and try to pick the most likely exit, then wait until she comes out and catch up with her. Also, she might be with somebody. If so, it wouldn't be cool if I asked to see her alone. I'll have to improvise.

As I head for the stairs, I feel a twinge in the heel of my left foot. There's a thumbtack stuck right in the middle. My feet are so tough it went in without my noticing. There are distinct blood spots wherever I've put my foot down. With some effort, I pull the tack out, and then it really starts bleeding. I should wrap it with something — toilet paper maybe. There doesn't seem to be a men's room on this floor. I look at my watch. Michelle's class will be over just now. I hurry down the stairs and out the door, and I spot a good vantage point next to a planter full of tall shrubs. I sit on the edge of the planter to wait, pressing my thumb against the wound to stop the bleeding. Ten minutes pass. Fifteen. Shit. I've come out the wrong door.

I walk across the courtyard to the coffee shop, order a latte, and sit down to think. It's probably just as well I missed her, trying to look casual and in control with my foot bleeding all over the place, plus now it's aching, and I'm starting to wonder about tetanus. How come I never wondered about tetanus when I was seventeen? I thought I was immortal. Right now if I really am the Zogon, I should have a jungle herb for this in my medicine bundle.

I look up and see Michelle standing in front of me. "Why did you leave?" she asks.

"Leave where?"

"You came to find me, right?"

"Came to find you?"

"Oh, come on, Professor Caldo. The minute I saw those blood spots, I knew it must be you. I was expecting you, sooner or later." She's more perceptive than I thought. I'm going to start wearing dark glasses. "Don't worry," she says. "I know you're a good guy." She sits down.

"Is that why you came after me?"

"Yep."

"Then all is lost." So much for the magnetic Zogon.

"You want to be the inscrutable wild man, don't you? I haven't forgotten the story you told us about Andy's Trail . . ."

"Randy's Trail."

"Whatever. What's wrong with just being your wonderful self Ashton? Can I call you Ashton? The bare feet are fun, though. You can keep them, just don't go around stepping on sharp stuff."

"Life is full of sharp stuff."

She shrugs. "Then maybe you should wear shoes, Dear Man." She devastates me for a minute with her eyes, then stands up. "I loved your poem," she says. "Will you write to me again?" I can't answer or look at her. "Please?"

It would be mean and stupid of me to say no. I nod weakly. She bends over and kisses my forehead. "Take care of that foot," she says. "You could get tetanus." And she's gone.

CHAPTER THREE

RANDY'S TRAIL

Despite everything, the Michelle adventure was really, when I stop and analyze it, a step forward. I certainly don't want to go back to being Professor Caldo. Professor Caldo would never have spoken to her and felt the joy and pain, never learned anything about his weakness. He would never have brought the seminar to its luminous height, or danced with the Hare Krishnas. Even my body is leaner and tougher than it's been in a decade or two. The lesson of Michelle is that some women, maybe most, lack insight into the power of the wild. They've been tamed to the point that their instinct is to impose their tameness on all beasts, and they've learned so well how to do it.

This strange transformation that's overtaken me would never have happened if it hadn't been for Randy's Trail and The Woman.

It was March 17, exactly seven weeks ago, an early spring day with morning fog turning to pure blue sky by noon. Sick with despair . . . no, not despair, only a nagging nausea at the recent chasm between my lechery and my aging body . . . I had decided to drive down the coast to the beach paradise of my youth. I don't know what I expected to find there, some magical effect by filling my lungs with the air that sustained me as an unself-conscious ocean satyr.

Highway 5 south from the Los Angeles area bypasses the beach towns — Oceanside, Carlsbad, Leucadia, Encinitas, Cardiff, Solana Beach, Del Mar. Dry canyons of red and buff sandstone speckled with sage and scrub pine alternate with vast tracts of tile and plaster homes built in the sixties and seventies. Far off to the right one glimpses the blue razor edge of the

Pacific horizon. I didn't really have a destination, just the urge to go south. Wherever I ended up, I might stay for a few days. Fuck the Dean's Lecture, from which my absence is a serious misdemeanor. Fuck UC Riverside and the Psychology Department and my students, none of whom has ever had their heart eaten by even a single lioness. Or the dean either, probably. Fuck him too. Fuck Delfin.

The smell of the sea and sagebrush pulled me back, back to my boyhood in Del Mar, some thirty-five years ago. Didn't know I lived in paradise then. You see, my heart was eaten in those days by something else, I don't know what. Maybe if I could remember that now, my heart would grow back from this lion eating.

I took the Del Mar exit at Via de la Valle and wended my way along the old coast highway to the spot where I used to cross into my place of peace and healing. I was remembering a place where I used to go to be alone, a little wild place where I felt safe. I parked on Seacrest Road at the top of the old trail and stepped out, breathing the nearly forgotten, now joyous fragrance of sage and eucalyptus. But as I started down the path, I saw this big house that wasn't there before. The architecture was self-consciously artsy. It was too damn big and tidy for a sensible person. Space in front for several cars. Lawns and hedges to keep the Mexican gardener busy. I tried to figure a way around it so I could find out whether the trail was still passable on the lower side.

This used to be where I walked to the beach when I was a kid. Yes, the memories were coming back. The dirt track used to start on the west side of Seacrest Road and wind its way for about a mile down to the ocean. The upper part meandered along an abandoned road and crossed a level place that looked like it had once been meant for a building site, but had long since given way to eucalyptus trees and sage brush. How that smelled on a hot day. About halfway down the trail you had to squeeze through a gap in the old chain-link fence that marked where a bathhouse had once been. Farther down, the trail passed along the bottom of a sandstone bluff, and you could begin to hear the sea, because the bluff worked as a sound reflector. That way you could tell how big the surf was down at the beach. When you heard that booming sound, you would get this tingle — part pleasure, part fear. Farther down, you would cross the railroad tracks and later Palm Boulevard, into the parking lot by the lifeguard tower.

My sister and I named it Randy's Trail when we were little, because this pudgy kid named Randy lived right across the street from the top of it, and he was probably the only other person we ever met going up or down. Even in those years, if I was feeling unhappy or just wanted to be alone with my thoughts, I would come down to Randy's Trail and take this one side path, a faint track through the brush that led to my favorite climbing tree — a Torrey pine whose upper branches gave me a view of the ocean. I was untouchable there. I was the intelligence of the tree. The tree held everything around it spellbound; the whole ocean was its ally. What was it, this longing for the sea? Was it anything like my longing for the scented silk of welcoming skin? No! The sea gave love promiscuously to anyone who had the capacity to feel it.

When I was in high school, I got into surfing. I never used to wear shoes in the summertime. Not even flip-flops. My feet had such humongous calluses then that I could carry my surfboard — a primitive forty-five-pounder — over any kind of rough or scorching surface. Gravel, asphalt, pine needles, whatever was there, I hardly felt it. "These days," I muttered aloud, "I can't even go out and get the newspaper without my shoes on. Losing the power of your feet weakens your whole body."

Randy's Trail. I had to see if it was still there. From time to time I still have these dreams that I'm walking it. The upper part had now become a long gravel driveway, lined with tidy rocks and mature oleander bushes — "freeway plants," Delfin called them. I shouldn't have been surprised that now there was this freaking house in the middle of the trail. I wondered if I should give up and go back, knock on the door, or just walk across the garden. I started across the front yard toward the south side of the house, just to see if I could get a look down where the trail used to go. This woman saw me from the window, I guess, and she opened the front door and said, "Can I help you?" She didn't step out, and I couldn't really get a look at her.

"Sorry. There used to be a trail here that went down to the beach. I was trying to get down there." I pointed. "Can I . . . is it still there?"

She didn't answer. She opened the door and came out, squinting at me in the bright sun. She was thirtyish, maybe well-preserved forty, dark haired, wearing a black leotard with sparkly leggings and a shocking pink miniskirt. I was the invader of her tidy lawn in my shorts and T-shirt and sandals, cursing my bony white legs, holding in my gut.

"How did you know about the sea trail?" she said.

I shrugged. I pointed to the hill. "I used to live up on La Costa. A long time ago."

"You can't get past the railroad tracks," she said. "There's a fence."

"You knew the trail too?" I asked. Again the silence, the suspicious look. "You guys built this house, I bet. It's very nice." I walked over to where she was leaning against the door frame. Her eyes were gray-green, not Delfin's pure blue, but wide set, sensitive. She was a bit more slender too.

"I designed it," she said, still not smiling. "So . . . you used to use this trail? When was that?"

"I left here to go to college . . . mmm . . . thirty-five years ago. Before that, I used to come along here just about every day in the summer time."

"Probably a lot of people did . . . I mean used it," she said.

"I don't think so. I never saw anybody. The trail was rough. There was a fence you had to crawl through back then too. We called this Randy's Trail."

She makes a face. "Randy? Who's Randy?"

"Just a kid who lived up at the top. He moved away ages ago."

"Randy's Trail," she huffed and, turning her back, stepped back inside.

"Ahh, can I go on down . . . ?"

"Like I told you," she said, "there's a fence." She closed the door.

My heart pounded a bit. Well, let her sue me. I really wanted to see what was left of Randy's Trail. I was going on down. I stood there and breathed deeply, but the tension didn't go away. Fuck it. I strode right across her garden, through a row of rose bushes, and down a bank of ice plant toward where the rest of the path should be. I crossed a footpath. It looked like it started at her backyard. I started to feel calmer as I walked in the general direction of the beach.

In certain places I think I almost recognized features of the old trail. There were stretches where the sandy earth was dotted with small anthills, I remember that. The big pine there might have been my tree, but now the lower branches were too far from the ground for climbing. Over here I saw a rusty bit of chain-link fence. I followed the railroad tracks to a place where I could cross and finally made it down to the beach, though damn it, now they'd built a park where the old rutted parking lot used to be. The pergola was gone. So was the broken-down old pier. The road had been widened, and now it was lined with big shiny SUVs and hybrids, invaders from the pampered present. Okay, I'd seen enough. I stood there for a while staring around, trying to find something familiar.

I started back up the hill along the two-lane street that leads to the town, but then I stopped. I had come here for one reason — to see the trail, to feel its power in me. It was a mistake. Like me, too much had changed, the power had been erased. Delfin would have laughed at my wistfulness. She was too young for me, too young and beautiful and bright to feel the encroaching darkness behind the midday sky. I should have known that about her; hell, I *did* know it, from the beginning. It was one of the things I chose to ignore, one of the things she forced from my mind with her lust that we agreed to call love, and calling is believing, and believing is the suicide of self-respect.

As I turned and began to retrace my steps, slowly, I thought about meeting the green-eyed woman again, and that goddamn panicky feeling came back. What was it? When your heart has been eaten, do you tremble at the smallest things? Well, that's bullshit, that's giving the lioness too much power. As I approached the house again, I forced myself to stay calm. Whatever annoyed her so much in the first place was going to give her fits if she saw me coming back, but fuck her. I climbed back over the ice plant, and this time I walked around the flower hedge and started to pick my way up the steep slope above her yard, and I saw her sitting right there in a white plastic lawn chair, wearing wraparound sunglasses. Seeing me, she stood.

"Excuse me!" she called.

Shit. I was trying to stay out of her way, but she had to do her little ownership thing. Everything that was once simple and beautiful shall one day be complicated and ugly. I stopped. I climbed back down and walked over to her. Before she could say a word, I said, "You have no idea what this place was. Some people think they can just buy anything they want, and just *erase* its history. Poof. So much for the places that were there for other people, the places they still care about. This trail is just a piece of real estate to you. You don't want to know what it is to me, but maybe you should." My fucking voice shook a little.

She stood there for a minute, facing me, inscrutable behind the sunglasses. Then, as though she read my thought, she took the glasses off and with something like shock I saw the soft eyes again. She tilted her head to one side. "Come on," she said quietly. "I want to show you something."

I'll show *you* something, I thought, as I followed her toward the house. There was an entry room with a pair of fine art nouveau ceramic cherubs holding up an orange neon sign that said *See Oh Tu.* To the left was the living room, with its huge west windows reaching up to the dark wood ceiling. On one of the grass-cloth walls was an oversized blue-neon line drawing of a computer, the screen of which was a mirror. On the opposite wall hung a large oil painting, a kind of impressionist rendering of a wooded glade. She stopped in front of it; this was what she wanted me to see. But I was looking at her, still feeling shaky. She *was* pretty, but it wasn't that. I'm a psychology professor, surrounded by pretty young women every day. Something about the situation made me feel *invaded* somehow. She was inhabiting, uninvited, a private place in my inner world, a place that I desperately needed right now. Like being charged admission to take refuge in my own oasis.

With effort I shifted my attention to the painting. It was somehow soothing. The colors dramatic, but not pushy. Intense sunlight playing through tall eucalyptus on dry leaf litter and sandstone and scrub.

"I painted it," she said.

She painted it. As if painting it made it hers.

"You're not looking at it," she said quietly.

"Where is this?" I asked.

She ran her finger lightly over the lines of the painting, then turned to me. "I grew up in apartments in St. Louis, Birmingham, Los Angeles. But when my granddad retired from the railroad, he got a little place up on the hill here in Del Mar, and I used to come and visit. He brought me to this wood twice when I was eight and a half." She started to pace the room. "When I got out of college, I knew this was where I had to live." She stared out the window. The front door slammed, making me jump. She smiled. "It's just the wind." I could see a puff of dust blowing past the bay window and, beyond that, the eucalyptus trees twisting and rustling, now chandeliers of silver reflecting the sun, now jade green where it shone through the long leaves. But it wasn't just the wind, you know.

Was she reading my thoughts? Explaining what she's doing in my inner space?

"You were only here once?" I asked.

"Twice." She started toward the front door.

My condition shamed me. She was the sane one, I was the lunatic. I could do better than this. "You're telling me that you feel as personally about this place as I do," I said. "I can understand that. You have your feelings, I have mine. Only now, you own it."

"Does that upset you? That I own it?"

"Well, it's not *you*, you know. What I see is that what I used to know is gone, no matter who . . . or no matter what happened to it." I tried to give her a warm smile. "Childish, maybe."

She leaned against the door jamb and looked me in the eye. "I don't think old memories are foolish or childish, do you?" She went on. "We lived in these little apartments when I was a kid, right in the middle of whatever city it was. If you wanted to play, you played jacks or hopscotch on the sidewalk, or went roller skating. You could always hear sirens. I used to dream about places where there were no streets or cars or lights. I used to beg for books about the Amazon jungle and the South Sea islands. I would hang my clothes on sticks around my room and pretend they were giant ferns, and my closet was a cave. I invented natives for friends, and we would have the most wonderful adventures together. I called them the Zogons."

Odd that she was so open about her childhood. Maybe she didn't have anyone to talk to. "About the trail . . . ?" I said.

"The trail. The first time I came here that day with my granddad, I felt like I was stepping into my dream. I had never seen anything like this place. The trees made you think you might see dinosaurs, or creatures from another planet. It had the smell of untamed life. What really thrilled me was, I could see that there were these big footprints on the path, from bare feet, and I asked my granddad who lived here, and he laughed and said nobody. But I knew that there were magic people, huge wild people. That night I named this place. I called it Zogon Wood. I begged my granddad to take me back, and just before I left to go back to St. Louis, we came back to this spot."

We had walked to the door. She stepped out onto the lawn and looked at the surrounding bluffs and trees. "That was the time I actually saw them, or him." She sat on the brick steps, her eyes closed. "It was hot. Granddad sat down against a tree and I think he was asleep. There were these holes in this cliff, and I was hiding in the brush so the animals that I imagined lived here wouldn't see me, and would come out, but they didn't come out. Then all at once, I saw him, right there, as close as that door. He looked like a wild animal walking along, only very tall. He was carrying this huge tree trunk on his shoulder. He was naked, his skin was dark brown, and he had this big shaggy mane of hair. I knew he lived here in Zogon Wood, and that there were others here like him. Big, powerful wild people. I held my breath. It was like being in Africa, or the Amazon. It was the most exciting day of my life."

She sat there, staring into space for a minute. "I didn't want Granddad or anybody to know what I'd seen," she said. "If he didn't believe me, it was okay, but if he did, he might tell other people, and God knows what would happen. I knew there was no way to get out of going back to St. Louis, so I just made a promise to myself I would come back here as soon as possible. But right after that my granddad left Del Mar. He moved to Mexico. I didn't get back here until I was twenty-one, but I have never passed a single day without thinking of this place."

"And the wild men," I said. I was thinking about telling her what, and whom, she actually saw. I knew she didn't want to know, but in a way she was asking me to tell her.

She smiled self-consciously. "Think I'm crazy?"

"You're not crazy. The wild man you saw? That was me. I carried a big wooden surfboard on my shoulder. I was always sunburned. I never wore anything but ragged shorts."

"*You*?! No. It wasn't *you*!" she laughed. She stood up and brushed the back of her skirt, made for the door again, then turned. "You don't even know what I'm talking about."

"I know exactly what you're talking about. I used to pass by here every day in the summertime thirty-some years ago. I was the only one who did. Nobody else could have walked this trail in bare feet. I had calluses like leather."

"Whatever."

"No! Not 'whatever.' You think I made this up?"

"Look," she said calmly. "You accused me of being on an ego trip about living here. I could see why you thought that. I shared my feelings with you. I told you private things about myself. You seem to care about this place, but it's really just yourself you care about, isn't it? Who is the ego tripper here?"

My self-centeredness. That was one thing Delfin was right about. "I'm sorry." I managed another smile of sorts. "We seem to have something in common. I'm not really a jerk. I'm under a lot of stress lately; it makes me rude at times."

She studied me for a moment. "Okay. You don't look like a jerk. And we have something in common — something *uncommon* in common. Would you like some coffee?"

We go back inside. While she made coffee, I looked around the interior again. The décor was unusual, but that's not all. There was a motif. Hardwood posts subtly fluted at the top, and above them slender joists spread out, a bit like a tree canopy across the ceiling. Wrought-iron door hardware suggesting the shapes of eucalyptus leaves.

She set out plain white cups that made the rich coffee look purple-black. She said, "Tell me about the Whoever's Trail. What did you call it?"

"Randy's Trail."

"Tell me about Randy's Trail."

"Right where this house is, there was a big sort of level place. In the winter the rainwater would run down this gully and fill it up, a huge puddle. My sister and I made rafts and sailed on it. We caught polliwogs. When I was thirteen and fourteen I used to come down here on moonlit nights. The shadows were so black I could make myself disappear from the face of the earth. Only the night birds and animals knew I existed."

"I never came here at night when it was wild," she said. "In my mind, this was the place I came to disappear, though. Somehow I thought if I owned it, I would feel peaceful here, but —"

"But what?"

"You can't own dreams. They own you," she said. My thoughts, again. Delfin used to do this, intuit and express what I felt. I thought that signified some sort of destiny, that we were meant to be soul mates or something, but it seems to have been one of those illusions that lie in ambush for men of my age. Or else women perfect it along with the rest of their clever arsenal.

"Listen, I've got to be going." She held up a coffee cup, but I shook my head. "Another time." She came with me to the door, but I kept walking quickly up the driveway, panting, dizzy with fear and confusion.

CHAPTER FOUR

NO COINCIDENCE

Since the episode with Michelle, I'm beginning to understand why Randy's Trail and The Woman have affected me so deeply that I can't put them out of my mind for more than a few minutes. The Woman is obviously cultured and intelligent, but somehow she's drawn to the primitive. Not just drawn to it: She's molded her life around it in a way, kept it in the center of her heart. Not the tame primitiveness of a travelogue, not the quaint simplicity of some remote tribe that flees in terror from explorers' guns, but the bold wildness in our midst, in our souls, the foundation of heroism and barbarity. I have to see her again. She has preserved in her heart the very thing that I have lost from my life. If I want to get it back, she's the only one who can guide me.

This will be difficult. She doesn't seem to believe that I am the actual Zogon — or rather, his faded remains. Even if she doesn't dismiss the idea, why should she be interested in it? Her fantasy is the thing that's precious to her. To press the mundane facts on her is like telling a child there is no Santa Claus.

Yes. But.

There's a huge difference between the child's Santa Claus and her cherished Zogon. There never was a real Santa Claus. There is no lost, old, fat, bearded man whom she once actually saw step out of his sleigh on her snow-covered roof and whom she kept alive in her heart until by accident he found his way to her. If there were, and if she could give him back his reindeer and his elves, why shouldn't she? To refuse to do it would be a shocking act of ingratitude, the mark of a deeply selfish person, wouldn't it?

Then there's the question of how she could perform this miracle of restoration. In the case of Santa Claus, it really would be a miracle, but in my case not at all. I don't want to fly though the air and be everywhere at once. I only want to recover the natural power of my animal nature. All I need is someone who knows what I was once, who understands the beauty of that, and who believes she can help me recover it. After all, it was she who cracked the shell of Professor Caldo in the first place, by showing me my inner self in the dark mirror of her dream.

What will my life be like if I can complete this rebirth? I begin with the person I am now — someone who longs to reach the limits of experience, to feel without restraint, to act without hesitation, who over and over sinks in the quicksand of shame and doubt instead. The story of the Fall is really the story of civilization. The parent is the serpent, and the apple is self-awareness. "Learn to become your own parent," they tell us, "and you'll own the power to command love." It's a vile hoax; becoming our own parent, we learn to judge our childish selves; we learn shame. To be reborn in nature, then, is to go back to what we knew before we knew shame, to look the snake in the eye and say, "Screw you and your goddamn apple; I've seen what it does, I remember who I was." The gift of civilized love — the love that's hoarded by the Michelles of the world and doled out in recompense for the loss of natural power — is the best that the Fallen can imagine. It's a laughable substitute for what was lost.

This monologue is a laughable substitute as well. To know one's original power only intellectually is to be a slave who suddenly remembers a remote freedom he once had in a wide green world. Such a slave is far worse off than his brother born to slavery and happy with his bread. The one who has remembered has only three choices — to end his life, to seize his freedom, or to become the object of his own loathing; and every day he wastes without action is a step toward the third choice.

The truth of this fills me with fear and hope, but mostly fear. Where to begin? As I say, I'm sure the first thing is to recruit her, the person who preserved my free self, The Woman on Randy's Trail. But how? The need for a strategy seems obvious, but maybe that's in fact the first thing to question. The fact that I had a "strategy" with Michelle should teach me something. In fact, becoming Professor Caldo is the result of years of strategies, one after another. To be intensely focused on a clear goal is the best strategy there is; let the action precede the plan.

Okay, I'm going down there again in a couple of days. Don't know how long I'll be gone, and don't want people looking for me, at least for a while. I have papers to write, but I don't have classes, so I can take vacation any time until September.

I call Ysabel and tell her I'm taking off for a month, maybe longer. Where? Wherever there's surf — I'm taking my board.

"Are you going to see Mom?"

"Probably not. You know we don't get along."

"Are you going with Blake?"

"Please don't tell him I'm going — he'll quit his job."

"He may quit it anyway when he finds out. Irresponsibility has got to be infectious in his case. So, you're going surfing by yourself for a month? You're not a kid anymore, Ashton, And by the way, your hair is way too long. You look like a Deadhead."

"I'll call you from time to time, Mommy."

"Don't bother. Just be sure your will is up to date; you promised me your books."

"You'll have to sell them to pay for my funeral."

"What if the shark doesn't leave any remains?"

"You think all this tenderness is going to keep me from going?"

"You wouldn't know tenderness if it bit you on the ass."

"Bye, Ysabel. Like I said, I'll stay in touch — I need the warmth."

Randy's Trail. Del Mar is a three-hour drive south when the traffic is light. I take my credit card, a few clean clothes, my laptop, and my surfboard. I drive at night, trying not to visualize the next few days. Whatever happens, I'll deal with it when it happens. My thoughts drift to September, when school will be in session again. I wonder if I'll even come back. I wonder who'll notice if I don't. Michelle? She might not be there either.

Here's this crap about the future again. I visualize the future as a big, fat steamship, sitting at the dock with its engines running. People are looking out of the portholes, to see who else is going to get on the ship. I see Michelle's face, and she opens the porthole and calls to me, but I don't move. Then I see Ysabel and Blake, and Ursula the Hun and our daughter, Thelma, and my department chairman. My students are there, too. I watch their faces as the ship pulls away from the dock, looking at me, bewildered, and I just watch them go and feel nothing. Then I turn around and the Randy's Trail Woman is there, waiting.

CHAPTER FIVE

NO WAY BACK

It's Tuesday morning. Del Mar is wrapped in one of those thin summer fogs that turns the rising sunlight smoky orange and coaxes rank smells from the earth. I've found a motel and eaten breakfast, but I haven't slept. I park my car next to her garage and knock on her door. I know this is going to be difficult, but I don't know just how. I lack a plan, but I don't lack determination. If things go badly, I'll find a way to come back. If someone stands in the way, I'll get past them. If she can't get my drift, I'll find a way to convince her. I've never sensed the correctness of a cause this firmly in my life.

No one answers the door, but I'm not about to leave. I start down Randy's Trail. As I walk, my tension lifts; I'm overwhelmed by the richness of the details teasing my nostrils and assaulting the tough soles of my feet. I walk some more, and I'm transported; tears blur my eyes. After twenty minutes I'm no longer here begging for redemption; I'm the natural proprietor of this place. It's as though she had already performed the miracle I meant to ask her for. My anxiety is gone, and my body is a furnace of desire for life, and for her. She's mine, as an essential part of this place that belongs to me.

I spend nearly an hour roaming the side paths, watching the fog melt and feeling the earth turn hot underfoot while the sunlight glints off the wings of insects stirring in the brush. My senses are so heightened I'm aware of her presence before I can see her, walking up from the direction of the beach. I can tell by her expression she doesn't recognize me at first, but when I approach, she relaxes a little. "Oh, It's you," she says.

"Not the me that you met last time."

She studies me suspiciously. "What do you want?" I can see that the pulse in her neck is galloping.

I step forward. "You changed my life."

"That's ridiculous," she says weakly, and I reach out and cup the nape of her neck softly and breathe in her rapid breaths and taste the slightly bitter, grassy flavor of her saliva. When the kiss runs its course, we walk awkwardly and silently together up to the house, and she opens the door and we step inside and kiss some more, and right there in the hallway I'm trying to undo her shirt and having trouble with the buttons, and then she's helping me. We stumble toward the bedroom, shedding garments, and then we're in bed and all one warm damp skin and she's sobbing beautifully, but with her eyes closed.

"Would you like to know why I'm here?" She doesn't answer. "Are you pissed?"

"No." But she jumps out of bed and starts to get dressed.

"What's your name?"

"Lisa. But listen, don't make too much of this, okay? We got excited."

"Okay, I won't make too much of it. You want me to leave? By the way, I'm Ashton."

"Please don't ask me a lot of questions."

"Can I tell you some things about myself?"

She has her back to me. "Not if it's really personal."

I've turned up my power too high. She really is scared. I can't relate to her in this state of mind. I'd better leave and come back later. She pulls up the blind, and I look out and see the heat waves shimmering on the dry leaf litter and hear the breeze stirring in the pungent eucalyptus leaves, speaking to me about my mission.

"Lisa, I didn't come here to make love to you — at least, not to do that and then leave. You've kept a part of my life, a part of my personality, that I lost over the years. The Zogon was me. After I met you, I realized how valuable that part was, and now I want it back. Your job is to help me get it back. I don't expect you to understand what I'm saying, but I think you do understand some of it. You're the only one who knows and appreciates what I was. It was more than a dream to you; it had to be more than a dream because you came back here to keep it alive. You see? You kept *me* alive, even while I let myself die. And I kept you alive, too. What you loved in me was a part of yourself; the natural intelligence of your young mind nourished you through your dream. Now I'm whole again, and you'll love me the way you did then."

She stares out the window. Did she hear a word I said?

"I'm glad you told me this," she says. "I knew it was a mistake to tell you about my dream, but I didn't know what a big mistake it was until now. You don't know me at all, not at all. I confess you got me very excited this morning, but that's because women easily mistake egotism for strength. What do you expect from me? That I'll crown you as my long-lost dream and kneel at your feet?" She shakes her head. "Mister, that's nuts. Now I have work to do. Would you mind showing yourself out?"

I close my eyes tightly, and I can see her tense face projected in the blackness. I make it into a child's face, an angry child of four. I feel calm. "Okay," I say to the child. "That's your head talking, and it's a good head. Your head feels ashamed because you let your guard down. When you told me about the Zogons, that was your heart speaking. Your heart was telling a high truth, a dangerous truth that your head doesn't like."

"Please leave now. Don't come back." She needs time to cool off. I pick up my shorts and reach in the pocket for my car keys, but they're not there.

"I'm going, as soon as I can find my keys." We look around the bed. We look under the bed. We go through the rumpled sheets and blankets.

"You must have left them in the car," she says. I go out and look, but they're not there. "Don't you have a spare?" she says.

"Yes, but that ring has all my keys on it. If I wait out here, can you please take another look for it?"

She glares at me. "You hid them somewhere, didn't you?"

I pull out my wallet and give her my professional card. "I'm going. Here's my cell number in case you find them. For now, I'm staying at the Coastside Inn on Ninth Street." Without looking at the card, she turns to go. "You're dead wrong about me, but go ahead and be angry. It won't change the truth of what I said, and you know it won't. You can decide to share yourself a bit, or you can keep right on with your perfect life the way it is." She doesn't answer, but she stops, with her back to me. I find the spare key in its hide-a-box under the bumper, and leave.

I'm definitely on the right path. Losing my keys was a sign from the Universe. I never would have thought of it myself. This morning was a natural first step, and I did well. What'll happen now? It'll be hard to stay away from her, but to do otherwise would be a mistake. For a while. Am I in love with her? I don't know yet. No two loves are ever the same. At the motel I immediately fall into a deep, dreamless sleep.

I spend the next few days driving around to the surfing spots, catch a few rides. When I go to the beach at the foot of Randy's Trail, of course I look for her, but she's never there. I think about asking the lifeguards if they know her, but decide against it. I would like to simply walk on the trail, but I rule that out also. Instead, I drive to the open backcountry and walk other trails through spicy sage and scrub pine and cactus. I buy a cheap spiral notebook at the local drugstore and start writing, diary style, with commentary. I've forgotten a lot already.

Mom lives a half hour away, and calling her is in the back of my mind, but I don't. Mom never had the slightest idea of who I was; she never made an effort to learn the first thing about me. As a child, I was her pretty toy, an extension of herself comparable to her fine high cheekbones and dainty hands. As I got older, I was a prodigy, who refused, out of spite, to live up to her hopes. If I tried to talk to her, to explain what it meant to be a flesh-and-blood man with feelings, she'd get physically ill. I should feel compassion for her now that she's old and weak of limb, but the fact is her personality hasn't changed one iota, and it never will. I could never explain about Mom and me to Ysabel, who apparently never had this problem. But with all her prickliness, Ysabel really knows me better than any other human being, and I need her. I call her, but luckily she isn't home, so I leave a message saying I'm fine and I haven't talked to Mom and probably won't.

The first three evenings I stay in and rent movies, but by Saturday I'm bored crazy with this. I keep having these vivid memories of making love with Lisa. Does she have another lover? Do they make love knowingly, intimately, as we didn't? I want to kill him.

Just to put a stop to this, I decide to go to this bar downtown called La Cantina. The bar is crowded with people of all ages, but there's a stool next to this couple in their sixties, so I sit down and order a glass of wine. Pretty soon we're on a first-name basis. Talking about how this town has changed, the rich Gen-Xers coming in, as if off some high-tech assembly line, not like the handmade cranks and weirdos of times past. I pick up that Sid is gay, that he and Louise are bar chums. She's a little overweight, but lively and clever, which makes her not at all bad to look at after a couple of glasses of merlot. I'm enjoying a nice vibe from her, but mostly I feel like talking.

"Speaking of the old days, what if you could go back there, back to when the things you miss were right in front of you, and bring one thing you wanted back here?"

"Any one thing I wanted?" asks Louise. "You mean something I personally had, or something everybody had?"

"Let's say you, personally."

"What an interesting question, Ashton," says Louise. "I used to believe in everything — in the world, in people, in God, in the future, especially in my teachers. That's what I miss the most."

Sid says, "It's a horrible question. Can't I please have it *all* back? Well, maybe not all. What I miss most wouldn't do me the most good now. There was this no-good bum that I cared about . . . What about you, Ashton?"

"Me? I miss living in the moment. I had no beliefs, no responsibilities, no values, no learning, only unlimited time, imagination, and raw energy. I made myself up hour by hour."

"Didn't you have dreams?" she says.

"Vague dreams. A different one for every mood."

He says, "You don't look like somebody who's weighed down, you know, by the weight of duty, my boy."

"I carry the weight inside."

"You must want to carry it," he says, "or you'd put it down."

"It's not a matter of desire," I say. "It's a matter of fear. Not knowing what will happen next gets more and more scary as we get older. Without knowing it, we give up little bits of freedom here and there. We pick up habits, commitments, attitudes, until one day we wake up and we can't get out of bed without a fucking blueprint. And it's getting late! Our needs are greater than when we were young, not less. Needs for comfort and security, and worst of all, the need for forgiveness, for the life we've created."

"Yes," says Sid. "Obligations. 'A married philosopher is a comic figure,' says Nietzsche. The ancients knew it too. 'When your kids are grown and the dog dies, leave home with a begging bowl.' I think that's in the Upanishads. My only promises are to myself."

"That's not in the goddamn Upanishads, and you know it," she laughs. "You just made it up! Anyway, what do you promise yourself?"

"I'll tell you one of my promises," he says. "That I'll never reveal my promises."

As the evening wears on, Sid's comments seem to set up camp in my brain. "A comic figure." "A begging bowl." Yes, I suppose I've become comic to myself, in the sense that Nietzsche was talking about — "married" to my job, my title, my rituals of respectability . . . unable to engage the world honestly, from my instincts, my heart. Full of intense emotion and afraid to show it. But what about the begging bowl? I thought I was willing to shed Professor Ashton Caldo, leave the trappings of social worth behind in search of something authentic. It never occurred to me that I would have to give up *everything*. But *wait*! Didn't I just say that's what I miss about my youth — having *nothing* but imagination and energy? Is that my real aim? If it is, what do I need Lisa for? To be a catalyst? To give me the courage to give up everything, to believe that my brain and my body are enough? That would mean to give *her* up as well. I look again at Sid. There's certainly nothing heroic-looking about him, a mild man with a sunburned bald spot and sandals, sitting in a bar. You would never expect those words to come out of his mouth — but of course, he doesn't care what you expect. His promises are only to himself. He *could* be someone without fear, without contempt. If I could make these words my own, I'd be free of Randy's Trail and of Lisa, even free of my contempt for Professor Caldo. The ship of the future would have left, and I'd be standing on the dock alone, with nowhere to go and nothing to do. Is that what I want?

I don't know. I don't know.

On my way back to the Coastside Inn, my cell pings me a text. It's from Lisa. It says, "I found your keys." It's almost twelve o'clock. I text back, "Okay if I stop by for them tomorrow six P.M.?"

CHAPTER SIX

GOOD-BYE TO RIVERSIDE

It takes a lot of work to quit a job you've been doing for twenty-two years. Back at my apartment in Riverside, I've been on email and on the phone for the best part of five weeks, and I think I'm going to get my final paycheck, severance pay, annuity, and vacation allowance eventually. When I tell Ysabel, she appears at my place within the hour. I think she's going to start in on me, but to my surprise she's only curious. She didn't know I was so unhappy, she says.

"I'm not actually unhappy. I'm going to miss my job quite a lot. I just think this 'me' who isn't unhappy is only half of what I could be. The other half has spoken up. He says, 'Now it's my turn.'"

"Sometimes half of me feels that way too," she says. "Only my other half still wants shoes and a haircut. Just what was it that touched this off?"

"One of these days I'll tell you all about it. You have to understand that right now I need some privacy. You know, to feel my way forward without too much, ahh, help."

"May I ask whether you have plans for making a living?"

"You may not."

"I see. You haven't told Mom, have you?"

"Of course not. Once I've sorted things out. I have to tell The Hun and Thelma, in case they have any ideas about help."

"This must actually be pretty tough for you. You've been secure here. Is there any way I can help?"

I never know quite how to handle sympathy, especially when it comes from my family. "Thanks, but security isn't what I want now. Which reminds me: this pile here is all stuff I'm not going to keep. Would you please go through it and take whatever you want?"

"My God! You're giving away your books? You haven't joined some sort of cult, have you?" I give her a dirty look. "Oh, sorry," she says. "I guess I wasn't supposed to notice. Anyway, what would somebody who looks like Robinson Crusoe want with books? Are you ditching your Bob Marley CDs?"

"Sorry, I'm keeping those."

"God, this is like when grandma died," Ysabel says.

"Grandma didn't even like Bob Marley."

She turns slowly from the discard pile, and I'm astonished to see her eyes are moist. "Ashton, I don't know what you want from life, or from me. Of course it's your decision, whatever it is. But there's something I want from you, if you can work it in. I want to be your sister. I want to know where you are and what you're doing, and . . . You know what I'm saying? Okay, I don't go around thinking about my family like I should, but that doesn't mean I don't care."

I suddenly feel guilty. I hadn't expected this, but I can't think of what to say except "Okay. I'm not walking out of your life, Babe. Try to think of this as my new adventure. You know I'm not an idiot. Anyway, I'll stay in touch and come to visit, and all that."

"I just feel so strange," she says, picking through the discard pile. She finally leaves with my box of cooking spices and my extra ski gear. I want to call her back, to hold her for a minute, but now doesn't seem like the moment, and I feel guilty about that, too. In our family, it never seems like the moment.

I call Blake and offer him the rest of the stuff. When he arrives, he's what you might call "pumped" that I've quit my job in order to live a freer life. "I never knew how you could put so many hours in, working, Prof," he says. "I mean, you weren't getting rich or anything."

I decide not to even try to explain my situation to him. "I liked my work well enough, but I spent way too much time thinking. Life was mostly in my head. I want to try just *living* for a change. I don't mean partying or anything like that, I mean just being there in the moment, using my senses and my body to the fullest."

"Totally! Like, if I don't have something to do, I start thinking, too. I can get seriously bummed, you know?"

"Well, there's that kind of bummed thinking, and there's something you could call cool thinking, I guess. But I'm not even into cool thinking. I'm talking about just living life as it happens. Anyway, I'm moving back to Del Mar. I don't know what I'll do there, but I'm sure something will come along."

"It always does. Anyway, Del Mar's a great idea. You'll be a surf bum again."

"And anyway, there's this woman."

"*All right! A Del Mar babe!* I'm starting to get the picture."

Blake is still exactly the same person he was when I left Del Mar thirty-plus years ago. To him the idea of going back there is like loading a favorite old song into iTunes. How could he understand that I've been living in a whole different genre? The Del Mar of my memories has been transformed by my life experience into something radically different; if there's a song for this, it hasn't been recorded yet.

But wait. At the same time, Blake is curiously accurate. He imagines that I'm moving toward my new life, pulled by simple, primitive ideas and impulses, and I am. The part he can't understand is that I'm also moving away, leaving my tended fields and taking up my begging bowl.

Surveying the pile on my living room floor, he says, "I can sell a lot of this stuff to the students in my building, I'll bet."

"Good. I'll help you take it over there."

Evening is falling when I get back, and I think about all the evenings I've spent alone here. To say good-bye to this place, there's one more thing I want to do. I sit down and log on to my email. I select all seventy-seven messages and hit "delete." Then I click on Michelle's address.

Dear Michelle, I hope you're having a good summer. I often think about you, and not in a sad or regretful way. You've had a real influence on my life, helping me make a huge decision.

I've quit my job here, and moved south, in search of a more authentic life. It would take me too long to explain that; but I wanted to tell you that you helped. Not that what happened between us was something unique, in fact it was fairly typical for me, except that you handled it more gracefully than I might have hoped. Rather, it was the intensity of my feelings for you, combined with the very familiarity of the situation, that triggered my decision. I don't know at all what the rest of my life will be like, but I feel optimistic, as it begins with a small bit of wisdom you unknowingly gave me: Unless our ideals match the life we live day to day, we force ourselves to live in a fantasy world; and when the fantasy comes up against reality, the pain can be devastating. Your loveliness and warmth were the catalyst of an explosion that was bound to happen. Thank you. No need to answer this. Ashton

When I'm through, the twilight has faded into dark. I unplug my router and laptop and put them in my duffle bag.

Lisa starts out being cautiously not cross, and after a couple of glasses of merlot, it appears I'm staying the night. She wants to know where I'm going to live (which means, of course, "not here"). I tell her that I've worked out a deal with the manager of the Coastside Inn. If I pay for six months in advance, I can get the room for a third of the regular cost, but I'm not to tell anyone about the deal. I know, or at least I suspect, that she feels a little awkward about kicking me out. Tapping her foot, she says she's still working on a project with a deadline. We make plans to go to Baja on the weekend.

The morning is foggy and cold. As I unpack my duffle bag and suitcase, and stow two cardboard boxes at the Coastside Inn, I'm trying to ignore this slight churning in my stomach. I suppose it's natural. I've taken a leap into empty space and have no idea where I'm going to land. I drive ten minutes to Torrey Pines Park. Besides the pocket sanctuary of Randy's Trail, Torrey Pines is just about the only small bit of wilderness still left on the coast. I walk among the pines that now drip fog on the sage and manzanita in the sandy gullies, so that their smell is animal. I don't remember ever being tired when I walked in this chaparral for days at a time as a boy, but now my feet feel heavy and the mist is cold on my neck and shoulders. I want worse than anything to be lying in Lisa's bed, feeling the heat of her skin.

The trial begins, I say to myself. If I give in to this fear and loneliness, everything is lost. My rebirth is still a distant goal, and the way forward depends on the strength of my will. It begins to come over me that I've taken on the job of constructing my life, and that leads me to a second thought: that I've always been a mere actor in someone else's play. As I walk, I become absorbed once more in thoughts of the dream that wants to become my waking world — the dream shared with Lisa of a vitality unbounded by any necessity but life and death.

The thought absorbs me; or rather, it focuses me on the here and now, on the colors of the chaparral and the steady rhythm of my footsteps on the path. I don't know how much time has passed when a jackrabbit startles me, bolting from the brush ten feet ahead. Now I notice that I'm walking fast, my body loose and full of energy. Turning off the sandy trail, I let out a howl and begin to run, zigzagging through the close brush.

This evening Lisa is in meetings, so I go to La Cantina to look for Sid and Louise, and there they are. Sid, I discover, buys and sells local art and handicrafts. He's moving his business to a new shop in La Jolla, and he could use a helper for a couple of weeks — minimum wage, of course. Fragile stuff needs to be packed, hauled, unpacked, assembled, installed; and he himself needs to be available to talk with customers, look at new pieces, keep track of the market. Maybe this could even grow into something. We agree that I'll show up at his gallery in two days. He seems pleased.

As it turns out, the work is appropriate — physical, leaving the mind and spirit free, yet with a touch of the spiritual too, involving, however vaguely, artistic values. Again, I feel as though a path is being cleared for me. What if Lisa were to end up painting stuff for him? Physically, handling art is a lot harder than I thought it would be. A lot of stuff is heavier than it looks. A chunk of stone or glass the size of your head weighs a lot more than your head, and those big paintings don't have handles on them. It makes a big difference that you don't dent, chip, scratch, bend, or puncture anything, and you find yourself straining to move delicately the same weight you could move easily if it were sheet rock or cordwood.

After my second day of work, I call Lisa.

"How's the laboring man?"

"Experiencing the mortality of the body."

"What's that like?"

"It's good. It's basic. If you make a mistake, you know it right away. You learn to think with your hands and back, and to feel with your bones and your butt."

"Would your bones and your butt like to feel some fettucine Alfredo tonight? I brought enough for two home from the deli."

We sit in her kitchen listening to a Nat King Cole CD, both of us too tired to talk much, but she wants to know about my job.

"The work reminds me of a summer slob job for three fifty an hour I quit after a week when I was a kid, except that when I was a kid I had a lot more stamina. A lot of Sid's stuff is awkward as hell to handle."

"Sid's stuff costs a fortune, as I recall," she says. "Does it make you nervous to touch it?"

"I don't think about the cost much. I just think about doing my work well. A lot of it is just like any other kind of fragile merchandise."

"I don't see how you can think of art that way," she says. "Mediocre art, maybe, but what about stuff that really moves you?"

"What do you mean by art that really moves you? I guess nothing of what I see in Sid's store really does that for me. I think people buy it because they want to own art, mostly."

"That's a great question. What really does move me? I have to feel that the artist has done something heroic — something that no ordinary mortal like me could possibly do."

"Such as what?"

She's frowning with concentration, her eyes closed. "I don't know. Bring real feeling into our lives. To do that, an artist has to care deeply about the meanings of things. That kind of caring can bring pleasure, I suppose, but most of the time I think it has to bring with it terrible suffering." She opens her eyes and smiles self-consciously. "It's a cliché, I know. Overeducated people like you and me have heard it so often. It's the stereotype of the great artist. Have we learned to scoff at it?"

"No, no. Go on." What she's saying fascinates and confuses me, scares me, actually. I'm not exactly sure why.

"But our cynicism really only makes it more beautiful, do you see? In a desperate world, to create is to resist despair. Art is an insurrection. Do you think that's silly?"

"No. Of course not." I want to ask her if she thinks dreams are an art form, that we can sacrifice our own complacency to a dream and become artists ourselves, drinking in the feeling from our own unlived lives. But I'm afraid of the answer. She seems very far away right now.

"Sometimes I wonder myself." She hunches her shoulders and toys with her fork.

I feel miserable, not just about the distance between us, but about my cowardice in the face of it. She's right about our being overeducated. A primitive wouldn't even notice that she's . . . she's what? The word *refined* presents itself. We sit here quietly for a while, and I can feel her begin to relax.

A faraway look comes into her eyes, the same look she had the first day we met, when she told me about her childhood. "I wish I was on the other side of this divide," she says, "this divide between the artist and the world. I wish I was free of the fear that keeps us cynics from going into our dream, from living it, from feeling the isolation and the pain that goes with being fully alive."

She looks at me. This moment is way, way beyond words. "That's exactly what I'm struggling with now," I say. "Meeting you forced me to face that divide, to throw myself against it. Will you come with me?" She looks away. Nat King Cole is singing "Walkin' My Baby Back Home." She says, "How are you at back rubs?" She gets up and moves toward the bedroom, and I feel the nearness of something that moves me to tears. I never want this moment to end. I want it to be here at my fingertips forever.

When we wake up early in the morning, she kisses my hands and says, "I believe you could make art with these."

You could make art with these. Nothing I could say would express the quiet elation that I feel right now. You could make art with these. The suffering artist is vanquished by the primitive man — the man who needs nothing but the simple action of his cunning on whatever is at hand. You could make art with these. I make a mental note: When your brain offers you something scary, smack it with a stick before it gets hold of your mouth.

I'm packing a group of colorful, fantastical human and animal figures in Sid's shop, among the last things to move. They're not quite life-size, made of something that feels like light plastic. They're kitschy, but well crafted. There's a pair of leering cherubs of the Victorian sort, but instead of the usual cornucopias of fruit, one holds a carrot and a diet book; the other, a squash racket and swim goggles. There's a send-up of Magritte's *Son of Man*, with the apple replaced by an iPad with an apple core on its screen. There's a unicorn with a microwave antenna instead of a horn, and a salacious-looking mermaid with a tattoo of a fat bald sailor in his skivvies over her entire chest. Sid comes in while I'm packing them.

"A local workshop makes those," he says. "They're getting to be popular."

"What are they made of?"

"Fiberglass."

"What do they sell for?"

"Let's see. This one's twenty-four five. They're all in that neighborhood."

"Twenty-five thousand each?"

"They're signed one-of-a-kinds."

What did Lisa say about the productivity of suffering? It disgusts me a little that people will pay that much money for something so trivial. They evoke no real emotion, only a certain smugness — smugness for being hip enough to get the joke, smugness for having enough money to buy and display it. In this sense, they're really useless. Looking at them, it occurs to me that uselessness is really what they're about. They're a statement. Envy me: I have more stuff, expensive and useless, than you have.

Sid is helping me with the packing. "We've only got a couple more days of work to do, Ashton. I'm glad you're here, I really am. Got plans for what you'll do after this?"

"Got any suggestions?"

"Just one. Don't try to make a living as an artist. If you're rich to start with, it might at least take you a while to go broke; but if you start out poor, as most artists do, you have to be lucky as hell *and* willing to whore in order to make it."

"I have no intention of that." I'm thinking: As an artist you have two choices — according to Lisa, a life of suffering that might lead nowhere and, following Sid's reasoning, a life of pandering to other people's vanity. Unless, of course, you're Picasso or Mozart.

CHAPTER SEVEN

THE TE MOKA TULA

After a week of this work, I no longer feel tired at the end of the day; in fact, I have a new kind of energy that comes from being more aware of my body and its growing strength. I'm going surfing after work most days, that mellow time of day when the low sun casts a dazzling reflection over the sea and backlights ragged black strings of shorebirds heading off to their night roosts. When there's no surf, I run for miles along the sand. I can do that in the semi-dark on a pebbled beach without stepping on a stone.

As I work, or run, or eat, or shower, I think about Lisa. I still don't really know who she is. I saw her at a distance at the supermarket one day, and I immediately knew it was her from the clothes — a striking yellow-and-blue-print skirt over gold tights, a wine-brown scarf thrown around her neck. She reads mysteries, poetry, translations of African and Latin American works, popular science, erotica. In bed she learns quickly what thrills me and how to do it, but she teaches me what she wants as well, and she can be demanding. She doesn't hide the fact that she's had several casual affairs since her divorce, but no serious loves. She has two friends, women who share her taste for British comedy and avant-garde art. She's happy being alone. Her father died several years ago. She's not religious, but she talks almost daily on the phone with her mother in St. Louis, who's the busy president of something called The Episcangels. She's sensitive about women's rights, but she doesn't like political conversation.

We haven't really talked about our feelings for each other. She often asks me what I like and why, what kinds of relationships I've had with The

Hun and Thelma, with Ysabel, my lovers, my students. It troubles her that I quit my job. I often tell her that I have no plans other than to learn to live every day to its fullest, but she either doesn't hear me or doesn't believe me, because she keeps asking what my plans are.

What's in the back of my mind constantly is that she'll get bored with all of this and end it, something I still don't know how to prevent. For now, her behavior is telling me that the main thing is not to seem too eager to see her. I call her a couple of times a week; we see each other most weekends. In the long run, it's a strain. I know that her dream of the Zogon is still tremendously important to her. The first time we met, she herself gave it as the explanation of her love for Randy's Trail. I know that, essentially, I *was* the Zogon of the dream. What she experienced as my power was real; it was the thing I lost when I left that place and that life. I know there's some connection between her dream and her feelings for me now; if that wasn't true she wouldn't have given herself to me. But it's a fragile connection, one that I must, must, must make stronger.

On the morning we're supposed to close out the old shop, I find Sid there conversing with a character whose looks are so odd as to invite close inspection. He's almost short enough to suggest the word *dwarf*, but sinewy, with a shaved head and what look like large opals set in his upper incisors. His eyes are watery blue-gray, but his skin is the color and texture of a saddle bag. He and Sid are contemplating a new delivery — a collection of primitive carvings, lying on the floor amid cardboard and plastic. There are powerful-looking masks and fetishes of various sizes, made up of dark wood, crude paint, shells, bright feathers, and worked bone. One piece is unusually large. A cigar-shaped object about ten feet long, its entire surface is intricately incised with grotesque animal figures and geometric designs. The point of it is adorned with a wicked-looking barbed spear the size of a carving knife.

Sid introduces the guy as Russell, merchant seaman by trade, collector by instinct, just back from New Guinea. I ask Russell what these things are called.

"In the old days, they were ritual and war items," says Russell. To my surprise, he has an Etonian accent. "Food hooks, spear throwers, lime tubes. Some of these may have been made for sale, but they're authentic. I got them from the Raapa Uu people of the Upper Sepik."

"Never heard of them," Sid says.

Russell chuckles. "There's no reason why you would. They're not on the art circuit. Anyway, many locals know them as the *Checheche*," he says.

"They have two names?"

"Many Sepik people do. *Checheche* means a certain kind of ritual, old boy — a rather, ahh, startling ritual the Raapa Uu are famous for."

"What is this big thing here?" I ask. "It looks a bit like my old surfboard."

Russell frowns. "A surfboard, yes. That piece is a real prize, the world's only *te moka tula*." He pauses, as if lost in memory. "A few decades ago, when head-hunting was still in full swing there, the Raapa Uu fled the Middle Sepik into the foothills of the Star Mountains, where they came in contact with the people of the Western Highlands. They kept what they could of their art and culture, but they had to adapt to the drier environment and way of their neighbors."

"Their highland neighbors were surfers?"

He frowns again. "No. There's a big difference between the floodplain and the mountains. While the Middle Sepik is pure Melanesian, the Western Highlands is a little like your idea of the American Wild West, if you substitute pigs for cows and longbows for guns. Like Tombstone in its day, the place is still too remote for law enforcement. Ritual warfare has never stopped. Even different villages of the same tribe can fall out and start killing each other over a small insult, or an unpaid debt, but most of all, over witchcraft."

"This thing is a weapon?" asks Sid.

"I'm coming to that, old boy. Indirectly, I suppose you could say it's a weapon. In some way or another, everything in that place is a weapon. War is the warp and weft of the culture. Villages try to protect themselves by trading. They build trenches to repel attacks, but they also build up networks of allies through the exchange of goods. Swine, mostly. One doesn't trade to get rich: the idea is to give away more than one gets. You gain power that way. This system, *moka*, is an obsession with certain men; they spend their whole lives becoming what's called 'big men,' building up political power by amassing and trading pigs, women, yams, and pearl shells."

"Aha. Shells. So this thing is some kind of water craft," Sid says.

"Yes and no. The Raapa Uu don't ordinarily go near the sea. A trip down the Sepik is a perilous thing, a journey through enemy territory. But they used to go there long ago, and in their lore, it's a great source of power. No, not a water craft. From what I could gather, a group of Baptist missionaries came through my villages a couple of decades ago. These chaps often bring their own magic to help with the business of conversion. They bring motion pictures." He pauses again. He has this unnerving habit of going absolutely quiet, then tensing, cocking his head to one side, and shooting his pale eyes around, as if he's listening for a faint sound. Meanwhile Sid has pulled an envelope from his pocket and is scribbling notes.

"From the stories the old villagers told me, I surmised that one of the movies they saw must have been a surf riders' travelogue. Shots of men riding those huge waves, like the ones you get in Hawaii. Well, the Raapa Uu had never seen anything like that — it created a lot of excitement in the village. For many days the elders sat in the spirit house and debated the meaning of it, and they came up with their own idea. To them, the film explained the wealth and power of the missionaries. It showed, they said, an episode from a Raapa Uu myth about the origins of pearl shells. In the myth, the sea god, Dukum, steals the beautiful nymph Kuibi, daughter of the river god, Ba, while she is diving for shells. Dukum transforms her into a shark. Ba is of course very angry. Using magic, he makes huge waves that kill the fish and animals of the sea, until finally Dukum is defeated and changes Kuibi back into a woman so that she returns from the sea with a great boatload of shells. This myth is enacted in the Raapa Uu war ritual called Ba Mataa.

"In the view of the elders," he goes on, "the surfboards in the film were the magic weapons that Ba used for making the huge waves that defeated Dukum. The meaning was clear — if they could obtain a surfboard, they would have its power. As near as I could make out, the village resorted to a familiar way of dealing with outsiders; they took one of the missionaries hostage, saying they would either kill him or release him in exchange for a surfboard. The government had to send troops to get him back, but that wasn't the end. There was a major 'big man' in the village by the name of Kasoi. He had his people build this object, to use in the Ba Mataa ritual.

Of course it was kept hidden in the spirit house. The male dancers would do a 'surfriding' dance in order to transform themselves into Ba's warriors in the ritual. See the arrow point on the end of it? That's made of cassowary bone, same as their war arrows."

"How were you able to acquire it?" asks Sid.

Again, Russell freezes and glances around. His voice drops almost to a whisper. "They were going to destroy it. It turns out the bloody thing is too powerful. You see, the trading system only works if it stays in balance. If one trader starts to acquire too much power, it frightens his friends and angers his enemies. After they built it, everyone wanted to trade with Kasoi, and he became enormously powerful. The system began to break down. Big men in other villages began to arrange attacks on Kasoi's people, and they were afraid. They tried to convince him to destroy the *te moka tula,* but he refused. Of course they ended up killing Kasoi — his own people."

"Why didn't they burn it or something?" I ask.

"They were worried about how to destroy it in a way that wouldn't anger the gods. They talked about this constantly, in fact. Ordinarily, I don't lie to these people; they're my friends. But in this case, I felt a judicious lie would be the kind thing. I told them I would take it with me down the Sepik River to Wewak, and offer it to Dukum, taking it far out to sea. That seemed to satisfy them."

"Why did they trust you?" I ask. The whole thing strikes me as a fantastic fable.

"I speak Raapa. I know their ways."

"And how do we know you didn't make all this up?"

He grins, flashing his opal-studded teeth. "You don't, old boy," he says. "But if I may, I'd like to give both of you a piece of advice. Treat this thing as if what I told you were true. Some of these ritual objects have uncanny properties." With that he stands and picks up his knapsack. "They don't, however, magically fill *my* hut with pigs and shells. I've got to get back to my ship." He and Sid walk out the back.

I squat down next to the *te moka tula* and examine it. The design seems to be an abstract human face, the details made up of smaller animals and humanoid figures. There's nothing particularly striking about it. But as I look, my attention gradually goes to the geometric designs that fill all the blank spaces. There is something strange about these designs. Far from being mere decoration, they're apparently the expression of some ineffable power, the language of spirits, and I can't seem to take my eyes away. Staring at them like this, I begin to feel an alien presence that I can't describe. It's not a pleasant feeling. I remember one other time when I had it: hiking in the Cascade Range, I looked across the valley below me at Mount Shasta. At the time, I didn't know that the Shasta Indians had worshiped that peak, but I had the overwhelming feeling that the mountain was watching me. Russell promised its creators that he would destroy this thing, yet here it is. Does it have a will of its own? If so, what does it want?

I look up and see Sid standing next to me. I don't know how long he's been there. "What's wrong?" he asks. "You look like you just saw a ghost."

"I don't know. I think I did."

Sid chuckles. "The ghost of Kasoi? Unless he can walk by himself, let's get him packed up with the rest of this stuff. The gala opening is in two days, remember. My van'll take the rest of this in one load, I think."

I don't want to lift this thing. Intimacy with it seems to require some communication, some formality. Besides, it must weigh about a hundred pounds. Lifting what appears to be the top end, with difficulty I balance it. "I know your power," I say under my breath. "I respect you. Please give me permission to move you to a more dignified place," and placing my shoulder at the center, I let the stern swing up so that my muscles are relaxed under its balanced weight, the way I used to do my giant surfboard. The long-forgotten feeling floods my body with strength and pleasure, and the *te moka tula* feels almost light as I stride easily with it toward the back exit to the parking lot.

Then something else happens. By the time I get to the parking lot, the weight of the *te moka tula* has become unbearable. It feels as though the twenty yards I've carried it has actually been twenty miles. Not only is each step a struggle now, but my mind has shifted into that state of fatigue — you feel it when you've driven all night — that state where time seems to slow to a creep, and movements that are usually automatic become matters of life or death. Should I place my foot here, or there, to avoid falling? Looking around, I can't recognize Sid's van in the lot, and I begin to panic. Can I put the thing down without dropping it? If I do, will I ever be able to pick it up again? If I don't put it down, eventually I'm going to fall underneath it. In this mental state, Sid's silver Jaguar convertible suddenly presents itself in front of me, seeming to offer me its hood as a resting place for my load. As I bend forward to ease the point of the thing gently onto the gleaming metal, my back simply folds under its weight, and with a sickening crash the *te moka tula* launches itself through the Jaguar's windshield into the driver's seat. Although this is not what I intended, still I feel some relief to realize that it's firmly stuck there, and I can actually let go of it without any further consequences. I'm struck by the fact that the windshield doesn't merely break like an ordinary window; the entire thing shatters into jewel-sized pieces, which adhere together and fold inward, imitating a flexible membrane or a suit of mail. I look inside the car. Incredibly, the soft yellow leather of the driver's seat has resisted the advance of the barbed cassowary-bone arrow point at the tip of the huge fetish. The whole scene strikes me as some kind of magic, the sort of thing that couldn't happen unless a supernatural force had intended it.

Now that I've let go of my load, fear of Sid's reaction seems to clear my head. There's no way I can extricate the object from the Jaguar and carry it to his van. It seems to me that if I can roll the car over to the van, with the terrible object stuck there as it is, I can then simply pull it out of the one vehicle and slide it into the other. I open the Jag's door, let the brake off, and begin to push, but without the power steering, it proves difficult to maneuver the car. I can, however, back it in the direction of the van, and I decide that this is better than simply giving up and calling Sid. Luckily, there is a slight downslope toward the van, and the Jaguar begins to roll backward by itself. Keeping pace alongside it with the door open, I can easily reach in and pull the handbrake when I get near my destination.

The Jaguar has its own idea about a trajectory. I'm struggling with the steering wheel as I hear hurried footsteps and look up as Sid comes alongside. "Holy shit!!" "Holy fucking shit!!" This seems like a good time to pull the Jag's handbrake, a move I haven't had occasion to practice. With a small screech of tires, the car stops so suddenly that I fall to the ground, but not before I see the *te moka tula* lunge forward, plunging its ugly arrow point deep into the leather of the driver's seat.

It takes Sid and me a good half hour to extricate the *te moka tula* from the Jaguar, and the result isn't pretty. One admires the artistry of the New Guinea tribes, whose barbed arrows are evidently designed to destroy their targets. Of course I tell Sid to deduct the damage from my paycheck. He is typically princely about it, noting that the artwork at least seems unharmed, and offering to file an insurance claim, but he's unusually quiet the rest of the day. I worry that it has taken the shine off our relationship. Beyond that, the meaning of the incident eats at me. Is there actually some malevolent power in the New Guinea fetish, or is my age mocking my intentions?

Lisa's coming to the gala opening of the new gallery. For weeks I've been eager to see her reaction, but now I regret inviting her. Before the Jaguar incident I also told Ysabel about the opening, and she told Blake. The two of them seize on this as an excuse to come and check up on me, which means they'll meet Lisa. I guess this was going to happen eventually, but the timing is bad. My mission remains far off, and they — or at least Ysabel — are baggage from the life I left behind. Besides, I'm now unemployed again. The expected request from Sid to stay on doesn't materialize.

The gala is on Friday evening. Ysabel and Blake arrive just after lunch, and we walk on the beach, reminiscing about the old Del Mar, catching up on each other's lives. They want to know about Lisa. I tell them we're just friends, and ignore the look I get from Ysabel.

"You look strong, at least," she says. "Disreputable, but healthy and strong."

"I can't afford a soft life."

Blake says, "Yeah. Looking at you, I gotta get back here, Prof. I mean, the college kids are nice and all that, but I feel like I've done that, you know? Like I'm starting to rot again."

Sid has hired a classical chamber trio and catered finger food and wine. His friends are the first to arrive — myself and my companions, Louise from La Cantina, a couple of guys I've seen around the shop. Then the artists and patrons trickle in. There's a glass blower — a black guy who looks like a pro linebacker, with hands the size of shovels. There's a sculptor couple, elegant white-haired people from Mexico whose work is already well known. I make friends with a painter, a wiry little man in disgraceful clothes, whose pupils, for some reason, are the size of half dollars. The sizable group of expensively dressed and coifed folks over fifty I take to be patrons.

After an hour I spot Lisa, talking with a couple of patrons she knows. She's wearing a cocktail dress of amazing iridescent silver-blue material that looks like shattered glass, set off by lavender suede purse and shoes, and her signature scarf coiled around her fine neck, this one of silver silk. Deciding not to intrude, I wave to her, and a bit later she finds me with my companions, just as Blake is shoving in his mouth a huge Vietnamese egg roll, which he seems to have dipped in hummus. Ysabel has had a couple of glasses of wine, and for a split second her jaw drops as I begin the introductions. Lisa picks up on it and smiles. "I always overdress, I'm sorry. Overdress, or underdress, or dis-dress," she says.

"You're stunning," Ysabel says, then pointedly turns and surveys me, from my tangled long hair to my bare feet. Blake, thank God, is speechless, his mouth immobilized around its international cargo.

As we wander through the gallery, I wish I were alone with Lisa; I want to study her reactions. "I'm glad you asked me here, Ashton," she says. "I should stay abreast of styles. Are you going to keep working with Sid?"

"I don't think so."

"I thought you liked each other, that he wanted you to stay."

"He hasn't asked me. Anyway, I'm not worried about surviving. When you're attuned to life, things work out." She falls quiet. I'm not sure she heard what I said.

Blake, who may never have been in an art gallery in his life, is the vocal one. "Look at this!" he gasps in front of a set of Hindu miniatures. "Smaller is better, just like with computers!" His lopsided grin has spread from ear to ear. In front of a whimsical wire sculpture he stops again and grins: "Three-dimensional doodle." At length we find ourselves looking at the satirical fiberglass statuettes I had discussed with Sid — the odes to uselessness. Blake looks at the price, squats down and studies their construction closely, then turns and looks at me. "Dude," he says, "these are made of fiberglass."

"I know."

"They're worth twenty-five K apiece."

"I know."

"I've built about fifty surfboards. I can do fiberglass."

"You need a studio to do stuff like that, Blake. Worse yet, you need ideas."

"Me and you could do this," he says. "We could start small. Small studio and big ideas."

"We're not artists, man. We don't know anything about making or selling art. We don't have space, or tools, or connections . . ." I look at Ysabel and Lisa. They're listening but I can't read their thoughts. Ysabel reads mine.

"Ashton, you want to be a free spirit, to take on the world with your bare hands and your wits, don't you? You have to take chances, don't you? Why can't you just think about it?"

"Right on!" says Blake. He's almost dancing. "We can borrow a few bucks to get started. We could make a mint. *A mint!*"

"Let's talk about this later," I say. "At the very least it's going to take some serious thought."

"Does it interfere with your *plans?*" says Lisa.

Sid and Louise walk up. I introduce them and say, "Sid, what was it you said to me the other day about getting into art? Something about having to be crazy to try it?"

"If there weren't any lunatics, I'd be out of business," Sid says. "Luckily, there are thousands of them within a twenty-mile radius. However, I can always use more."

"Show us your favorite things, Sid," says Lisa.

"The stuff you're looking at isn't bad, from a dealer's point of view. It's unusual: it's exciting, it's contemporary."

"What makes it exciting and contemporary?" asks Lisa.

"The fact that people with money want it," says Ysabel.

Sid laughs. "People with money *and taste.*"

Sid takes us through the gallery, talking about the works and the customers. Lisa drops behind and I join her. "You're not even going to think about it, are you?" she asks.

"What? Going into the sculpture business with Blake?"

"It's a compliment that someone with craft skills wants to work with you."

"Don't you think that stuff is vulgar?"

"It's fun! Self-conscious kitsch, satire."

"I prefer sincerity. When satire becomes too easy, it's simply fake. *Real* kitsch at least is cheap."

"So. It's beneath you to produce art that people will pay for? You're more arrogant than I thought."

"Are you trying to *reform* me? You talked once about the artist as hero. What do you think of one who makes stuff he doesn't believe in, just for money?"

"Lots of great ones produce knock-offs of their popular stuff so they can live for the real work. Even a so-called commercial artist is better than someone who's too proud — or too something — to produce anything at all."

"What is this? Why is my productivity suddenly an issue?"

She turns and glares at me, searching for words. "It's not sudden, Ashton. You seem to think that you project some mystical power, some charisma, that you can draw people to you just by breathing in and out. Well, I won't be part of that. I don't want to play. People are what they do, Morse. Get a life." Turning away, she walks quickly through the gallery and out the door.

Should I run after her? No, let her go. This is not the Lisa of the Zogon dream. This is another Lisa: the missionary, the savage-tamer, the evil twin, the one I thought I had defeated the day I arrived and took the real Lisa by surprise on Randy's Trail.

CHAPTER EIGHT

NEW GUINEA?

Nothing piques a hangover quite like waking to the smell of burnt chili beans. Blake has apparently left a pot on my hot plate and passed out on his sleeping bag. I can barely keep from heaving as I get up and put the pot in the bathroom sink, throw open the door, and stagger onto the veranda of the Coastside Inn. Yesterday's conversation is already on my mind, an imaginary morning front page: *Sleeping Beauty, Still in Coma, Beheads Rescuer. Man Who Can't Heat Canned Food Seeks Fortune in Art.* The sun is high and the heat is damp and sullen. Gradually my nausea subsides and my head clears a little. I need to get away from everybody. Here comes the motel manager. He looks like he's already smelled the chili. Now he sees me standing here in my BVDs, and it's too late to retreat. He asks if I can stop by the office when I'm dressed. Well, I'm tired of living here anyway. I go pull on my trunks and walk down to the beach without waking Blake.

Lisa might have just been in a bad mood yesterday, but I don't think that's it. There was a lot of steam behind what she said. I've been through breakups before — Delfin, The Hun, that crazy student what's-her-name. The task at hand is to remove the spell of Lisa's wicked missionary self and reawaken her to the truth of her dream, which must become our shared truth. No. Somehow the dream truth has to be transformed, to be made real again in the present moment; and that can't be done by dealing with the missionary in her. One thing she said is true, though: we are what we do. My sin has been the lack of action. Not any bent-kneed action at

the altar of respectability as the missionary imagines, but the opposite —
convincing insurrection.

Damn, I can still smell those beans. I wade into the cool water and
push my way past the breakers. As I turn on my back and drift on the
swells, above me I study the complex patterns in the cirrus clouds. I seem
to recognize repeating patterns; yes, like those of the great New Guinea
talisman, the *te moka tula*. I feel a strange foreboding. Something stirs in
the back of my mind, but I can't bring it forward. I'm tired and my head
aches.

It dawns on me that my so-called conquest of Lisa was nothing of
the kind; she's taken me as a plain sex object, keeping her feelings under
close guard. I'm just a passing, if passable, screw to her, unconnected to
the power of her Zogon dream. It's an ancient and often-told story, my
son. In the Norse sagas, Sigurd first finds Brunhild dressed in the battle
gear of a warrior. With one stroke of his sword he splits her armor, setting
her free as a lover and a sorceress. The Lisa whose sweet body I've come to
know is still wearing the armor of convention, interested in her work, her
comforts, what passes for culture and refinement in a humdrum world,
almost unaware of the imaginative child that crept out for a moment the
day I met her on Randy's Trail. I have to find and wake that child at any
cost, not just for my own sake, but for hers as well. If I fail, I abandon
both of us to slow death: drifting, passionless, toward our barren and
complacent old age.

Now, for the first time, as I see this, I'm deeply disturbed to find that
I love her, or rather, I love the child who keeps me in her dream. Too alive
to thrive among the Missionaries of Cool, that child has allowed herself
to be kidnapped by the Lisa I saw yesterday, the one who dreams, if at all,
the collective dream of bankers and their proper wives. That child is my
salvation, and I will find a way to bring her back to herself.

In the meantime, I have to survive. My work for Sid is almost finished
and I haven't looked for a job. I leave the water and go back to the Coastside
Inn. Blake, mamboing around the room with my Maná CD at full blast,
spoon in hand, stops long enough to offer me the last of the burnt beans,
into which he has apparently stirred a can of sardines in mustard sauce.
"Do you know Gordo Toole?" he asks.

"Sure, it's a pornographic machine shop, right?"

"Everybody knows Gordo, man, he's the dude who builds Greenberries."

"Greenberries?"

"Greenberries! The hot green boards! Down in Mission Beach! I worked for him for a while. In his workshop he's got the stuff we need to build fiberglass sculptures. If we cut him into the profits, he might help us get started."

"Listen, I gotta look for a paying job, starting now. So do you, unless you go back to running your whorehouse. The sculpture idea sucks. If you were really, really lucky, it would take you at least a year to see any profit from that. Unless you find a genie in a bottle, it'll end up being a costly hobby."

He almost chokes on a sardine. "Unless *I* find a genie? You're not up for this? If the two of us do it together, man . . ."

"Wait, wait. Right now, this is nothing but a pipe dream, it's not a plan. A lot of work needs to be done. Convince me that I should even think about it. Prove to me it'll work. What'll it cost to get started, where are you getting the money, where are you getting your ideas? I want to see examples of the work. I want to hear people with money say they'll buy your stuff. Geez. Lisa's at me, you're at me, Ysabel's at me, about what? I don't see it."

He stiffens. "Okay. I thought you were all into making things happen for yourself."

"Making things happen and chasing rainbows are different things. What's happened for *you* lately, anyway?"

As soon as I say this, I regret it, but it's too late. He sits there with his head down for a minute or two. Then he says, "You know something? You're right. You changing your life was like an example to me, you know? I been thinking, Hey, if Ashton can do it, Blake can do it." He gets up and starts pacing around the room, stops and looks out the window. "Now it looks like you're not exactly doing it, Prof. But that doesn't mean I can't do it, does it?"

"Of course it doesn't. Hey, I know that what I said just now sounded, you know, smartass. You can do whatever you want, if you know what it is and put your mind to it. I just know this isn't what I want to do right now."

"Think you might change your mind?"

Now I'm feeling like a shit for not encouraging him from the start. It wouldn't have cost me much. In fact, it would have saved me that scene with Lisa. "I don't think I'll change my mind," I say. "But Blake, follow your own dream. I'm behind you, man. If I can, I'll help you. Go find this Greenberries guy. Maybe he *can* help you get started."

So we look up the number, and Blake calls Gordo Toole, right there and then. Toole remembers him, and when he invites Blake over to talk, Blake looks scared. "Don't worry," I tell him, "this is just your first shot. If it doesn't work out, try another tack. Maybe Sid will help, who knows?"

It's ironic, isn't it? I start off with a plan, a plan to reinvent myself, to find that vital center that somehow got away from me way back when. Now I'm at a standstill; I have no ideas whatsoever. In the meantime, Blake, the original *mañana* man, is actually taking steps to reinvent his life. He has an idea, at least. And who am I to snicker at a crackpot scheme? If anybody's flying on blind faith, it's me.

That afternoon I go back to Randy's Trail, starting at the bottom to avoid Lisa's house. As my feet retrace the familiar ground, in my mind I can see Lisa's face when she talked about the Zogons — that enchanted expression. She had it again when she showed me the painting she did of the trail. What am I brooding about? Our meeting was a clear sign, and I'm following it. I thought this journey would be harder than it's been, for Chrissake. At every turn, I've felt doors open for me, and they will again. Maybe the next door has already opened, and I only need to walk through it.

An intoxicating smell fills my lungs. I look up and see a huge, ancient, wind-blown pine I hadn't noticed before. Its branches are twisted into fantastic forms. I'm drawn to it, and as I approach, I see that the deep grooves in its bark suggest some kind of runic script, like the figures on the *te moka tula*. The thought gradually comes to me: My vision has been to recapture the spontaneous strength of the primitive life, but my vision of the primitive has been too simple. People who haven't lost that openness to experience, to unvarnished sensuality, are aware not only of their own power but of the power of the world around them as well. Their ability to engage that magic is what I've overlooked. Everything is related. People who are attuned to it can *read* the bark of ancient trees, the patterns in the cirrus clouds, the embers of a fire.

Now I realize why I met Russell and heard the story of the *te moka tula*. My mission is to save Lisa, the child dreamer, from the civilizing missionary who confronted me in the gallery yesterday. All right: In Russell's story the river princess has been transformed into a shark by the sea god. Her father (was his name Ba?) uses his magical powers to force the sea god to free her. Russell's people use this story to gain power over the human world by way of the *te moka tula*. The very outrageousness of it fills me with joy. What I need now is an outrageous plan. I've got to find Russell.

It's now about noon. Sid doesn't answer the phone at the store, so I call his house. I tell him I find the New Guinea art fascinating (which is true) and want to talk to Russell. He gives me the name and phone number of Russell's ship — the New Micronesia. The number proves to be the office of the shipping line in Oakland, but they put me through. I explain who I am to the ship's operator, and ask to speak to Russell. He says Russell's at work on deck, but agrees to pass the message. In the evening, Russell calls.

"Your stories about your New Guinea people were fascinating," I say. "I want to learn more about them."

The Raapa Uu?"

"Yes, the people who made the *te moka tula*. Can I come down and talk to you?"

"That would take some doing right now," he says. "We're three days out of San Diego, due to arrive Hawaii tomorrow, and New Guinea a week from Wednesday. Anyway, there are books on Melanesian art and culture. What do you want to know?"

It hadn't occurred to me that he might be at sea. His voice is perfectly clear, as though he were sitting next door, except that I can hear an intermittent mechanical whirring noise in the background. "I . . . I'm not sure what. It's not any commercial thing. I don't care about trading. I just want to learn something about their way of life."

He's silent for several seconds. "It's deeply interesting," he says. "Do you know anything about the highland people at all?"

"Nothing, I'm sorry to say."

"Well. There's nothing like going there. My partner didn't ship out with me this trip, as it happens. You don't seem like the sort who worries about things — sickness, snakes, spiders, occasional violence, are you? We'll be in Port Moresby for a few days. I suppose if you want to fly down,

I can take you to the highlands. This will be my last trip this year, and I was wanting to go up the Sepik anyway."

"That's really good of you, Russell. I'll meet you in Port Moresby. A week from Thursday, you say?"

"Call me at this number if and when you get there. Meantime, you might visit the library."

I go to the main branch of the library in San Diego the next day. With the exception of some fine anthropological reporting here and there, most of the writing about Papua New Guinea culture is along the lines of *Heart of Darkness*, short on facts and long on cannibalism, strange rituals, and other rarities that Westerners have always loved to imagine lying just beyond the fringe of the Coca-Cola distribution grid. Clearly, I must go there myself.

Looking up flights to Port Moresby, I find there's a discount seat available in two days. With the little money I have left, I reason I can probably hang out cheaper there than here anyway, so I buy it. There's only the question of what to do with my stuff — minimal though it is. I don't have the nerve to ask Lisa if I can leave it at her house, and I haven't even called my mother in a month. I ask Blake if he would mind selling my car and wiring me the money, and keeping my stuff with him till I get back. Good old Blake. I guess I had better write a letter to Mom and an email to Lisa.

Dear Mom, I hope you're well. Of course I am a horrible son for not having contacted you. The main problem has been that I really don't know what to say. You and I have never been able to talk about deeply personal things, in a way, we've been too emotionally involved

[meaning, of course, that she's been too touchy . . .]

to do that comfortably. I've known for some time that I want some major changes in my life, but I haven't known exactly what. I'm on a path of exploration. I'm writing to you tonight because that path is taking me to New Guinea

*for a short while. I want to experience a very different way
of looking at the world, and my study*

[what a distortion!]

*has convinced me that this will be valuable. I promise I'll
contact you as soon as I get back. Try not to worry about me.
I love you. Ashton*

Now for the hard part. I must send Lisa an email. Somehow I doubt
that I can rely on a good internet connection in Port Moresby. I haven't
opened my messages in several days — there's rarely anything but spam
in there anyway — and when I do, I find to my surprise there's a message
from the student siren, Michelle, a voice from the dungeon of my teacher's
conscience.

*Dear Morse, I hope you're doing well, as I am. Your last
email had a pretty major effect on me. At first it made me
sad, because I liked you the way you were — kind, humorous,
idealistic, shy. I didn't want you to go change yourself. I
didn't see how your values could be so different from the way
you lived. Then I realized what an honest thing you were
doing, striving to get rid of things you didn't really believe
in. I hadn't seen that side of you before. That has made me
think about my own relationships and behavior. I realize
now that a lot of people, including me, aren't able to look at
themselves clearly at all, let alone completely change their life
in order to live more idealistically. That's really amazing, I
think. Thanks for saying that I helped, but I wonder if you
give yourself enough of the credit. Taking your course, and
knowing this about you, I feel you are a fine person. I really
regret that we didn't get to know each other better. I guess
you have a whole new life now. I'd like to know about it. I
admire you a lot. Best always, XOXOX Michelle*

P.S.

I actually tried going to school barefoot the other day, just to see what it felt like. Man, the looks I got — but I sort of liked it! There's a rebel in there somewhere.

Of course Michelle belongs to the past, the life I've left behind. It irritates me that this old life comes chasing after me, and I decide not to answer her e-mail. I sat down here, after all, to write to Lisa.

Dear Lisa, Now that I'm about to leave for a month in New Guinea, I realize there's so much I want to discuss with you, and I'm so sad that our relationship isn't okay . . .

No. Too apologetic. Delete.

Dear Lisa, I'm about to leave for a month in New Guinea. This is a part of my journey of self-discovery that I know I have to take. I know it looks to you as though I lack a serious direction or plan in life, but you're wrong . . .

No. Too defensive. Delete. What are the strengths of our relationship? Is sex all? If she loves me, wouldn't I know it? Or is her anger a sign that part of her feels threatened by her feelings for me? Does she know that I love her? Actually, what I feel for her is clearly a kind of love, but it's not what she wants — or rather, not what she *thinks* she wants. And just what is it that she thinks she wants? Someone *responsible*? What did Michelle's e-mail say? I open it again and look. "*. . . kind, humorous, idealistic, shy . . .*" Surely nothing could be farther from the qualities that attracted Lisa to me — both her previous incarnation as the dreamer-child and those few weeks ago, when I took her more or less by storm.

And what, after all, is Michelle saying to me in this e-mail? That she *liked* me as the mild professor, but she feels *moved* by me as the man of action?

Maybe Michelle actually does belong to my new life as well. At any rate, she's offering me friendship, and it would be churlish to turn it down.

Dear Michelle, Thanks for the affirming words, I'm glad to hear you're well. I'm intrigued by your message. You liked the gentle old prof, but now you admire the rebel misfit — in yourself as well as in me. What does that say? I still don't have the life I'm seeking. Tomorrow my search takes me to New Guinea for a month or so. I'll contact you when I get back. Meanwhile, set your rebel free. Feed her with meaningful acts. Good hunting, Ashton

This message pleases me. Why am I unable to speak to Lisa this way? It dawns on me that I've given her my power, and I have to take it back. Again I click on her address, and this time I write:

Dear Lisa, Tomorrow I leave for a month in New Guinea. I go to explore the knowledge of the tribal people, not as a curiosity, but as a basis for a richer life. I take with me treasured feelings for you, and a belief that our relationship is something that will bear fruit in the end. Love, Ashton

This seems to me stilted and self-protective. I want desperately to tell her how I long for her love, but I can't do it. I hit "send," then exit my e-mail and open Word. After an hour I've written a poem:

Our tongues field easily
the everyday un-special
pawn words moved
along the grooves
we follow in to tea.
Likewise we agree
by scanning brows
how far to mark
in words the dark
things anyone must know.

With miracles, not so.
Out of the billion
shutter frames the one
that somehow caught
and holds condensed,

engraved on every breath
pure eloquence,
can never be expressed;
above all alchemy,
we masked and goggled dread
the steel of destiny
whose ore is fired
in the crucible of text.

The fact
of having found
my image bound
in archives of your dream
is now, will be,
my liturgy — fuse lit,
spring cocked,
lips, tongue locked
around a voice whose rise
will ever be unfit
for speaking sanity;
and yes the little madness
in the way you look
at nothing
gives me ecstasy.

I think about sending it to Lisa, but decide against it. I shut down my laptop, unplug it, and put it in the box that Blake will hold for me until I get back.

CHAPTER NINE

UP THE SEPIK

R ussell tilts his head back and lets the warm beer flow down his throat, some of it trickling out the corners of his mouth. "This is a good place to gear up for the Sepik," he says at length, leaning over so that I can hear him over the roar of the surf. The waves aren't large, but they're less than twenty yards upwind of the house, and what a wind blows here in Wewak, scented by the warm sea and the great arc of palms and mangroves crowding the white sand. The shack Russell has rented is little more than a tin roof and a grimy glass windbreak, but a more substantial structure would be out of place here. Wewak's scattering of casual shelters and flyspecked stores seems to say that the mighty Sepik needs no introduction. "Rest up. You can get a mosquito net and quinine in town this afternoon — and iodine for water. The bus doesn't leave till three, from right in front of the general store. We won't get to Pagwi till dark, but we can buy gas and kerosene there in the morning."

With luck, I add to myself. Already I know that everything one says in New Guinea has to be qualified like that. "And you're sure we can get a canoe?"

He shrugs. "It might take a couple of days. I've got rum and playing cards. There are women there, but one has to be careful. Honor packs a sharp machete."

"The women I've seen here have orange teeth and purple gums."

He studies me for a second, then shrugs again. "Yes, the betel nut. Suit yourself. I find them interesting." He takes another long drink of beer. "Have you ever been to Cuba?"

I shake my head.

"The Kararau people of the Sepik here remind me of Cuban cars, you know. Nineteen fifties Chevrolets and DeSotos, dented and painted with kitchen enamel, but running like new. They're the real thing, steel and chrome in a plastic world. Don't be fooled by the orange teeth or the thirdhand T-shirts; the magnificence lies behind their eyes. No Kararau woman would sleep with a man for money. They want to know what you're made of."

"The Raapa Uu — are they Kararau too?"

"They speak a dialect and follow the main social forms."

"Then why go up there? From the way you talk about the Middle Sepik people, I feel they could teach me a good deal."

"The older men still might. They know the words, the medicines. But for all that, the lowland is Christianized. Up there in Raapa Uu country, the spirit world keeps its power pretty much unchallenged." He puts his beer down and does that listening thing with his head cocked to one side. "Of course, this purity has a price. Few strangers go up there, and even fewer come back alive."

I've heard about the violence in the highlands, a vast world almost unbroken by roads and unpatrolled by the agents of what is loosely called civilization. Wiwak might be an indication that a lot of naive thinking went into this adventure. I had visualized a real town with paved streets, sidewalks, and telephones, not this eddy of threadbare humanity around a sparse collection of crude necessities.

The highlands? It surprises me to realize I had painted myself a mental picture of a tribal Eden — a dangerous Eden, but still one where a strong and well-prepared traveler with a good guide might want to stay for months at a time among people of unspoiled simplicity. Now, I'm beginning to see that the contrast between my world and theirs transforms us both: To them I'm an inscrutable being — remote and foreign in thought and speech, amazingly wealthy. To me they are suddenly the unlucky victims of history, whose arduous and narrow lives are reproduced endlessly thanks to the lack of almost everything I take for granted. Now I can see why strangers like me might be foolish to go into the highlands. True, Russell is not completely a stranger, and neither of us has much to tempt a gang of bandits, but we are, after all, white men.

The bus engine smokes and screams as we climb into the coastal hills. It's jammed to the gunwales, and many were left behind with their burdens on their heads — sacks of sugar, machetes, patent medicines in string bags, iron adze blades, stacks of old newspapers, lengths of plastic hose around their shoulders, bundles of used clothes, parts for an outboard motor, magazines. I guess few white people ride the bus, but our fellow passengers regard us with a kind of idle curiosity, as though we were a couple of unusual hats. I instinctively like these quiet people of the Middle Sepik. I do feel I could learn a great deal from them, although I have little idea what. Russell points with his chin at the back of a young man standing next to us. The entire back is covered with an orderly pattern of heavy scars. "Initiation," he says. "They do it with a bamboo knife."

Two hours out, we stop at a market. Fresh coconuts, mangos, bananas, peanuts, cigarettes of local tobacco rolled in old newspaper (aha!), stacks of betel nuts, cooked plantains with coconut on banana leaves, tomatoes, onions, squash and many greens I can't identify, eggs, net bags made of rough hand-rolled string. To my astonishment, a dozen more people wedge their bodies and their bundles onto the bus; but soon it begins to stop more often along the winding ridges, and in threes and fives the riders step down, until half the seats are empty.

Pagwi is still another surprise. Something that appears even as a dot on a national map must be at least a village, must have at least a post office, a police station, or a church. Pagwi is a small clearing next to the mighty Sepik, which now stretches dimly silver under a half moon. The road ends at the river, near a corrugated metal building with some sort of government sign on it, and a few native huts. The jungle is alive with sounds, the air full of hurrying birds. A great flock of something — very large bats, I think — passes quickly, erratic and low over the water. This is another world; I stand on the muddy bank and feel myself pulled in two directions: On the one hand, another sinking realization of how far I am from my known world; on the other hand, a sense of awe at the great current of life that passes here, a power and majesty that mocks my little comprehension, my puny human powers. Although the surface of the river is serene, it gives off an overwhelming sense of motion, of energy: a great dynamo, a consciousness that one might appease, but never understand or resist.

Some of the bus passengers climb into waiting dugout canoes that silently disappear on the current; we join a dozen others who will wait for dawn, stretched out on a split palmwood platform under a thatched shelter. Russell is instantly asleep, but under my mosquito net I can't escape this turmoil of emotions. If I am to thrive — even to survive — in this haphazard reality, I'll have to become a different person somehow. I'm willing to try, but what will that mean? At the same time, this here-and-nowness, this innocence of expectation, is exactly what I set out half a year ago to find. I knew somehow that this drama was here, waiting for me; I've captured the lead part in it, and whatever happens next I have no choice but to play it out. Here, listening to the jungle frog and bird calls and to the rustling of wind in the roof leaves, one moment I wonder apprehensively what the script is like and how I will learn it; the next moment I embrace the thought that whatever I might have to suffer here is simply a part of the script that I have; I have long since chosen the end of it, without knowing what that end is.

I wake to the smell of wood smoke and the low murmur of voices in early light. I climb out of my net and go find a spot to pee in the tall grass. Several canoes nose up to the bank, their passengers walking quickly to the road where today's bus for Wewak is already idling. When I get back to the shelter, Russell has procured a green coconut and some chewy tortilla-like things without flavor. "Sago cakes, the staple," he says. He borrows a machete and hacks off one end of the coconut. We drink the sweet freshwater, then he breaks it in two and shows me how to use a piece of the husk to spoon out the soft oily meat. Others around us are eating as well.

A middle-aged man sits down cross-legged and offers us a large piece of papaya. I dig in my pocket for something to give him, but Russell is now speaking with him in pidgin, and motions to me that there's no need to pay. I find I can understand a phrase of their conversation here and there. "Git big fella moto makim kano i go fas," for example, isn't too hard: "He has a big motor that makes the canoe go fast." I could learn this language in a couple of weeks. After the two have talked a bit, the man rises and moves off. "There's no life on the river without cooperation," Russell says. "This man says his clan brother has a motor. He will go to Kanganaman and speak to him, and he might come to take us up as far as Yigei. No Kararau will go past there; we'll have to find friends of the Raapa Uu for the next leg."

"When will he come?"

"Maybe tomorrow or the next day. He has a good motor, so he can get here in a few hours once he's ready." One phrase in their conversation needed no translation: "forty-horse Yamaha." That other wizardry, the magic I thought I was leaving behind.

I'm soon glad that Russell brought playing cards and rum. We sit in the shade of the shelter and watch the canoes come and go on the river. Russell makes sure the guy who sells gasoline from the back of his flatbed truck will be here tomorrow. We purchase peanuts and bananas from passing women, and I buy a betel nut and the required pinch of the lime — calcium carbonate — that activates it. Russell explains that the men along the Sepik all carry quivers of bamboo charged with this lime. Each quiver has a dip-stick, usually of cassowary bone, to carry the lime to the bearer's mouth. A man will bang this dip stick in its quiver to show great agitation.

The betel high is mild, and it wears off in a few minutes, but it's quite pleasant while it lasts. I can understand why people discolor their mouths chewing it day after day.

In the evening, we fetch crackers and canned tuna from our packs, and as we eat, a young woman appears from the thatched houses and shyly sets in front of me some kind of cooked meat with plantains, then without speaking, retreats toward a thicket of bamboo at the edge of the river. "She's interested in you," Russell says.

"Yeah?"

"Only women cook, but unless you're at a market stall, men are generally served either by a kinswoman or by a man. If a strange woman prepares food and serves it to you, she's inviting you to lie with her."

"And?"

"It's not manly to refuse. That means you're afraid of her kinsmen."

"What if you don't find her attractive?"

"It's not manly to refuse sex with a young woman."

"Do I have to wrestle a crocodile too?"

He hands me the rum. "Drink. Eat."

Drink, eat, screw. I've given up my hypercivilized life to pursue simplicity, but I feel that I've jumped into the deep end without learning how to tread water. There's nothing in my experience that has prepared me for the rawness of actual primitiveness, and I'm suddenly filled with anxiety, with dread. I try to imagine having sex with this silent young woman, but the scene is absurd, not because there's anything wrong with either of us — our bodies are healthy and well proportioned — but because my senses, my limbs, are tuned to follow a different path. Human sex is profound, complex, subtle, or it isn't somehow human.

The mosquitoes are thicker now, beginning to irritate me. Maybe my entire flirtation with the idea of the primitive has been a fantasy — an illusion that New Guinea is about to shatter. Yes, the breaking of civilization's conceits on the rough stone of unadorned human nature. Isn't that the idea that brought me here? If it isn't, it should be, and I should be embracing the lesson that now stares me in the face. I take another swig of rum. I should be pleased. I'm experiencing the point of no return. I fill my mouth with the strange stew she set in front of me, and wash it down with swallows of rum.

It's almost dark when I enter the bamboo thicket, and the sound of frogs and night birds has begun in earnest. I see her — I think it's her, the rum has clouded my perception a bit — sitting in her simple shift on a gnarled branch of driftwood next to the water. She has created a beautifully romantic scene, and I feel my heart pound as I draw nearer. She doesn't look at me, but hearing me approach, she lets herself slip slowly into the dark water up to her chest, still holding on to the branch. In the twilight I can see the thin shift clinging to full breasts that rise and fall with her quickened breath. A primeval Venus: the ultimate erotic drama, provocative yet demure. "I see you but I don't. I flee but I don't." The heat of the rum pulses in my limbs. I can do this. I feel my cock rise tentatively, and I quickly drop my pants to the ground and follow her into the water.

Surprise! Immediately I sink to my ankles in the thick mud. I can barely move. She turns toward me, her expression somber but serene. Is this the invitation? I'm dizzy with excitement. I want to approach her, but when I try to lift my feet, I lose my balance. I make a grab for her to keep from falling, but to my horror I only manage to catch the neck of her thin shift, which easily tears away in my hand as I fall headlong into the current. She shrieks, then begins yelling something in her native tongue, as I drift downstream, toward the area where the canoes are beached. My head is suddenly clear. I try to swim toward shore, where I can hear men shouting, but the current is swift here, and my left arm is tightly tangled in the girl's shift, making it hard to swim. I'm past the canoes before I can reach them. I think it's best to relax until I have a plan, but that's not so easy when it occurs to me that there are crocodiles in the Sepik, and they are most active at night.

What would a primitive man do? He would resort to magic, a thing I've learned nothing of yet. I begin to pray generically to whatever spirits inhabit this stretch of river. "Spirits of the Sepik, of the sago palm, of the cassowary, of the betel nut; help me and I swear I'll build you an altar. I'll sacrifice a pig a day. Two pigs. I'll . . ." This is idiotic. I'm beginning to feel exhausted, but then a terrifying thing happens: The shift that still clings to my left hand is suddenly caught by something below the water. Gasping for breath, whimpering with fear, I'm sure I'm finished, but nothing happens. No giant jaws clamp my thrashing body. The dress must have caught on a snag. In a moment I hear the sound of an outboard motor and see the flash of a light. When the men pull me naked from the dark water, with the remains of the girl's dress still wrapped around my hand, they're laughing, and in relief I laugh too. They have my pants and sandals with them.

"You've distinguished yourself, old man," Russell smiles when we get back. "To chase a woman into the river naked is not a bad start. You might have to pay a fine to her kinsmen, though; in fact, that might have been her plan from the start."

"What would have happened if I'd caught her?"

"Ah, that we'll never know."

I would gladly have paid the relatives of that river Venus whose dress saved me (I now realize) from a strange and terrible fate. I have this odd feeling that the whole episode was orchestrated by an unseen force. Did she herself take pity on me and will my rescue, or were both of us the instruments of spirits that inhabit this wild place? But when our canoe arrives the next day from Kanganaman, there has been no confrontation with her kin.

The first couple of hours up the river to Yigei enchants me. Egrets, herons, eagles, kites adorn the trees or take wing at our approach; we exchange greetings with occasional fisherwomen and with the people who come down to the bank from their thatched outposts at the sound of our forty-horse Yamaha. In addition to us two foreigners, the long dugout carries clothes, cookware, kerosene, seashells, and pharmaceuticals, in hopes of trading for highland products — yams and smoked pigs, beetle grubs, healing and aromatic herbs, gemstones, fish poison. We also carry a huge man with an even huger head and godlike gray beard, an elected councilman from the Middle Sepik, who comes to talk with his counterparts up the river. "The mark of civilization, for sure," says Russell. "In the old days, he'd have had to take several canoes of armed men." The canoeman, whose name is Kamawi, and the councilman have already heard the story of the week — the story that Russell says has become Ashton's Death-Defying Assault on the Lovely Maiden, and I guess this is why they seem to be treating me with some deference.

Yigei is a settlement of about a dozen stilt houses, and what seems like a hundred pairs of children's eyes. Kamawi has traded here before, and we are invited to stay in a house that's still under construction but has a good roof. At night we hear the boom of thunder and the roar of a tropic downpour. I rise at first sunlight to greet Kamawi as he climbs the steep stairs of the house, soaked to the skin. "Canoe almost fill up, tip over," he says good naturedly, dramatizing with his hands, "all night, bailing, bailing."

Three of the men from Yigei who regularly trade with the highland Arambak know the people along the river upstream from here. While they select a few of our things to trade, there is much conversation in pidgin. Russell explains, almost with a straight face, that they have agreed to send word upstream that he, Russell, and Ulupariaminja, which means, "The White Man with the Hard Prick," are coming to visit the Raapa Uu, in a long canoe with a big motor. "I have things they've asked for," he says. "Sandpaper, carving tools, wire." A few more hours of discussion and the promise that Kamawi can have first choice of the highland goods, and he agrees to make the three-day trip, after another day of preparation.

The next morning I'm a bit alarmed to see Kamawi seated on the palmwood floor of our host's hut, bent over an array of outboard motor parts, which he appears to be adjusting with the point of a machete. I have a very fine Gerber all-in-one tool in my backpack, and I give it to him. It belongs in his hands, not in mine. I wander through the village and begin to wonder where the Middle Sepik people get their energy. The ordinary houses are large and sturdy, built with hand tools from great hardwood timbers, artfully woven together with sago palm and bamboo, and they have to be replaced about every twenty years even when they don't catch fire, which happens with great regularity. The men's "spirit house" is a tremendous work of art, five times the size of their family homes and elaborately decorated with carving and paint. Virtually everything they have — stoves, bowls, fishnets and rope, spears, string bags, tools, baskets, ornaments and toys of all kinds, musical instruments, canoes and rafts — is made, and finely ornamented, using local plants, animals, and earths.

Then we're away. The motor is running like silk; the breeze of our passage cools the humid air; the hamlets where we stop are curious but quietly respectful. Everyone knows who we are; no one asks the why of our journey; no young ladies come forward to serve us food; and no one asks payment for what they give us, although we're careful to leave a donation of trade goods. Along the wide Sepik, the swampy lowland begins to give way to hills, the baking sun to patches of sullen mist. The river runs clearer and more rapidly here; a floral spiciness flavors the jungle air. Russell points out the bows and shields carried in the canoes we meet. "We're approaching the Raapa Uu," he says. "When we reach our destination, stay with me, or with other Raapa Uu who know you. Some of the people along this part of the river are afraid of white men; they call us *laleo,* pale ghosts. A frightened Raapa Uu is a very dangerous thing."

CHAPTER TEN

THE RAAPA UU

H aving heard our motor, five or six men have come down from the village called Komoko, the Raapa Uu site where Russell is best known. The greetings are quiet, but the ease in their movements shows pleasure. We follow them for a half hour uphill along a narrow stream, until I see through the trees the high thatched gable of their spirit house. To enter the clearing is to wonder at this structure, and at the strength of the shared imagery that has built it. At least forty feet tall at the peak, it dominates the collection of sturdy stilt houses around it. Its huge posts are elaborately carved and painted in dusky reds, tans, and yellows. Finer carvings decorate the stairway to the upper floor, and high on the gable is an immense wooden spirit mask richly adorned with bone, string, shells, palm fiber, and feathers. Russell has explained to me the layout of these spirit houses; only men are allowed to enter. Along the walls of the lower floor, we will find the sitting platforms, where clan membership and social status dictates each man's place. In the center will be the perpetual hearth fire and next to it, the "talking stool," where they compete for honor with passionate oratory. The upper story is even more sacred; here will be the sacred flutes, drums, and bull-roarers that are the voices of the spirits; and here the young men will undergo their long and painful initiation into manhood, with its education in the magical secrets of their clans.

Within these high palm-branch walls are kept the secrets I myself have come here to learn. For the first time I realize the gravity of those secrets, and the greatness of my arrogance in seeking them. Each clan guards its knowledge fiercely from all others, and betrayal is a capital offense. This architectural magnificence, this eloquence of great labor, announces the value of the lore that's kept in it. Why in the world should they share it with a stranger who doesn't even speak their language or know their laws? If they will even entertain the notion, I'll have to do whatever they ask in return. I think back to the bus trip, to the young man's back with its fierce initiation scars, and I feel a twinge of nausea. Russell has explained that we have to wait until our hosts bring up the question of my purpose.

As the idle days pass, I watch the men carve masks or butcher pigs, the women cook yams and plantains and bathe their children at the stream. Attending the construction of a dugout canoe, I pick up one of the primitive adzes and join in the laughter as they watch me hack ineffectually at the bone-hard wood.

A wiry old man named Matthew who was raised by missionaries speaks broken English, and at night we sit by the fire in the spirit house and I learn to endure the mosquitoes as he translates the long stories of his clan — tales of astounding magic events, treasured details of their wars and migrations. I ask for the story of the River God Ba, and his daughter Kuibi, and the one of the Big Man, Kasoi and the magic surfboard, the *te moka tula*. On this subject, the elders fall to arguing over the details.

One of the younger men takes up the three branches of sago palm that lie by the talking stool, and strikes the stool three times. As he speaks, his face contorts, his voice rises to a scream, flecks of saliva fly from his mouth, and he gestures mightily with his hands, causing giant shadows from the firelight to fly around the walls. Some in the audience roar with approval while others shout and gesture angrily. Bending close to my ear, Matthew translates: Kasoi's power as a trader was not that great, the speaker says; he was simply a braggart and a buffoon. What power he had, he had stolen by black magic from the speaker's clan. The *te moka tula* was inhabited by bad sprits, who injured the power of the Raapa Uu.

At length the speech is interrupted by a loud clacking noise, and the assembly falls quiet. Someone is pounding his lime stick in its bamboo quiver, a signal that might mean a fight. I've seen the stick pounder before, sitting silently in the shadows while the others talk. He has the sinuous frame of an athlete, with prominent veins on his powerful arms; his hair and beard are cut short; his face has the sharp features and intensity of a hawk. He takes up the sago leaves and strikes the talking stool.

This, whispers Matthew, is the man who killed Kasoi. The man speaks quietly, looking intently into the eyes of those around him. Let me remind you, he says, my kinsman Kasoi was the incarnation of our ancestor, Cassowary. He had knowledge that no other Raapa Uu has, or ever has had, or ever will have. If I had not shot him with my magic arrow, he would have taken everything. All of you would be nothing more than his pigs, to trade or slaughter as he liked — his dogs, to fetch him game and bite the heels of his enemies. Where are the Raapa Uu men today who could stand up to such as Kasoi? Our youth have grown soft; they fear the missionaries who tell them the Christian god is more powerful than their ancestors; they fear the soldiers who talk of hanging a whole village if they find trophy heads on the spirit house walls. They carve the masks, not to increase their power, but to trade for the liquor, clothes, and motors that foreigners bring up the river.

There is some murmuring of agreement. Then the speaker turns to me. Why have I come to Komoko and the Raapa Uu? I don't trade for masks as Russell does. They have heard that I attack women strangers with my hard prick. That is only to be expected of a man, but look, the women run away; I have no magic. Are there any men in this village who will teach me sex magic so that I can copulate with their wives and sisters?

No one seems the least amused. This is the moment I have been preparing for, the questioning of my purpose. I've prepared carefully what I should say. I look at Russell. He points to the sago leaves lying next to the talking stool. My throat is dry, but I pick up the leaves and strike the stool as my predecessors have done.

"Many generations ago," I manage to say, "the people of my clan were great magicians, but we have forgotten their magic. In my home across the great ocean there are no longer any sorcerers who know the names of the powerful ancestors, or who can speak the language of the spirits." Russell is translating. "We have no sex magic, no trading magic, no war magic, no magic to make children, and only a little to cure sickness, in the land where I live. I have a dear friend who is possessed by an evil spirit, yet I cannot help her because I know nothing of the spirit world. Where I live, I heard that the Raapa Uu still know these things. My great hope is to be able to learn them from you. Although I have come here on a journey of many days, that is no reason why you should welcome me or consider my request. If you help me, I will always be your friend; my heart will be as if I were your clan brother. I know nothing of the enemies of the Raapa Uu, and they know nothing of me, so how and why would I use this magic to harm you?"

After a moment's silence, the fierce-looking man comes forward and strikes the stool again. "What do you want with this magic, then? You white men have many things. You can fly around the sky like flying foxes. You can make rays from the sun shine in the night. You can make spirits speak from a little box. First, teach us how you do these things." There are shouts of agreement from the others.

I had expected some argument like this. High on adrenalin, my mind is racing. "This is not difficult to answer," I say. "These things are not real magic, they are mere tricks. Only a few people know these tricks, and our enemies have those tricksters too. Our power is useless, only good to amaze those who do not know the tricks. Anyway, I cannot teach you the white man's useless tricks because I have not bothered to learn them. But I can teach your young men not to worship the so-called magic of the white men, to believe instead in the wisdom of their ancestors."

Another man seizes the leaves and strikes the talking stool. "Remember, the spirit of the crocodile sometimes takes the form of a man in order to seduce women. Perhaps this stranger is not really a man; perhaps he is a spirit who has taken this form in order to take our magic and sell it to our enemies. Even if he is not a spirit, if we teach him our magic, soon other white men will come and ask for the same thing. Perhaps his enemies will come and will be angry with us. What will we say to them? We must send him away at once, and if he comes back, we must take his head and bury him under the stones at the entrance to the spirit house."

Far into the night, speaker after speaker addresses the issue. One says that I am a clan brother of Russell, who has been adopted into the Cassowary Clan; my death would require revenge, and where would the head-taking stop? Another has heard the missionaries say that the evil Christian spirit Satanu often appears in the form of an ordinary man and tries to lure people away from the will of the supreme god by flattering them and making them do evil things. A third says that the shaman in another village can see spirits, and they should take me to him to find out whether I am human. If I am, let me be fully initiated into the Cassowary

Clan. This touches off a long and disorderly debate over which of the three village clans should do the teaching, until dawn begins to break and some of the men drift off to their houses to catch some sleep, while others simply stretch out on their clan platforms and doze.

Another sultry day. I have this eerie feeling of vulnerability, as if I'm barreling along a road where I not only don't know the rules and can't read the signs, but don't know where I'm headed either. Should I ask Russell to get me out of here? Nobody has actually threatened to kill me. Everybody I meet seems as friendly, and as enigmatic, as ever.

There's a young woman in the village who seems to be handicapped somehow: She never takes part in regular women's activities, and nobody pays any attention to her. She might be mentally ill or retarded, or she might just be deaf. I catch a glimpse of her from time to time moving along the paths or working by herself next to the stream. The way this girl moves is altogether different from the other women. While they are shy and awkwardly self-conscious in the presence of men, she seems to live in a world of her own, and moves with an easy grace that reminds me of a wild animal. She doesn't seem to notice other people either, including me, and of course I've been careful not to approach her, although I'd like to — in fact I find her silent, graceful solitude exciting.

So today I'm dozing in the shade of our host's house wondering what will happen next, and suddenly I have the sensation that someone is near. Coming awake, I see her. She approaches the house, fixes her eyes on me for a moment, then stops and kneels down about fifty feet away. Now she stands and makes an odd sound, a deep gutteral purr, then simply turns and walks away with that liquid walk of hers that would draw looks from strange men anywhere. There seems to be something on the ground where she knelt, although I didn't see her carrying anything. I walk over and see that it's a wooden bowl with a papaya and something — fish, I guess — wrapped in banana leaves. The place has a musky animal smell.

As if I weren't confused enough already by last night's events, now this. Did she mean this as a gift for me? Did someone order her to bring it? Is this her declaration of desire in the local language of sex? If so, how should I respond to it, if I dare to respond at all? Or maybe her impairment exempts her from the rules about serving men? Could her act be a signal that my status in the village has changed, or that I'm being prepared for some ritual ordeal? Or again, this could be some sort of test that the men have cooked up, and if it is, what's the right response? What reward or punishment is in store?

I had imagined the primitive as an alternative reality that was simple, uninhibited, innocent; I had imagined that the way back to my Zogon youth on Randy's Trail led through this other, simpler, reality. It's another reality, all right: one where the demand for complex and subtle knowledge leaves the stranger powerless and afraid. A mighty respect for Russell comes over me. How has he endured this for months at a time, years, even? I turn this over in my mind. I've followed my instincts here, and my instincts have been right. I'll not only endure this test; I'll master its riddle and emerge annealed by its fire, a real-life Zogon, a blade of a man. No alternative is imaginable, other than death or madness. I'm not hungry, and for now, I decide to leave the bowl there and try to sleep again.

Russell says he hasn't noticed the strange girl and has no idea what was meant by her act. He says it's time for him and Kamawi to pack up their goods and return to Pagwi; the men here will soon make a decision about my request to learn magic, and if their answer is no, I can go back too. I tell him I'll stay if the Raapa Uu will let me, regardless of what else they decide. To go back empty-handed now is not an option.

That night there is no storytelling, and spirit house is almost empty. I don't feel like sleeping and there's a full moon; it's light enough to walk the paths. "Only spirits and crazy people go out at night," he says. "I don't think you should attract attention that way." So I sit on the veranda of our house, brushing away the mosquitoes with a palm fan and listening to the bird sounds in the jungle, thinking about the strange girl. Who is she? She has to belong to a family, or at least to some man in the village. I have to pee, so I climb down and walk to the usual clump of banana trees at the edge of the house clearing. I stop at the spot where she put the bowl down and see that it's gone. On my way back, I see someone walking at a distance along the village path. It seems likely that it's her; the person's gait is fluid and musical, and who else would be walking here at this hour? I try to follow her, but she quickly disappears, and I go back to the house and crawl under my mosquito net to get relief from the biting. Russell and Kamawi are sound asleep.'

It seems as though I've been lying there in the dark for hours when again I feel the nearness of someone. Sitting up, I see her at the other end of the room, seated by a window where the setting moon casts a broad beam of blue light. She is naked to the waist, and I can see the lovely smooth contours of her shoulders, arms, and breasts clearly. She is looking in my direction, and begins to move her hands, talking with them. As I watch, she repeats the same motions over and over, and the message becomes clearer each time: "If you will come with me, I will show you the way to the spirits." I nod my head, and she lets her hands fall to her sides and makes the purring sound again. I raise my mosquito net to approach her, but as I do she moves out of the light and I can't see her. I'm afraid that if I turn on my flashlight, I'll wake the others. I creep to the place where she sat, and there again, I smell the strong, erotic musk of her body, but all other traces of her are gone.

Then in the distance, I hear the purring sound again. Looking out the door of the hut, I can dimly make out her form, standing at the edge of the clearing. I climb down the ladder and approach her, and she moves away into the trees, with that undulating feline step, and I follow. Soon we're deep in the jungle. I keep expecting her to stop or to come to me, but she moves on, looking back, making sure I'm there; when I stop she stops, when I approach she moves on.

After what must be an hour or more, a feeling of exhaustion comes over me. I find a mossy log and sit down, and when I look for her again, she is gone, and at that very second I realize I'm lost in the jungle, far from the village. I have nothing with me, not even water. If I wait until sunrise, I can at least orient myself to the compass points, but then I realize I have no idea which direction will take me toward Komoko or any other human settlement.

Gradually it grows light. I get up and inspect the forest around me, looking for a path, but I see none. I listen for anything resembling human sounds, but all I hear are the sounds of birds and insects on all sides. I'm pushing back against panic. Russell, at least, will be concerned, but the men of Komoko have no idea where to look for me, even if they're inclined to do so. I cup my hands to my mouth and call as loudly as I can, now in this direction, now in that. My throat already feels dry, and I realize I'm panting with fear. Should I look for a stream? Will the water be safe to drink if I find it? I sit down again and try to control my emotions, and my mind clears a bit. Coconuts. Green coconuts contain clean water. I look around me, but I don't see any coconut trees, and I realize that they only grow close to ground water. And what if I found such a tree? Could I climb it? And if I could, how would I open the coconuts without so much as a pen knife? My stomach is growling as well.

Slowly the sun mounts into the tree canopy, and the heat grows oppressive. I try to find deep shade, so that I will sweat as little as possible, but the shadiest spots are swarming with mosquitoes. My hearing seems to have become hyper acute; my attention is riveted when I hear a crashing sound far off, as if something or someone were moving through the brush. There are wild boar in this forest. If I were to build a fire, the men from Komoko might be able to find me by following the smoke; but again, I have no matches, no dry wood, and I never joined the boy scouts. Besides, what if I should be discovered by people from another Raapa Uu village? They would see only a lone *laleo*, a pale ghost, who speaks neither Raapa Uu nor pidgin, and they would be foolish not to kill me.

As the sun slants low in the west, I'm searching for any kind of vegetation that looks like it might be succulent. Without exception, what I find is either too tough to bite into or so bitter I'm sure it must be poisonous. I begin to feel dizzy, and it occurs to me that I'm already well on my way to death. Oddly, it's a liberating feeling. I still have the strength to walk, and I set off through the dense growth to see if I can find a stream or a pond. But soon it's too dark to continue. Deeply exhausted and disoriented, I lie down against a log and sleep.

When I awake it's midmorning. I'm in my hut in Komoko, and Russell and Matthew are bustling about, packing his artifacts and chatting in Raapa Uu. When they see that I'm awake, they come and stand over me. "Okay," says Russell. "What the bloody hell happened?"

"How did you find me?"

"Our dogs found you," Matthew says, and waving his arm. "You were just over that hill. Why?"

"The young woman who doesn't speak, the one who's always by herself. She led me there."

"Ah, the deaf seductress?" says Russell.

Matthew sits down and examines my face for a long minute, then says, "Where have you seen this woman?"

"Here in the village. Several times. She brought me food."

"What does she look like?"

"She's young, pretty." I draw a voluptuous woman in the air. "Big eyes, small hands and feet. When she walks it's like . . . like an eagle gliding."

He glances around and lowers his voice. "Has anyone else seen her?"

"Not that I know of. Russell says he hasn't."

"Did you tell this to anyone else?"

"No."

"She brought you food. What else?"

I'm starting to feel uncomfortable. I trust Matthew with his wrinkled, kind face, but maybe I shouldn't be telling him this.

"That's all. She came to this house last night."

"Did you eat the food?"

"No." Somehow I already know what he's going to say next.

"Good. She is not a human, she is a spirit."

"What kind of spirit? What should I do, then?"

"That's all I can say. It's okay that you told me; the Christian pastors taught me things about how to protect myself. But some of the men might not like to hear this story of yours. Don't go near her or eat from her hands. Don't tell anyone what has happened. Tomorrow you and I will go to the shaman called Sosi, in Sangrapa, to learn more. For now," he reaches under his ragged shirt and pulls out a cross on a thong, which he hands me, "wear this, but if anyone asks you, tell them you brought it here with you." I don't like this idea, but it's important to keep his friendship, so I put it on and button my shirt over it.

Is this a huge practical joke? Has the heat, the odd diet, the mosquitoes, the confusion and fear pushed me over the edge? Or have I actually entered a place where dreams and reality blur into each other? Any sane person in my shoes would go back to Pagwi with Russell tomorrow, so what does it mean that I have no intention of going back? I throw back my head and laugh.

"What is it, Ashton?" asks Matthew.

"I don't wear shoes anyway!"

CHAPTER ELEVEN

SANGRAPA

Each man or woman carries a bundle to put in the canoe with Russell and Kamawi. It's early in the morning, and the whole village seems to be here. On the bank of the Sepik many hugs and promises are exchanged on all sides. Kamawi puts his long arms around me and we hug for a long time. As for Russell, I hand him a page from my notebook with a scribbled note for Ysabel — "Tell Mom, and Thelma, and Blake, and Sid, and Lisa that I'm fine, I'm glad to be here, and I think of them daily." There's that awkward moment between white men who are about to say good-bye. I've thanked Russell at various times for bringing me here, but I've never told him how much I admire him or given him any token of affection. We squeeze hands and look in each other's eyes. He flashes his opal-studded teeth. "You're a crazier fucker than I am, you know that?" he says. Then the roar of the Yamaha drowns out the benedictions, and in a moment the canoe is just a speck disappearing around a bend of the great muddy current.

Everyone in Komoko knows I'm interested in shamanism, so there's no need to hide the fact that Matthew and I are going up river to the village of Sangrapa, where the healer lives. Matthew puts two large smoked fish into a string bag, and in my backpack a thick package of sandpaper and a pint of rum. Having no motor canoe, we'll go on foot along a trail that more or less follows the course of the stream through the trees. There's a huge variety of vegetation and bird life. After about three hours, Matthew stops and listens silently for a minute, then cups his hands to his mouth and shouts, first a long drawn-out "Oooh," then a few words in pidgin.

He squats on his haunches and waits. Hearing no answer, he repeats the call, and in a few seconds we hear a similar call in the distance. Matthew shouts again in reply, then turns to me. "You say hello too."

"Ooooh! Hellooo! I am Aaaashton!"

Matthew nods approval, and we continue for another five minutes through the jungle, arriving at a more open area where a few houses can be seen among the trees. Three men stand glowering in the path, dressed in the traditional G-string and penis sheath, two of them carrying bows and arrows; but when they see Matthew they flash betel-red smiles and come forward and hug us both, the oldest one speaking in pidgin, the other two silent. Soon we're standing in front of their spirit house, and two of the men disappear inside, leaving us in the company of the old one. "Sosi," says Matthew, indicating our companion, "is the healer. Usually they would beat the drums and have a feast for us, but I told Sosi we are not staying, that we have come for a healing and must leave today."

Sosi's gaunt, stooped frame seems to struggle under the weight of his huge halo of hair and beard, and a great necklace of beads, feathers, and shells. He walks with a limp and looks very old indeed, his face a mass of deep furrows and pocks, his jutting brow hanging almost down over his eyes. What is startling is his voice, which is youthful and strong, as though it came from another body altogether. He hobbles into the spirit house and emerges with a string bag of fruit and a smoking branch from the fire, then motions us to come with him. We follow him to a small house in the jungle some distance from the village and climb the entrance ladder. Hanging from the rafters are dozens of intricately carved and painted masks, the necks of which end in broad double hooks, rather like the points of spears, and which I recognize as "food hooks" of the sort that Russell had sold to Sid back in Del Mar. From the hooks hang bundles of herbs, feathers, strings of shells, crocodile teeth, boar tusks, animal bones, and many other things I don't recognize. Using the brand from the spirit house, Sosi makes a small fire on the open stone hearth and offers us betel, which we decline, and bananas and papaya, which we accept.

He listens intently while Matthew tells him the story of my vision, though he asks no questions, and I can't read his reaction at all. When Matthew has finished, the healer reaches up into the rafters and selects a generous handful of herbs, then almost smothering the fire with them, sits and closes his eyes. Like this he stays, almost motionless, the acrid smoke swirling around him, moving only his betel-red lips from time to time and nodding slightly, as if in conversation with unseen others.

The ritual goes on and on, for perhaps an hour, and now and then the glowing ashes swirling up from the fire drift onto his hair and beard, and I half expect to see him burst into flame. Little by little his limbs start to tremble and twitch, sometimes violently, so that his shell necklace rattles and the palm floor shakes beneath us. I can scarcely breathe in the smoke-filled hut, but Matthew seems oblivious to the problem, and we sit quietly. Finally the herbs have burnt up and the smoke ebbs away. Sosi stops whispering and twitching and opens his eyes, and at that moment the hair on my neck rises, as I hear the sound of something, or someone, howling pitifully in the distance. It must be a dog, I assure myself, although the sound seems too human. Sosi stares at me intently now; does he read my anxiety? He speaks in pidgin to Matthew, who translates.

"He says your life is in danger, but he cannot heal you with his magic. You must leave the Raapa Uu right away. The deaf woman who possesses you is a spirit, but she is not an ancestor of Sosi's clan or any of the clans of Komoko. She is a spirit that followed you here from far away. You must not stay here, and you must not go back to Komoko. The people might kill you to protect themselves."

So it comes to this. I sit for several minutes, my mind racing. How can I leave? Who would give passage to a man possessed by a dangerous spirit? What an ass I was, to let Russell and Kamawi leave — to think that I could face whatever horrors this strange place held for me! What an idiot to ask Matthew if he had seen the girl! Much better to take my chances with a spirit of any kind — and this one seems so gentle — than to face the arrows of actual men! I look for sympathy in the faces of Matthew and Sosi, but I see none. Calm yourself, Ashton. Think. Slowly, searching for words, watching his reactions closely, I begin to speak to Sosi via Matthew:

"People say you are a great healer. Can you not bargain with this spirit?"

"It is a foreign spirit. My ancestors do not know it."

"Then how do you know that it intends to harm me?"

"No one knows the minds of the spirits, especially foreign ones. That's why we cannot take the chance of caring for you."

Panic is once again beginning to make me dizzy, but somehow the words keep coming out of my mouth. "If this was a spirit whom your ancestors know, could you command it?"

"Yes!"

"Perhaps *my* ancestors know it."

"If they can speak for you, you must ask them."

"This is just the problem. My people have forgotten how to talk to the ancestors and spirits. I came here to learn that from you. If you teach me, I can command this spirit."

There is some rapid conversation between the two of them. Matthew says, "He cannot teach you. It is too dangerous, and besides, you don't speak Raapa Uu."

A ray of hope? He's almost saying that he would teach me if I knew his language. "You speak pidgin. I can learn to speak it in a few weeks."

"That's too long. It's too dangerous."

"If I am dead, what will this spirit do? No one here will be able to command it. How do you know it will not turn on the Raapa Uu? Who will protect them?"

They talk some more, and then Matthew turns to me, his face grave. "Ulu, you say your elders have forgotten about magic, yet you knew that this was the place to become a magician. Tell me the story of how you came here. Were you commanded in a dream?"

"I will tell you exactly as it was, but there may be many things that are strange to you.

"It began when I met a woman, let's call her a sorceress, her name is Lisa. She told me a magical story, a story that made me realize that I had lost my power, and my life had become meaningless. I was working as a teacher, not a teacher of magic, or of reading and writing, but a teacher of my people's lore, stories about why we do things the way we do. This woman made me understand that the lore I was teaching is only a small truth, that there is a bigger truth that I must learn."

"We teach our boys the small stories first," says Matthew. "It makes them curious, and it doesn't matter if they tell the women. But how did this woman know the big stories?"

"How did she know? In my country, women go to school with men and learn the same things. But not even the men know the great stories. I think the spirits brought them to her in dreams. Anyway, when I met her, I stopped my teaching, and I become a kind of wanderer. I went to work for a man named Sid, a man who trades in art goods, all kinds of carvings and paintings. With this work I was able to be near Lisa, and to keep my mind open and free for whatever teaching she, and the spirits would give me.

"But everything was not well between Lisa and me. She didn't trust my belief, that I would find my way to true knowledge by myself. She was afraid that I would somehow injure myself, and possibly her as well, because of false knowledge. This trouble between us made me very sad at times.

"These thoughts were heavy on my mind. One morning when I came to Sid's trading place, I found him conversing with a person who looked very strange to me. It was Russell. They had some carvings from the Raapa Uu. I asked Russell what these things are called, and he told me about them and about the Raapa Uu. There was a big wooden thing, that looked like something we use in my country to ride the waves of the sea. He called it the *te moka tula*."

I see that Matthew and Sosi recognize the word at once. The atmosphere in the hut has grown electric.

"Russell told me the story of the *te moka tula,* the story of how the Raapa Uu fled to the Upper Sepik from downstream and took up the highland way of life, trading pigs and shells, a manly and warlike way of life. He told me about how the Big Men build up power by using magic to build up their trading networks, and how jealousy over their success often leads to killing, sometimes by war, but more often by witchcraft."

"He told you about Kasoi also, and the magic of the missionaries?" Matthew asks.

"Yes. The Big Man Kasoi, the great trader."

Matthew tilts his head back and narrows his eyes. "The missionaries," he says. "The Baptist Brothers came to Komoko with many strange things. They had a metal box, with electric light inside. We had never seen electric light. The box told stories and made pictures appear on a white cloth they hung on the spirit house. One of the stories showed how the Baptist Brothers became so powerful and rich. It showed men like them making huge waves in the sea and riding on them. For many days, the elders of

Komoko talked about this, and finally they understood. The film showed how the missionary people were able to harvest as many canoes full of pearl shells as they wanted."

"Yes, Russell told me the story of Kasoi and the missionaries. He said that Kasoi became too powerful, and that the other villages began to attack Komoko more and more. The people told Kasoi to destroy the *te moka tula,* but he refused, saying it would enrage Ba and bring ruin on the Raapa Uu."

"There was no other way but to kill Kasoi," Matthew says. "Russell promised us that he would take the *te moka tula* far out to sea, where the gods would forget about it. But now you tell me he did not keep his word." Here he translates for Sosi, and the two of them sit glowering at me. "You have brought the danger of the *te moka tula* back here. This spirit that threatens you is a sign of it."

"No. It is not like that. The *te moka tula* spoke to me in my own tongue. It taught me that the Raapa Uu alone have the wisdom that I was seeking. It told me I must come here and learn from you if I want to have my power back. I have put my life in your hands, in order to learn the way of the spirits. If you force me to leave, or kill me, I and my people will continue forever without your knowledge. I think that might be safer for you, but it will be a great tragedy for my people. They mean you no harm. Hardly any of them even know you exist. They have lost the magic of their ancestors and become confused and unhappy. For this reason I am willing to risk my life by coming here."

Matthew and Sosi begin to converse in rapid Raapa Uu, their voices rising. From time to time Sosi bangs the floor with his open hand in emphasis. When they've talked for what seems like an hour, Matthew turns to me.

"The spirit woman who possesses you knows why you came here, and it does not want you to learn to speak to our spirits, because they are its enemies. This means that all of us will be safer if you learn. Sosi will teach you some of the songs, maybe for hunting or for trading, but he will not teach you war songs. If you want to leave here alive, first you must become a member of his clan, the Crocodile.'

With this news I suddenly feel exhausted. "I will do as you teach me, and I will be as a kinsman to both of you" is all I can think of to say. I can see that Matthew picks up on my fatigue. He speaks to Sosi again for a few minutes, then rises to go. We do not embrace as is the custom. As he mounts the ladder to descend, he turns and looks at me — an intense look, as though it might be his last.

CHAPTER TWELVE

CASSOWARY

U sing gestures, Sosi instructs me to stay within a few yards of the healing hut, which he has protected with spells. He will bring me water and food, and most important, he spends a couple of hours teaching me a song, which I gather I must sing to my ancestor spirit if I see the deaf woman spirit again. He indicates that he learned in his trance that my ancestor is one that is known to the missionaries, a spirit named Mekiimos. By the time his teaching is finished it is midafternoon, and Sosi leaves. Again I find myself not just physically but psychologically alone.

At home alone gives me a sense of freedom, but as the trees merge into blackness, I begin to feel something far worse than anything I've felt since I was four years old — the same terror of the dark that used to drive me wailing into my parents' room. I add sticks to my little fire. I try talking to myself out loud, but my own voice sounds insane in my ears. I strain to focus my mind on my professional knowledge of irrational fear, and I realize that Freud never found himself alone in a jungle where his actual flesh and blood was a beacon to murderous spirits and men. I find no weapon in the hut, so I hold my flashlight in one hand and one of the painted wooden food hooks in the other. I'm afraid to close my eyes, and I sit shivering with my back against a post, cursing the dawn whose absence tortures me.

I don't know how long I've been sitting here — certainly several hours — when I detect a subtle change in the jungle's chorus of night bird and insect song. My heart accelerates. Where the fuck did I put the scrap of paper with Sosi's song on it? No, not that! The cross! Where is the fucking cross that Matthew gave me? As I'm scrambling for my clothes, I feel the hut shake, and I distinctly hear the purring sound that I heard her make.

The next thing I know, it's daylight. I'm alive. I seem to be lying facedown on the floor. My neck aches like hell. The air is full of herbal smoke. With effort I sit up and see Sosi a few feet away, rocking, his eyes closed, gesturing, conversing with the unseen. Next to the hearth I see the burnt remnants of my pants, and I realize they must have fallen on the fire when I passed out. The thought drifts through my head that it might have been the burning of Matthew's cross that saved my life.

Sosi seems unaware of my movements until he has finished his song. Then he stands and takes up a handful of sago palm leaves, holds them over the fire for a moment, and brushes my entire body with them. He takes up a half coconut shell that contains a white liquid and hands it to me, brusquely making a drinking gesture. I wonder what the bitter stuff I'm drinking is.

In a few minutes I begin to feel disoriented. I've smoked weed, taken LSD, breathed nitrous oxide, and eaten psilocybin, but the feeling I have now is unfamiliar. Instead of sensory intensity, I'm getting the opposite; my senses gradually shut down. Sounds and shapes around me become indistinct and distant, my body somewhat numb. At the same time, I seem to be seeing and hearing things inside my head: not abnormal things, ordinary things like faces, landscapes, human voices, flowing water, all of them unfamiliar, giving me the sensation that my mind has quite left the scene and is wandering somewhere far away, bewildered and lost. On top of this, I feel a rhythmic swelling and ebbing of inchoate sensation. It seems harmless enough at first, but its persistence begins to terrify me. I feel that "it," whatever it is, will swallow me, and I cry out in alarm. Eventually, little by little at first, this experience — the flow of strange imagery and the consuming rhythm — is punctured here and there by snatches of Sosi's voice speaking softly and steadily in Raapa Uu, and this calms me a little. There is no sense of time.

Then quite suddenly I pop back into my old self for a moment and, with tremendous relief, see and hear Sosi and sense the hut and the herbs. I notice that it's now dark except for the ritual fire; many hours must have passed. Before I can gather my thoughts, I begin to drift back into the drug state. This repeats itself several times, the altered states getting shorter and the normal states longer, until I begin to feel impatient and wish it was over, and then, finally, it is over. When I realize I am not drifting back into the drug state, I feel great relief again, as though I've been set free from torture. I hold up the drinking bowl, questioningly, and he nods and says, "*Wegura. 'e maykim gos' 'e kom bak.*" I'm beginning to understand a little pidgin. I nod. This drug, *wegura*, "*makes a person's [wandering] spirit come back.*"

Sosi sits silently, but the look on his face, his posture, wants to tell me something, or perhaps command me. "What should I do?" I ask, adding gestures. He hands me my backpack and indicates that I should take things from it and put them on the fire. One by one, I take out the burnable things — a T-shirt, underwear, socks, shorts, and put them on the fire. I stop, but he indicates I should continue, and I find myself eager to please him. Passport, airline tickets, and wallet go next. I put my notebook and toilet kit beside me on the floor, and hand him the now-empty bag. He looks in it, then takes these two remaining possessions and throws them in the fire as well, followed by the bag itself. All this is acceptable. He is the master and the healer.

For the next three days I am not to leave the healing hut. Sosi brings me a gourd attached to a string, of the sort the Raapa Uu wear as penis sheaths. He also brings water, cooked yams, and a little fruit, and teaches me a new song, which I must sing repeatedly throughout the day. During the daylight I feel excruciating boredom, and I sleep a lot. The first night I lie wide awake, listening to the jungle, glad that Sosi is nearby. He does not stay in the hut with me, but he enters many times during the day and night to sing with me, and he never seems to be far away. The second night I sleep fitfully, but wake up long before dawn, faintly aware of something unusual. Then I hear it, the same purring sound that stunned me with fear three nights ago, but this time I'm able to listen to it calmly, and as I do, I begin to recognize it clearly as an insect sound, one I've heard many times since I came to New Guinea, and I laugh, and go back to sleep.

By the evening of the third day my boredom has given way to a kind of weary calm. I hear the drums in the spirit house, and when Sosi comes around sundown, he brings a headdress and leg bands of bird feathers, and a grass skirt for me to put on. With white, black, and red pigment he paints my face as well. As we approach the center of the village, I can smell roasting pig. There is a fire in front of the spirit house, and the women and children sit silently while the men in their spirit masks dance to the sound of the sacred flutes and bull-roarers, music coming from inside the spirit house. Throughout the night I am required to dance with the masked figures, while pieces of roast pig and bowls of sago palm beer circulate among the group. When finally the eastern sky begins to pale, I'm led into the spirit house by the drunken men, and laughing and embracing, we finally settle on the clan benches and fall asleep.

Weeks have passed, I don't know how long. When your life depends on it, pidgin isn't hard for an English speaker to learn — or at least something enough like pidgin that Sosi and I are soon conversing in it. Sosi has shown me how to arrange an altar on the earthen floor beneath the healing hut — the selection of sacred objects and plants, a circle inside a square facing the cardinal directions. Every morning on rising I build a new altar and offer herbs and a song to the spirit whose aspect is the deaf woman, and it has not come back. He has me practicing many different songs, and I find it extremely frustrating, as they are in Raapa Uu, which makes no sense to me at first. Some of the songs go on for twenty minutes, and not the slightest variation is allowed. There are songs to bring game, to weaken an enemy or ward off his magic, to straighten the path of a spear or arrow, to remove various kinds of curses, to diagnose and cure diseases and injuries. Some of the songs require water, and most need burnt offerings as well — herbs, sanctified objects, animals. He shows me the procedure to sacrifice live chickens, pigs, and jungle game.

By now I can even get up and walk after sitting cross-legged for hours, but I still haven't mastered the voices. Each spirit uses a particular tone of voice, and these have to be copied closely. Te voice of my ancestor spirit Mekiimos is the most difficult — a high-pitched falsetto that makes my throat ache after a few minutes.

I learn that Raapa Uu healers do not use drugs, other than the *wegura* that I drank for the exorcism, plus of course betel and the smoke of the herbs. I ask Sosi to teach me the songs for the exorcism and for calling a soul back to the body, but he tells me I'm not ready. I have no notebook to write down the songs, so I have to remember them as best I can. When

I ask him how long this will go on, he only says, "I'll tell you when you are ready."

After weeks I've mastered the words of the principal songs, but I know from watching Sosi that this is only the beginning. Before he sings, he uses the herbal smoke and imagery to put himself into a trance. Each time he does this, I watch him closely and try to imitate everything — his posture, his breathing, his movements — and I do begin to feel a certain alert calmness, so that the words of the songs take on color and weight. I can see and feel them, but I'm not sure that I have even come close to the state I need to succeed with the spirits. Over and over, Sosi stops me in the early verses of the songs and tells me to watch him again. I've completely lost track of time; I think I've been here for several months. I'm allowed to go with Sosi to his house to eat, to help him with his carving and other chores. I'm even beginning to understand the Raapa Uu words that I sing, over and over. But the lack of progress is depressing me to the point where I can no longer concentrate on the task at all — my mind simply goes blank when I begin to sing. I seem to have come to a wall.

I have indeed come to a wall. I can feel it with my whole being. There is no way around it, my patience is exhausted, my despair is complete. I try to forget the struggle, let my mind wander back to California and Lisa, remind myself why I'm here, but it's useless. When I woke up this morning and thought of yet another day of fumbling with the trance thing, I decided I absolutely can't take it. I won't do it again, not today, maybe not ever. I've survived the spirit attack; I've learned the songs. I decide to tell Sosi that my apprenticeship is over; as soon as I can arrange for transport, I'm going back to Pagwi. I do feel guilty about this. Sosi has spent hundreds of hours working with me, and I have failed him. The best I can say is that I seem to have learned to protect myself, and I'm no longer a threat to the community.

As soon as Sosi arrives in midmorning, he asks me to come with him to catch and slaughter a pig that must be offered at the marriage of his clansman tomorrow; I'll have to tell him my decision later. The work takes until late afternoon, and we return to the healing hut to eat.

"Sosi, I have a big thing to tell you." He understands my bad pidgin (broken version of a language that is itself a broken version!), but shows no sign of surprise. "I'm sure I do not have the ability to become a healer. At first I tried to learn your way to enter the spirit world, but lately, I have no heart to try. It is too difficult. I would like to go back to Pagwi."

"This is a big decision," he says without emotion. "We must ask the advice of your ancestors. Let us call on Mekiimos." He throws a handful of herbs on the fire and sits next to me. "Together, as one," he says.

All right, this one last time. Everything is familiar — the smoke, the posture, the breathing, the words of the song to Mekiimos. My frustration is relieved by the thought that it will be over very soon. As we sing together, I begin to feel something very unusual, a sensation that my body has disappeared, or rather, that it has become the vivid words and rises into the air along with them. I see no imagery, but I feel that the words are fully alive, that they are the embodiment of my consciousness, my spirit. When I finally open my eyes, I realize that Sosi has stopped and allowed me to finish the whole song, and I see a gleam of satisfaction in his eyes. I feel exhausted, but after a few minutes' rest, he commands me to perform another song, and then another, and each time the result is the same — the sensation of my own vanishing into the soaring words.

I feel tremendously excited, but Sosi simply gets up and leaves me to think about what has happened.

There's nothing to think. I've mastered the trance. I'm so tired I soon collapse into sleep without eating.

At last I know I'm ready for the most important skill, the one I came here for. When Sosi comes in the morning, I say to him, "Teach me how to cure a person of spirit possession, *way Ulu 'e makim gos' 'e kom bak.*"

"You learn much," he nods. "*Ulu gos' e kilim all sik. Sosi teachim now.*"

The next several days are filled with excitement for me, while he teaches me the songs and explains the meaning of the steps. The first phase is the destruction of the possessing spirit by the ancestors, with *wegura* and war songs. He shows me how to make the *wegura* by mashing the vine with water and lime. By drinking it, the victim forgets the thoughts that the possessing spirit has planted in him. This is extremely dangerous, because the victim can lose his own thoughts as well, another way of describing madness, and in order to survive it, the possessed person must go into the second phase, complete isolation in a quiet place, repeating his ancestral songs and watched over constantly by the healer for three days. The third phase I experienced is of course the rebirth; here the patient must put on new jewelry, paint his face in a new way, and dance and share food and drink with the whole village.

It's the day after the exorcism lesson. Sosi enters the hut looking more serious than usual and tells me that the men of Sangrapa need feathers and bird bones for new masks and costumes. I will be allowed to go hunting with them, provided I will stay quiet when they approach their prey. He sits me down and has me watch him once more as he goes into trance and performs the magic that will bring to us the eagle, the bird of paradise, and the kookaburra. By now I'm sure I can follow his actions and his words almost exactly, and he does not test me.

Back at the spirit house, six of us go with bows, but without the dogs. The men shoot a few parrots and two whistling kites.

Before daybreak the next day, Sosi comes carrying a bundle of herbs and takes me to the village, where we find several men with dogs waiting in the lower level of the spirit house. Sensing high excitement, the dogs are prancing, whining, tussling. The men sit quietly on their clan platforms, but their eyes are dancing with the dogs. I recognize the names of the men and hold them in my memory as Sosi has taught me. I already know they are members of Sosi's clan, the Crocodile. We mount the entrance ladder to the sacred second level and he turns to me. "Do you remember the magic for cassowary?" he asks.

Cassowary! This is the most difficult game — fast, smart, dangerous. Dogs, and sometimes men, can be easily killed by the birds, whose huge razor-sharp spurs have been known to shatter the shields that stop war arrows. Can I remember the long ritual — the ancestor names, the formulas? Can I dissolve myself into the words and ride them into the spirit world? The men take down the sacred flutes and masks as I put the herbs on the fire, sit cross-legged, and breathe the smoke, the familiar smoke, the bright smoke that rises into the world of the spirits. I begin the chants, barely aware of the lightening sky outside, the monotonous notes of the flutes, and the slow dancing of the masked men. The words, not I — I have become the words — the words see and smell Cassowary, become the names of his ancestors and his allies, introduce him to the men around me, and name their ancestors as well. Together with the words, Cassowary enters the spirit house and takes part in the dance.

When the songs are done and the men put away the flutes, I'm still in the spirit world. I don't want to leave. I sense a disturbance. The men are talking urgently in Raapa Uu. The one named Ranjima is angry, shouting, gesturing at me, and banging his stick in his lime gourd. Sosi bends close to my ear, saying something. I struggle to understand him. "You are singing in the voice of Mekiimos, not the voice of our ancestors. These are not our songs. These are the songs of another magic."

"My songs came to Cassowary," I say calmly. "Let us go to the hunt. Let us see."

We hunt all day, and although we shoot a fine kookaburra and see cassowary tracks, by evening we have not found the prey, and we turn back to the village. Everyone is tired, and the dogs run ahead toward home. I myself am in deep gloom; my chance to win the respect of the people is deeply damaged. I didn't even realize during the singing that I had completely departed from Sosi's text. What comes next? The idea of several months' more apprenticeship to Sosi — if he himself would tolerate it — is too depressing to think about. Maybe I've even damaged Sosi's reputation as well, dragged him into my own outcast state. No wonder he was reluctant to teach me! Worse, if I, or we, are disgraced as shamans, does it mean that we're again seen as a danger to the village, a danger that must be dealt with in the direst way? I don't want to be with these people now, or ever again, and I see no way out of this hole I've dug myself.

I'm deep in these black thoughts when suddenly in the distance we hear the furious yapping and yowling of the dogs, and the men draw their arrows and run forward on silent feet. Following the commotion, I see we're approaching the village itself, and we begin to hear the shrieks of women and children. There in the path, sprinting towards us on their long legs in front of the dogs come two huge cassowaries. The one in front seems to be headed directly at me. I've been told not to retreat in such a situation but to kneel behind my shield; but in my panic I fling the shield in its direction and turn to flee. Leaping into the air, the bird gives the flying object a tremendous kick, and its death talon sticks fast in the wood. In the hopping and clawing that ensues, the dogs are immediately on the bird. The hunters are able to approach and finish it off with a hail of arrows, but not until one large tawny dog lies squirming and chittering on the ground, its intestines spewing from its groin. A very pregnant woman with a machete waddles up and with three strokes beheads this dog, then drags its edible carcass away. Its life will soon be recycled. Meanwhile the other bird has run off into the jungle, but with at least two arrows in its side as well, and several dogs and bowmen hot on its heels.

As the women and girls gather in the dusk to begin butchering the bird, the men and boys come to stand around Sosi and me. "*Raapa Uu ol' father fella e tell 'im longtime pas' story belong cassowary e come Komoko,*" Sosi says. "*Longtime pas', longtime.*" Then he lifts the heavy necklace from his shoulders and slips it over my head.

CHAPTER THIRTEEN

MEKIIMOS

Tonight I sit in the spirit house with the men of the Crocodile Clan. Sosi is at the talking stool. When he finishes his speech in Raapa Uu, he turns to me. "*Sosi not teach im Ulu time come, Ulu belong ally Mekiimos. Mekiimos e no belong im Crocodile fella. Ulu e mus finish, time come e look im all Mekiimos.*"

I still have no clear image of my spirit ally. "*Sosi now e finish teach im Ulu songs Mekiimos. Now teach im Ulu Mekiimos story. Teach im all Mekiimos . . .*" I don't know the word for *heart*, so I point to my chest.

His eyes half closed, Sosi delves into his memory, speaking in pidgin, pausing here and there to translate into Raapa Uu.

"I learned from my grandfather. He learned the story and the songs from a missionary named Boos, when our clan lived on the Sepik. Boos had a magic light that showed the deeds of the spirits. It showed the deeds of Mekiimos, who has the shape not of a man but of an animal. One the size of a dog, with a black body and a white face. He can leap like a spider and run like a cassowary. He lives with his ally spirits, Donno and Polotu, in the village of Apibali. Mekiimos's bow has many strings, and it can speak. It sings. This bow's song makes the rain fall. One day, a giant named Uili came to Apibali and stole Mekiimos's bow, and took it to his own village. Mekiimos and his allies were starving, because there was no bow to make the rain fall, to grow food. They had nothing to eat. They did not know who had stolen the singing bow. Mekiimos made magic with three betel nuts. He planted them, and a huge tree grew up, a tree that reached all the way to the clouds. The three allies climbed the tree to find food. Instead, at the top of the tree they found the village of Uili. Everything in the village was very big, but they went in. They found that Uili had the singing bow hidden inside a drum. When the giant found Donno and Polotu, he put them inside another drum, but Mekiimos hid from him. Then he made the bow sing from inside the drum, and the song made the giant Uili sleep. While he was sleeping, Mekiimos opened the drum that held his allies, and they took the singing bow out of its drum, away from the giant's village, down the tree. The giant woke and tried to capture them, but when they got to the ground, Mekiimos cut the tree with a magic machete and it fell. The giant Uili was killed. After that, the singing bow made the rain fall and everyone had food.

"This happened in the village of Apibali, a long way from here, a long way from the Sepik. Now, when a foreign spirit threatens us, we sing to Mekiimos. I have taught you the songs, and they have protected you from the deaf woman spirit."

One of the men, whose name is Muriu, speaks excitedly in Raapa Uu. Sosi answers him, then turns to me. "*Muriu e say, Ulu e command im Mekiimos e callim cassowaries. Ulu mus' stay longtime Sangrapa; Crocodile fella not command Mekiimos.*"

Sosi translates my bad pidgin into Raapa Uu: "I will ask Mekiimos to make peace with the ancestors of the Crocodile Clan, Sosi has taught me their names. Then, you can make offerings to him through your ancestors, and he will help them. I must leave Sangrapa because I am called to heal a woman in my own village who is possessed by an evil ghost. Also, I am a danger to you if I stay, because the spirits of my village might be envious, and you do not know them." Sosi continues speaking for some time, and finally I can tell by the quiet in the spirit house that the men are satisfied.

Back in the healing hut I hear the sounds of the night jungle as usual, but tonight they seem to have an altogether new meaning. It's as though they want to converse with me to learn my story, and to tell me theirs. How could I have experienced this any other way? I had no idea what I was seeking when I came here; I had to be frightened out of my civilized sanity and badgered beyond endurance before it came to me. I feel sorry for my American tribesmen, the people who believe they can force the cosmos to reveal itself with their measurements and their machines. They're pathetic, actually.

I know, too, that having the knowledge I now have opens a tremendous gulf between me and them — most of them, anyway. I wonder whether any of the people I used to think of as New Age nut cases actually share some part of this knowledge. I doubt it, actually, having read some of their books. Most of it is deeply self-absorbed, concerned with spiritual "development," not with humility in the face of the dangerous and power-charged unseen world. My semi-literate Irish grandmother was closer to this wisdom, with her trembling awareness of ghosts and leprechauns. Nana, I'm sorry I laughed at your stories.

And then of course there's Lisa, and there's the young Ashton, the Zogon whom she met in Randy's Trail so long ago. Our youthful dreams — hers and mine — were precocious understandings of things we were forced to leave behind, but we had the intelligence, or the depth of spirit, to build a special shrine for them in our hearts. I kiss her spirit, I embrace it — if it hadn't spoken to me, I would never have come here, this other world would never have been revealed to me. I rededicate myself to her. I've risked my life for this knowledge, I will risk it again to bring her back to the wisdom that lies buried in her dreams. With the help of Mekiimos, I will exorcise the missionary of mediocrity who has stolen her soul.

As for Professor Caldo, I smile to think of the comfort he took in his science, his earnest seminars, and his admiring students. But he's not to be laughed at any more than he would laugh at the naked shaman who has replaced him and lies here now. He had the gift of curiosity. In fact, he would have found this shaman fascinating, and Sosi too. He would have poked and prodded us with his questions, pickled and diced us with his theories, written tracts and given lectures on us: all, of course, without ever coming near the truth of our understanding.

There's nothing much left for me to do here in the foothills of the Star Mountains or on the watershed of the great Sepik. My thoughts tonight tell me that my spirit has already begun to leave. Can I pack this knowledge and bring it with me? I must, but how to be sure. There are things other than the songs I'll have to take with me — herbs, for example, icons, and of course the exorcism drug, *wegura*. I've never seen an icon of Mekiimos; do the Raapa Uu have them? I must ask Sosi in the morning.

But wait, there is one unfinished thing — my relationship with the spirit of the deaf woman. Although I haven't seen her since that night her presence might have killed me, she's never far from my mind, and as I confront her memory now, the hair on my neck stands up again. Her influence on my life has been profound. Though out of sight, she might in fact be necessary to my knowledge and power. Where did she come from, and why was she attracted to me? Something tells me I can't claim the title of shaman until I know these things; until then, my work will remain flawed and incomplete. But how am I to learn them? I've got to ask for help from Mekiimos, ask him to lead me to her, just as he has kept her from me thanks to Sosi's songs, and I resolve that I'll do it soon.

In the days that follow, the thought of going home becomes a great restlessness, a feeling of urgency. I have to acquire the trappings and materials of an independent shaman, to arrange transport back to Pagwi, to pay my respects to the Raapa Uu, their spirits and their traditions — and to get a new passport in Port Moresby.

I find that there are no carvings of Mekiimos, but Sosi sets about making two of them — one to remain here in the spirit house in Sangrapa. Together we also forage for the herbs I will need, and he shows me how to prepare them.

This morning when Sosi greets me, I can see he's troubled. "Talk of your success with the cassowaries has reached Komoko," he says. "Some of the men there are claiming you as their clansman, saying that it was they who introduced you to Sosi, and that it was in their spirit house that you first made your plea to learn the secrets of the Raapa Uu."

"What should we do?"

"I sent word to them that you have decided not to continue your training as a shaman, that you are lonesome for your home village and will leave without knowing much. I told them that you have been freed from the spirit of the deaf woman. I also told them that your spirit helper is Mekiimos, an ancestor that does not belong to their clans. This will keep them calm for a while, but you had better leave soon, before this becomes an issue between the villages."

At last the masks of Mekiimos are finished, and they are distinctive — a round white face with a pointed, upturned nose, black on the end, and large, round black ears. Rather than the usual cowries, the prominent, staring eyes are set with big round whelks. Holding it, I feel its power speak to me, just as I felt the power of the magic surfboard, the *te moka tula*.

It's time to go. There is no farewell ceremony for a shaman — to hold one would invite all kinds of mischief, supernatural and human. One morning before dawn I simply walk with Sosi and two canoemen from Sangrapa down to the place where the trading dugouts are kept on the Sepik. I wear the shaman's necklace Sosi gave me, and a tattered pair of his shorts in place of my penis sheath. I carry a string bag with food, my Mekiimos mask, and two other well-made masks the men of the Crocodile Clan have given me to trade for cash in Wiwak. There I can buy clothes and a bus ticket to Port Moresby. The others bring their bows and shields for protection on the river, and goods to trade at Yigei, from where they will come back up the river. There is little talk, but I ask Sosi if he has any last advice for me.

"You are not yet a shaman," he says. "You do not know where your ancestors hold power and where they do not; you know only a few of the many clever beings, the many wide places, the many twisted paths of the spirit world. You must use your little knowledge very cautiously. Do not draw attention to yourself. Make allies with men and spirits both; don't forget to give gifts and speak kindly. Save your knowledge for serious things.

"There is another thing. The spirits are not men. They have their own ways. Often they will test you and play with you. They will fool you just to show their power. They will lead you to expect one thing, then do another. They will give you power one day and take it away the next. They will make you look foolish, and laugh at you."

"What about the spirit of the deaf woman? Will it come back? If so, what should I do?"

He nods gravely. "Don't forget to offer herbs and songs every day, both to your ancestor and to this spirit. If you pay attention and practice what I taught you, some day you will know the meaning of this woman, whether it is lucky or unlucky."

"You have been like a father to me, Sosi. I will not forget you. I will not forget the Raapa Uu. If I live, someday I will come back to Sangrapa, I promise you." The Sepik glistens golden in the rising sunlight. We embrace; I step into the canoe.

CHAPTER FOURTEEN

THE ZOGON SHAMAN

Disorienting as Wiwak was when I first landed there, now I find walking through the LA airport even more bizarre. Why is everything so big, so shiny? Why is everyone overfed, overdressed? The Raapa Uu would call these people *laleo* — pale ghosts. I must look terribly strange to them, with my long beard and hair and ragged clothes. But they don't look at me. They don't look at each other. They seem absorbed, possessed by something far away.

We're funneled along stainless steel corridors with silent escalators to Passport Control. The young agent looks like two people stuffed into one huge, neatly pressed blue uniform. She examines the temporary passport I got from the American embassy in Port Moresby. "One moment, Sir," and she taps something into her computer. What a strange word, *sir*. Once a title of respect, it's now used precisely to strip a person of his identity, exactly as if she had said, "One moment, Number 5482." An older male agent appears, examines my photo as she did, then eases her aside and clickety-clacks on her computer some more.

"What's your social security number?" I give it to him. "How long were you in New Guinea?"

"Two hundred and twelve days."

"What were you doing there?"

"I'm a professor of psychology," I start to say, then realize that this will sound ridiculous given the way I look. If I say "adventuring," he'll take me for a drug dealer. If I tell him I'm an art collector, he will want to see my purchases. In desperation I say, "I'm a missionary," thinking that's true enough, I'm bringing the supernatural knowledge of the Raapa Uu to these shores. But he interrupts my thought. "Welcome back, Brother Caldo." He stamps my passport.

On the way to baggage claim I go to the men's room. After I pee I stare in the mirror. I've lost a lot of weight. My skin has the same leathery look I saw on Russell when we met in Del Mar many months ago. I did wash my hair and beard in Wewak, but I didn't really realize how long they are, and how curly. I look like a skinny, brown, aging Wavy Gravy.

As I enter the main terminal, I'm struck by a new sensation — the savagery of this world. It's not just that these people fail to see each other. Whether they're talking on a cell phone or staring at a TV screen, their eyes are blank, like those of actual ghosts. They have no names, no tribal markings except for the occasional Sikh turban or cleric's collar. In the gleaming terminal hallways, they seem like the unmourned dead, wandering their nameless land, and I wonder who has murdered them. Far better to be eaten by one's killers, as the Raapa Uu would do. For a second I wonder if the Del Mar that I left was just an illusion, that the real one is just a suburb of this ghost world, but I shake off the thought. There, surely, people still have names, their eyes have souls, and they speak to one another.

I reach San Diego at noon. Having burnt my cell phone, I don't have a number for Blake, but I remember Ysabel's, so I phone her from a booth, and get her answering machine. I ask her to call Blake and tell him I'm looking for him in Del Mar, at the beach park. I have a few dollars left and I remember Lisa's number, but decide it will be better to hitchhike. After a couple of hours of fruitless thumbing, I sit down by the on-ramp, place my Mekiimos mask on top of the knapsack I bought in Port Moresby, and begin to sing a trading song. Almost at once, a new Ram pickup stops. The driver is young and wears a goatee and a baseball cap. "You selling that?" he asks, indicating the mask.

"This is Mekiimos, my ancestor. I can't sell him to you, but if you give us a ride to Del Mar, Mekiimos and I will share our knowledge with you."

He scowls. "Don't have time for that, Dad. Anyway, Del Mar's like, waaay out of my way."

I nod. "Good luck to you, then."

"Thanks. I need it." Instead of driving off, he leans back in his seat, rubs his face with large calloused hands, sips slowly from a paper coffee cup. "Let's go," he says at length, nodding toward the passenger seat. When I get in, he sticks out his hand. "My name's Chilly," he yells. I can hardly hear him over the CD he's playing — a routine by some stand-up comic. In a frame on the dash is a photo of a gentle, homely woman holding a boy of about ten, who looks like a clone of herself.

"My name's Ashton."

"So the mask is your ancestor. Did you carve him?" he shouts.

"No. He came to me in my dreams. A New Guinea carver made him for me. They understand about spirits and dreams."

"I dreamt of my grandmother a couple of times," Chilly says. "She died when I was twelve. In this one dream, I was looking down at this stream from a bridge, and she floated by in her long dress, smiling up at me."

"She's here with us, then."

He sighs, like he's heard this before. "I don't know if I believe that stuff."

"Who knows? It's odd, though, isn't it? I ask Mekiimos for help; you stop and give me a ride. You tell me you can use some luck. Then you tell me a dream about your ancestor, your Mekiimos, giving you a blessing."

He turns down the stereo. "Yeah, I guess it's a little strange. What do you make of it?"

"I don't know. Maybe the dead know a lot of things we don't. Maybe they can hear us."

The comic is saying, ". . . and being heavier than air, crashed through the roof of the carnival freak show, crushing the dog-faced boy, and destroying many of his chew-toys . . ."

Chilly laughs. "Yeah, and maybe our ancestors are as full of shit as we are!"

When we reach Del Mar, Chilly asks me if I need money to eat. I tell him no, I have friends here, and besides, I have Mekiimos. I ask him to drop me off at the foot of Randy's Trail, thinking I can find a place to sleep in the eucalyptus trees.

He says, "I guess I don't need to wish you good luck, then, do I?"

"Doesn't a gift return to the giver?"

"Well, good luck then." He smiles and drives off. When he's out of sight, I walk up the trail and find a shady spot in the trees. I had forgotten that there are very few birds here, no frogs. I have nothing to eat, but I've learned that hunger is a normal experience, like fatigue, not something to struggle against. I take my water bottle from my backpack and make a place at the base of a great tree where I can set Mekiimos and build a small altar of stones, pine cones, and flowers of broom and Indian paintbrush that I find at hand. Here I bless the spirit of the tree with a few drops of water, then mark off a square on the ground, about three yards by three, the corners facing the cardinal directions, and bless each corner with water while asking the spirits of the grove for their permission to stay here. I gather up a few twigs and pine needles, and sit down cross-legged in front of Mekiimos. I light a small fire and place a sprig of herbs from my string bag on it. Then I sing Mekiimos a song, a song of farewell and blessing for Chilly. It pleases me to find that learning the formulas of Raapa Uu magic songs has many uses I hadn't thought of. Translating the names of the spirits and places to English, the blessing song formula goes like this:

> *Mekiimos, rest in the company of the spirits of thunder and yams.*
> *Mekiimos, rest in the company of the small spirits.*
> *Mekiimos, rest in the company of the human souls.*
> *Mekiimos, eat and enjoy the blood of my pig.*
> *Mekiimos, eat and enjoy the smoke of my fire.*
> *Mekiimos, eat and enjoy my song.*
>
> *Mekiimos, speak to the spirits of thunder and yams.*
> *Mekiimos, speak to the small spirits.*
> *Mekiimos, speak to the souls of the Big Men.*
> *Mekiimos, tell them to eat and enjoy the blood of my pig.*
> *Mekiimos, tell them to eat and enjoy the smoke of my fire.*
> *Mekiimos, tell them to eat and enjoy my song.*
>
> *Mekiimos, tell them to eat and enjoy the blood of Chilly's pig.*
> *Mekiimos, tell them to eat and enjoy the smoke of Chilly's fire.*
> *Mekiimos, tell them to eat and enjoy Chilly's song.*

Spirits of thunder and yams, don't forget you have enjoyed Chilly's pig blood.

Spirits of thunder and yams, don't forget you have enjoyed Chilly's smoke.

Spirits of thunder and yams, don't forget you have enjoyed Chilly's song.

Small spirits, don't forget you have enjoyed Chilly's pig blood.

Small spirits, don't forget you have enjoyed Chilly's smoke.

Small spirits, don't forget you have enjoyed Chilly's song.

Souls of Big Men, don't forget you have enjoyed Chilly's pig blood.

Souls of Big Men, don't forget you have enjoyed Chilly's smoke.

Souls of Big Men, don't forget you have enjoyed Chilly's song.

Mekiimos, Spirits of thunder and yams, small spirits, souls of Big Men,

Let this song gladden your hearts until Chilly's descendants sing this same song to their Mekiimos.

I have no sooner finished my song than I hear a deeply disturbing sound. It's not loud, maybe a quarter mile away, but it's unmistakable: a bulldozer, and a big one too. I hide my pack in the brush and head toward the sound. As I approach, I hear the crash of a tree going down, then the sickening crackle of breaking limbs as the dozer crushes its victim. From my hiding place in the brush, I see that the dozer has already cut a road from Seacrest down to the heart of the trail, and is clearing and leveling an ample building site. The raw yellow earth is piled with the debris of trees and brush, twisted roots now pointing skyward, piles of limbs, their shredded flesh reeking of sweet sap, tangles of trampled coyote brush, manzanita, and sage. As I watch, a man wearing a yellow construction helmet fires up a chain saw and begins ripping into the carnage.

First thought: Counterattack. Second thought: Where, and how, is Lisa? Counterattack will take some time and thought, but Lisa's house is a few hundred yards from here, and I start at once to make my way there, staying out of sight. I'm sure her horror at this assault matches mine, and that the moment she sees me she'll know that I'm her strongest ally in this struggle. Ironically, this catastrophe is my good fortune. Once again, Mekiimos has dealt me a winning hand.

Still, I have to prepare myself spiritually before I confront her. She's still angry with me, and mistrustful, maybe even more so, since I left at a time when I might have been a help to her. Months of strenuous work have prepared me to deal with this through the patient path of spiritual knowledge, not through the heroic path of open conflict. I've put away the poses of ordinary men: the masks of glittering intellect, smooth refinement, generous wealth. To add to their altars the Raapa Uu seek out the rare sharp stones among the river pebbles; I've become such a sharp stone.

I have to accept the risk that I might fail and that my failure might mean death. That's right, a kind of death, because like a warrior committed to victory, I can no longer imagine a life in defeat. Everything will be wagered, and everything might be lost; without the wager, everything is already lost. My fatigue and hunger leave me. I feel light, powerful. Here on Randy's Trail was where Professor Caldo met Lisa only a few months ago.

Lisa's house comes into view through the trees. It seems bigger and more elegant than I remember. A wind chime, hanging from a corner of the eaves, is sending out small, clear tones. This house is a kind of idol, an image of the omnivorous spirit of wealth. For a fleeting instant, I feel a tremendous urge to destroy it, to bring the huge bulldozer up the trail and assail its placid walls in a great shrieking of pulled nails, cracking of timbers, crashing of shattered glass. Calming myself, I picture Lisa inside.

The Raapa Uu say that the spirit house is the body of the community, and the men inside are its vital liver, brain, muscles, heart. Ugly as it is, this is her spirit house. Inside its body, Lisa is the heart of Randy's Trail; I am its muscles. I will bring the spirits of this trail, and Lisa's with them, into the circle of my power.

I climb the slope to the corner where the wind chime hangs and, in full view from the bay windows, unfasten it and bring it to the place where I sang the blessing for Chilly. In the small clearing the sinuous red branches of the manzanitas look like blood vessels. I hang the wind chime on one of them. I gather a few more yellow flowers of broom, red Indian paintbrushes, blue Ceanothus, and arrange them in radial lines on my altar below the wind chime. Sitting cross-legged in front of it, I'm selecting herbs from my string bag when I hear Lisa's voice behind me,

"Hey! What are you . . . Oh my God! Ashton? Is that you?" I want her to witness this tremendously important song. I turn around and motion her to sit down. "Ashton, It's you, isn't it? It's Lisa! Don't you recognize me? Holy shit, you look like a . . . like a goddamn ghost or something. Oh dear. You're in bad shape, aren't you? What happened?"

"I'm fine. I was about to call you, but you got here too soon."

"All right, Ashton. You go ahead with that. I'll be back in a little while, okay?"

"Wait! I want you to see this."

"No, no, I'll be right back." And she disappears quickly toward the house.

Okay, I look bizarre, maybe even crazy, but no matter, the battle has only begun. I understand that the spirits are playing with me. As if to make the point clear, the wind brings me again the distant snort and diesel smell of the bulldozer down the trail. Sosi warned me of the spirits' playfulness, and I won't be fooled — it's just a matter of joining them in their game. The prayer will not be one of calling magic, then, it will be one of thanks. I will offer the wind chime in sacrifice, and sing the prayer twice. Again, I gather sticks and pine needles, and make a small fire. Singing to the great spirits and Mekiimos, I lay the chime on the fire and watch its strings and wooden frame dissolve in the flames, leaving only the blackened metal tubes.

I find a skull-sized rock nearby, and I'm about to hammer the tubes into the ground to finish the offering, when I hear footsteps on the leaf litter up the hill. Lisa approaches, this time holding the arm of Blake. He calls out in his familiar way,

"Hey, Prof! We didn't know you were back. What's up, dude?"

Careful, his face and his greeting don't match. But Blake is my friend and ally. I stand and embrace him, then I simply gesture in the direction of the bulldozer.

"Yeah," he says. "Major, major Shitsonville."

"We can talk about that," says Lisa, "but first, what did you do with my wind chime? Do New Guineans greet someone by burning their possessions or something?" Again she takes Blake's arm. There's something subtly different about the way he looks. A bit heavier, maybe? A bit tidier?

"Papuans understand many things that Westerners don't. It may be useful that I've learned some of their ways."

"Prof," says Blake, "have you seen yourself in a mirror? We've got to get you some hot water and a barber — not to mention a little food."

Lisa murmurs something about a psychologist.

Barbers. Baths. Doctors. How can they be thinking about that, here where we can hear the sounds of someone raping Randy's Trail? I study Lisa. I'm beginning to understand that my job is going to take tremendous patience, wisdom, and power. Ordinary measures won't be enough, I'm certain. Lisa stoops down and one by one picks up the blackened tubes of the wind chime before heading back to the house.

Blake is avoiding my eyes. "It's okay, man," I say. "Better see if she needs help." He grips my shoulder, finally meets my gaze for an instant, then nods and goes after her. I fetch my backpack and head up the trail.

When I reach her house, they're sitting in the kitchen talking, but fall silent when I walk in. "So," I say, "are you going to tell me about this bulldozer business?"

"First," says Lisa, "are you going to tell us what you were doing down there?"

"In time I'd planned to explain the ritual system I learned in New Guinea. It's quite sophisticated, and it works, but I wouldn't expect anyone to accept it who didn't know the philosophy behind it. Especially not a Westerner who's been trained in so-called rational thinking. I can help you with this bulldozer problem."

"You believe you can influence events with primitive magic?"

"Do you know anything at all about magic, primitive or otherwise?" I ask.

"I don't have time for that. Please, just don't help me with my problems, okay?"

Blake reaches over and puts his hand on Lisa's arm. "Whoa. Just a second. The Prof is just trying to be helpful, right, Ashton? He's not going to mess things up. Shit, we've known each other since we were in high school. You've always been kind of an oddball, Prof. Go ahead."

"Thanks, Blake, but I don't need your defense. Lisa, do you honestly think I'm nuts?"

She stares at me for a minute, then looks at her hands. "I don't know. Anyway, I want you to promise not to try to help unless I ask you to."

"Okay."

"Okay?"

"Okay."

CHAPTER FIFTEEN

BULLDOZER

Lisa seems fairly calm about the bulldozer people. "When I bought my property, I thought that no one could build there, because I controlled road access to the whole slope. But the owners have dragged me into court over it. They have this diabolic strategy. If they start construction without legal clearance, they hope the court will give them a kind of squatters' rights. And once they've already gutted the forest, they hope I'll give up and accept a cash settlement instead of an injunction."

"I can't imagine why you're so calm about it," I say. "You dreamt about this place for so long, you worked so hard for it. It's part of you. Nobody deserves to be treated this way . . ." She nods now, and her eyes finally fill with tears. Since I've known her, I've never seen her cry, and the sight stirs a parade of images and sensations: Could I have prevented this if I'd made up with her and stayed in Del Mar? Her love and mine for Randy's Trail isn't just nostalgia. This miniature wildness isn't just the symbol of a juvenile dream, some treasure of a half-remembered past; it represents something every sane person loves — the beauty of wildness, a past that was simple and innocent. This attack on the trail is a symptom of our culture's diseased condition — the immense destructive power of the selfish rich; the ignorant disregard for nature and community; the contempt for the "weak" values of sympathy, reverence, patience.

Has her unhappiness, and my absence, driven her farther from me? What is this bond that seems to have grown between her and Blake? Looking at him now, his craggy face with its crooked smile, I'm realizing that I've never been able to read that face, that I don't really know the guy. Up to this moment, I never cared.

"Blake," I say, "what are your thoughts about this?"

"I was gonna ask you that, Prof."

I look at Lisa. "The two of you must have talked about it."

"Blake's offered to help cover the legal costs," Lisa says. "He has his own business now. It's doing well."

"It's doing *great!* Remember my idea for fiberglass art? Well, Gordo Toole and Lisa have been fantastic. They financed my first couple of pieces; they fed me some great ideas. Now I've sold some stuff, and I have a show coming up at Sid's."

Lisa brightens a little. "I've got one of his pieces here. Come and look."

In the corner of the living room stands a well-crafted nude figure of a woman. The figure leans forward, a bit off balance, with head turned slightly to one side, arms raised in front, fingers spread, the pose suggesting a mixture of eagerness and fear. The skin is a speckled pale gray, looking a little like stone. Lisa lowers the living room lights with the dimmer switch, then picks up a remote control from the side table and flips it on. The figure emits a bluish light, focused in the head, and as we watch, the focus of the light moves to other parts of the body and begins to change color. The breasts, the loins glow purple, the hands orange; the color of the head shifts in a red direction, slowly undulating. A small white strobe begins to pulse between the breasts, accompanied by the sound of a heartbeat. The effect is uncanny — the figure seems to be moving slightly. Then the light and sound fade gradually, revealing the stone-like skin again. In a few seconds, the tableau begins to repeat, and we watch it again.

Lisa turns it off and brings the lights back up. "This is a prototype," she says. "Blake's got some orders for new ones that are programmable; you can design your own sequence, add your own sound track. They'll sell for fifteen thousand apiece."

"I've got this one now that projects films on the skin from the inside," says Blake. "You know, any kind of detailed moving images. Think of the possibilities of that, Prof. We just got to solve the focus problem."

The possibilities, indeed. I'm surprised at Blake's mastery of this peculiar medium — if he's actually done it himself — but not by the gimmickiness of what he's doing. He's avoided the serious labor of a real artist — the work of perfecting, through personal struggle and patient trial, new ways of expressing deep truth. His work is a shabby shortcut that relies on the viewer's childish fascination with novelty itself. I want to say, "I thought you wanted to be an artist, not an interior decorator," but obviously Lisa has other thoughts, and this doesn't seem like a good time to insult the two of them. "Very, very original, Blake. Really interesting. Really well done, too." I'm actually sincere about the last part. His work has the stamp of craftsmanship.

We all agree it's been a long day. It's been at least twenty-four hours since I've eaten, and I feel light-headed as well. It's getting dark as Blake and I head out, stopping to pick up a frozen pizza, a jar of peanut butter (for Blake's pizza) and a six-pack of beer on the way. His place is a tiny cinder block room with a kitchen and toilet, attached to a huge three-car garage. The garage reeks of polyester resin, a smell every surfer knows well. It's a jungle of sculpture molds, rolls of fiberglass, drums of resin, cans of pigment, tools, stacks of electronic equipment, and projects in progress. One wall is papered with images of all kinds — print media, photographs, sketches, even a children's doll and a teddy bear, hanging from pegs.

While Blake heats the pizza, I look closely at the wall, trying to ignore my stomach's gnawing response to the kitchen smell. There are several snapshots of pretty women scattered throughout the mix of magazine ads, art posters, scenic photos, and carnival masks, and as I scan these, my eyes is caught by something familiar. I look more closely, and sure enough, there's Lisa in her iridescent dressing gown, looking radiant.

Well, well. Well, well. I feel dizzy. Hands shaking, I take the picture down and turn it over. On the back, in Lisa's writing, it says, "Is that you? Is this me?" and there's a drawing of a heart. The feeling I have is like one I had a few times when I was a kid and I woke up from a nightmare, only the nightmare kept going, as if it were there in my room: it's a situation that would seem to call for action, but you aren't really conscious, and you have no will to make your body act. You can't even call out for help.

I find myself carefully pinning the picture of Lisa back on the wall. The smell of the polyester resin is oppressive, nauseating in fact. I want to get out of here, but I feel my knees giving out . . .

The roaring sound rises and falls, just like the voice of a bull-roarer. I must be waking in the spirit house in Sangrapa. But there's too much light here. I lift my head and look around, and I see I'm in Blake's bed. The sound is coming from his workshop. It must be some kind of grinding tool. Slowly my head clears, and I remember last night. I sit up, still dizzy. I'm in my shorts, and I look around for my clothes but can't see them anywhere. The smell of weed in the apartment sharpens my senses and makes me realize I need food. Have to think. No money. No place to live. My only friend within a hundred miles is screwing the woman of my universe, who in turn is about to have her dream shattered, the dream that ties me to her.

Yet I feel strangely calm. I brought myself to this situation, slowly and deliberately. I'm lying here retracing my steps, inch by inch. My life had become meaningless, devoid of self-respect. I broke my bonds and threw myself into a void, led by the vision of Lisa's dream. I embraced humility, poverty, danger, fatigue, and hunger to become worthy of that dream. I've now reached the place where my worthiness is to be tested. It makes perfect sense. Fearing the loss of Randy's Trail, of losing the dream at the core of her life, Lisa has run in panic away from that dream, away from me. As the only true representative of the dream, my presence has even added to her confusion and fear. Once the threat is defeated, she'll be herself again — more so than ever in fact, since the fear of loss clarifies and strengthens whatever is precious to us.

The meaning of my journey is becoming clear. I was led to Lisa, then to Sid and Russell and the *te moka tula* and Sosi and Mekiimos, then back here at the precise moment where only someone who had taken this exact path would have the needed knowledge and spiritual development. The spirits chose me, instructed me, for this. Lisa and Blake's relationship is a vital part of the plan, a signal calculated to ignite my soul. All the symbolism fits. In her fear, Lisa has embraced a false champion, a clever actor who poses as a shaman — since a shaman is what a true artist is — but who only uses tricks transparent to the spirits.

I finish the remaining half of the cold pizza, wash it down with beer. I go in the bathroom to take a shower, and I get a look at myself in the mirror. Holy shit. No wonder people ask me if I'm sick or something; I look like a Tijuana panhandler. A couple of my ribs are visible over my shrunken waist. My hair and beard belong on a Hindu holy man. I shower, wash my hair, and shave.

I find a stub of a candle in a kitchen drawer, light it, and stick it on a plate with a few drops of wax. I sprinkle a pinch of herbs from my pack on the flame, set the plate on the floor, place Mekiimos on top of my pack facing it, and sit cross-legged in front of it. The bull-roarer sound comes again from the garage. In the flame I see the yellow bulldozer and the smashed forest, but I make my breathing and my mind calm, and concentrate on the face of Mekiimos. In the finely carved surface I see new forest crowd in around the machine and strangle it, until it dies and then disappears completely in the underbrush. Now in the candle I see Lisa's face. At first it's stained with tears, but as I relax and breathe, it too begins to relax and then to smile a little. I hold the image for several long minutes, then blow out the candle and put the things away.

My body is loose and my mind crystal clear when I step into the garage workshop. Blake is applying a coat of resin to what looks like the back half of a nude figure, clamped horizontally to a metal jig. His clothes, his eyebrows and hair, are covered with white crumbly material. "Jeez, I'm glad to see you're alive, Prof," he smiles. "You scared the shit out of me, passing out like that, but you look okay now — anyway you look more or less human."

"Thanks for taking care of me. You're a good man. Can you tell me where my clothes are?"

He points to a washer and dryer in the corner of the garage. "You were pretty grungy, Man. Have you had anything to eat?"

"Yeah, thanks. Look. I know I can't stay here. I have to get a job and find a place to live."

"I stayed on your couch in Riverside, dude," he says. "You can stay here until you get settled. I was even hoping I might talk you into helping me in my workshop for the time being."

"I thought you might say that. Sure, we can talk about it. However . . ." At the tone of my voice he stops, looks at me eye to eye. "There's something else we have to talk about first." He straightens, still holding his brush.

"I gotta get this coat on, before the resin gels."

"This won't take a minute. It's that I know you're, ahh, *seeing* Lisa."

He bends over his work, avoiding my eyes. "She needed somebody."

"It's okay . . . Well, it's not exactly okay, but I probably would have done the same thing if the situation was reversed. You guys must have talked about her and me."

"Yeah. At first she wouldn't, ahh . . . you know . . ."

"wouldn't get it on with you."

"Yeah. I was consulting with her all the time about my artwork, and we talked about stuff, you know? She liked helping me. She said you never asked for her input on anything. Said she cared a lot about you, but you confused the shit out of her. She didn't know what you were up to, or when you were coming back, or even whether you loved her. Then this thing came up with her property, and I was over there helping her with that, and one thing led to another . . ."

"I understand. You figured I didn't really care enough about her to make an issue of it, or I wouldn't have left the way I did. You figured that when I came back — *if* I came back — the three of us would just sort it out. Like I said, I don't blame you. But here's what I have to tell you. She's the one I love, Blake. *The. One.*"

"Wow, Prof! Where are you going, dude? Are you asking me not to see her?"

"No, that'd be useless in any case. She has to make up her own mind. She might be finished with me now, I don't know. I'm just telling you that I'm staking my life on having her. You know me, bro. You know what I mean by it."

He stops his work again and stands quietly for a minute, then says, "I think she loves me, man."

Silently I thank Mekiimos and the spirits. I've won. If he was in love with her, he'd have told me, politely or not, to go fuck myself — that she's his. As it is, he's probably telling me that he's told *her* he loves her. "Has she said that?" I ask.

"Ashton. Let's not get into who said what, okay? Anyway, are you going to see her?"

Again I thank Mekiimos. She hasn't said she loves him. "Not unless she starts it," I say. "I'd like to help her defend the forest, and let her handle the man-woman thing. For now, I won't say anything about this unless she asks me, Blake, but she just might ask. If so, I have to tell her what I'm telling you."

He dips his brush in the resin and bends over his project again. "She's more likely to ask *me* these days, I'd say."

"And?"

"It depends on what she says, right, Prof? Bummer this all happened this way."

"I think it's just begun. Look, I don't want to lose your friendship, man. Let's keep talking, okay?"

"Yeah. For sure. Let's keep talking. Fuck! The damn resin's starting to gel already."

"Still want me to work with you? We could keep an eye on each other."

He shrugs. "We can give it a try, see if it works, I guess. I gotta throw this batch away and make a new one."

"Sure, let's give it a try. Can I have today off? Still kind of strung out, you know."

Actually, I feel full of energy, but I need time to think. A lot of time.

The first thing, of course, is to begin the counterattack on the bulldozer people. My deepest study with Sosi was the lifting of curses and the liberation of captured souls, aiming as I was on the task of freeing Lisa's child spirit from possession by her missionary identity. In the process, though, I could hardly avoid learning a fair amount of the Raapa Uu specialty: war magic. Most of it doesn't fit my purposes too closely, having to do as it does with killing people, but they can also mobilize the spirits to weaken and distract the enemy. It should be fairly easy to do that to those I now face, who surely have no knowledge of the needed countermagic. It will be wise, of course, to keep my own presence and identity, and my background, well hidden. I have magic for that as well.

I need to know everything I can about everyone involved — the owner, the contractor, the financer — who they are, where they work, and how to get direct access to them, to their personal belongings, and to the places where they live and work. It would help if I could simply ask Lisa and Blake what they know, but then I'd have to explain what I'm going to do with the information, and Lisa almost certainly won't agree if I tell her the truth. I can get what I need with a combination of public records and creative guile. I'm a bit surprised to find that Blake has a high-speed router and a fancy computer for his graphic design work. I really don't know him at all, do I? Transportation is critical for my task, but he also has an old pickup truck in addition to his car, and I might be able to borrow one or the other for the time being.

Today he's working in his studio, and he lends me his car plus a hundred dollars. I drive to the public library and find that they do indeed have databases of local deeds, building permits, and court proceedings. I love the irony of this: My New Guinea magic comes from a human environment where people know the details of one another's lives intimately. Knowing exactly who, where, what, why, and when, over a wide stretch of jungle, are things one can scarcely escape knowing, since they are the daily material of talk and observation. Every act has social reverberations over which people have very little control. It's for this very reason that they go to great lengths to hide the details of their magic within the spirit house, but the fact is, even many of these details are known widely as well. Such social transparency sounds preposterous in our so-called civilized world, where we feel protected by the fact that nearly everyone we meet is a stranger who has no business knowing anything about us at all. And yet this is an illusion. Our lives are, in a different way, as regulated and as transparent as those of the Raapa Uu, and their magic will work as well here as there. By nightfall I have the names, ages, home and business addresses, phone numbers, and Social Security numbers of the owner, one V. (for Virgil) Prentiss Harmon, and the contractor, one Bjørn Flysted.

With this information and internet access plus a phone and fax machine, it takes me another three days to find out the makes, models, and license numbers of their cars; their educational histories; the names, numbers, and addresses of people and businesses they've phoned lately; and how much they've charged lately for what. Using this and a map, I know almost as much about them as the men of Sangrapa know about their neighbors. Harmon is a financial analyst, divorced, with two grown kids; he lives in a condo near the La Jolla Cove and drives a black 2006 Lexus SUV, with vanity plate IHRMNYU. Flysted, who is married and has three kids, spends a lot of time in motels within thirty miles of his home; he uses his work phone to call the home of a woman named Luna Estrada almost daily, usually for periods of less than five minutes. Estrada works at a restaurant in Encinitas called Ruby Blue's and takes computer skills classes at North County Junior College two nights a week.

And I've never even tried this before or studied how to do it.

The next step is trickier. To enlist the spirits against these people, I need to bring them in person, as it were, into my rituals. I find a photo of Harmon online and print it out, but I find none of Flysted. I need things that bear what the Raapa Uu call their *kuesu*, the signature of their mortal presence — what we might call their DNA — nail parings, hair, clothes, and artifacts that they use all the time. In the case of Flysted, I think Estrada might prove helpful if I can be helpful to her, meaning if I can build up a bank account. The case of Harmon is more challenging. Apparently he frequents a health spa called LifeLift in San Diego. I only need to find out what his schedule is and, of course, to raise a bit of cash for a membership.

CHAPTER SIXTEEN

STALKING THE ENEMY

Ysabel phones a couple of days later, to talk to Blake. He tells her I've been back for four days.

"I thought we were going to be friends, Ashton. I thought we were going to outgrow all that family shit and treat each other like human beings. Or did you put yourself up for adoption in the rain forest? Did you trade your family in for a set of real-life cannibals . . . ?"

"I was going to call you. I wanted to get settled first. You're not the type to worry about things, anyway."

"How would you even know what type I am? Anyway, that's not the point. I feel like you just don't give a shit. Do you?"

"Of course I do. It's a struggle for me to get my own life under control, can you understand that? I need to work things out in my own unique way, without having to explain myself."

"Do I *ever* try to tell you what to do?"

"You have Supreme Court opinions about everything, Ysabel."

"Well, excuse me. Since we're here, though, I think you ought to know that Thelma called me — you do remember Thelma, your daughter?"

"What did she want?"

"She wanted you, Morse. She wanted her father. She didn't even know you were in New Guinea."

"I'll call her. Listen, don't stay mad. I'll write you a big email tonight." I want to tell her I love her, but as usual, I don't. It sounds too strong, somehow.

My research on Flysted and Harmon is duly reported to Mekiimos and the spirits in my nightly songs. I also report my need for sustenance, to prepare for the battle ahead, and the results are almost immediate. Sid, ever sensitive to his clients' habits, has dreamed up something new called "art piñatas." These are beautifully designed, one-of-a-kind works of art, used the way ordinary piñatas are used, except their smashing doesn't require a children's or even an adult's birthday party. They have the tremendous advantage over ordinary piñatas of being valued at well over a thousand dollars in themselves, filled not with candy, but with smaller works of art worth forty or fifty dollars a pop. Having sold this idea to a dozen clients already, Sid now needs the goods to start coming in a couple of weeks from now, and he wants Blake to make them.

Working into the night, first we try building a few basic shapes of fiberglass, but this doesn't work. Even the extra-thin structures take a mad pounding with a baseball bat before breaking. When they do break, shrapnel-sharp pieces fly around the room and get underfoot. Most ordinary piñatas are made of clay or papier-mâché, and although neither of us knows how to work with this stuff, we begin to experiment. We try various grades of paper and stiffening agents, and discover that plain old newspaper and wheat flour work best. They're cheap and available, and you can make them do almost anything. Blake comes up with a way of hand shaping modular plastic forms, covering them with papier-mâché, letting it dry, then cutting it off in sections, which we just stick together with more of the same material. The modular parts can be rearranged and modified to produce an unlimited variety of finished shapes. Giving a high-tech smoothness and luster to the paper piñatas is a challenge, but with heavier papers and laquers we're soon making figures that look very much like Blake's fiberglass ones. We can't make them translucent, but we get a unique effect by fitting them with motion-activated electronics — fiber optics, tiny strobe lights, and even thumb-sized digital voice boxes that we can easily program.

It's a new and surprising experience to work with Blake. His offhand, loose-jointed manner never seems to vary much, but he gets things done somehow. He knows how to get information from people — about where to get stuff, about the merits of various materials and technologies, and he has an amazing memory for these details. He's incurably optimistic, and when he makes an unsuccessful decision, he never broods over it, but moves smoothly to a new plan. His manual skill is the really amazing thing. His hands often rush ahead of his mental grasp of a problem, making things work as if they had brains of their own. A lot of our work is trial and error, but Blake works so fast that results are never long in coming.

The work is demanding and absorbing. We eat take-out, often working right through meals of pizza or Chinese or sandwiches, to which Blake generally adds some bizarre condiment — especially sliced avocados and pickles — and always beer. I find I have little time to think about my Randy's Trail project. In odd moments when a new construction is drying or Blake is out searching for parts, I can spend a few minutes making notes. It shouldn't be too hard to meet Harmon at his gym. I can identify him from the photo I got online. As for Flysted, Ruby Blue's, where his girlfriend works, must be a small world, and I should be able to locate her there. Maybe the staff wear name badges. Anyway, Estrada obviously sees a lot of Flysted and will lead me to him wittingly or not.

After a couple of weeks, Blake and I are producing magnificent piñatas. The first finished one is a sleek, powerful Jules Verne submarine with glowing portholes that makes "emergency dive siren" noises when struck. On the drawing board are a glowing green crocodile with a ticking clock that chimes when beaten; a jewel-studded Cheshire cat with a diabolical snicker; a sort of W. C. Fields politician who can give a bombastic speech, punctuated with boos; a realistic coffin that groans; and an antique Chinese vase that emits smashing sounds. For more risqué tastes, we design a fat pink couple locked in sexual congress, who oooh and aaah under the force of the baton.

It's midafternoon and we're tired. Blake, stripped to his skivvies, is hauling cold pizza out of the fridge. "I'd like to have a break, man," I say. "Do you mind if I take the afternoon off? We're making good progress."

"I guess you're right," he says. "I need a rest myself."

So I scrub the dust off my face and comb the plastic bits out of my hair, and I'm off to Ruby Blue's. The place is downtown and has business lunch written all over it. In a gesture toward elegance, the floors are carpeted and you have to wait to be seated, but the menu is average and a bit overpriced.

The waitresses wear black skirts and cobalt blue blouses (no name tags), and they start by offering you a cocktail. I ask for a glass of white wine. Business looks awfully slow today; the room is less than half full. In two minutes my waitress is back with my drink. "Excuse me," I say. "Doesn't Luna Estrada work here?"

"Oh. You know Luna?"

"Ahh, sort of. I was in her class at North County for a while. I hear she worked here."

"Can I tell her who's asking?"

"She probably doesn't remember me. I was only there a few times. My name's Mike." She takes my order, and I watch her as she goes about her rounds. In a couple of minutes she stops and talks to a short, busty woman with black hair pulled back in a bun. This woman isn't what you'd call beautiful, but her skin is warm café au lait, and she has an open, gentle face with huge dark eyes. She fixes said eyes on me for a moment, then picks up a tray and marches off. I think Flysted is a lucky man. I know intuitively that she'll come and talk to me even though she's never seen me before.

"Your name is Mike?" she says cheerfully, with a light Latin accent. "Have I met you?"

"Actually, just once, just briefly, in class. You were in kind of a hurry, but you made an impression on me."

"When was that?" Now she's giving me this very strange look, as if I had a banana in my ear or something.

"Oh, a few weeks ago, I guess."

Her look changes to amusement. She's suppressing a laugh. "How did you know I work here, Mike?"

"There's another guy in the class who knows you, let's see, Asian guy . . ."

Now she can't stop herself, and she's actually laughing. A couple of guys at the next table turn and look. "I don't know any Asian guys," she giggles. "Here, let me help you with this." She takes a cloth from her waistband and starts to wipe the table in front of me. What the hell is going on? The table is covered — I mean covered — with little flakes of something that looks like miniature wheaties.

"If you wanted to get a girl's attention, there are other ways to do it, you know," she laughs. It finally dawns on me that the flakes are wheat paste from the papier-mâché I've been working with all week. I look at my clothes and realize that they're crusted with a thin layer of this, which has dried and is now crumbling and falling on everything around me. All I can do is put my head in my hands, but then I feel her warm hand on my shoulder, and she says, still giggling a little but gently, "I'm sorry, Mike. Anyway, you're very original. I won't forget you this time, really!" and off she goes.

Okay, the spirits are still playing with me. What have they got for me next? I go out in the parking lot and brush my clothes off the best I can, until I seem to get most of it off. I'm about to head back in when I see this big tan pickup pull into the driveway. In maroon gothic letters on the door it says, "FLYSTED CONSTRUCTION." Out of the truck climbs a heavy, florid man with thinning yellow hair and pale blue eyes, a lit cigarette stuck in the corner of his mouth. Talking into his Bluetooth, carrying a battered black ring binder, he strides into Ruby Blue's. I go back to my table and watch as Flysted, without waiting for the hostess, sits at a table near the back. Estrada is there in a moment with a cup of coffee, waiting for him to finish his phone conversation, then setting the coffee down, smiling, talking quietly. He puts out his half-smoked cigarette on the coffee saucer. I feel a surge of sympathy for her. Flysted gulps his coffee as they talk. She goes back to the kitchen, and he gets up and goes to the men's room, leaving his cell phone clipped to his binder. A minute later, it rings.

The phone must be his heart and soul. If I can take possession of it, I can bring him under control. But wait, there's a difficulty. Unlike a primitive enemy, he can replace the physical tool. Ah! Now it comes to me. What's needed is to take possession of his *cell phone number* — to place a curse on the spiritual essence of his power. But I need a sample of his person as well. I get up and go toward the men's room. As I pass his table, I snatch up his half-smoked cigarette and slip it in my pocket. I take a second to look at his phone, noting that it's a large silver Android. No one seems to notice me, so I return to my table. Flysted comes back, checks his phone, clicks call-back, and dives into another lengthy conversation.

As I'm paying the bill, Luna passes me and smiles. "What was that stuff on your shirt, if I may ask?" she says.

"Sorry. Some construction material I was working with. I'll change my clothes before I come in next time."

"It's okay. Sorry I couldn't help laughing." And she goes back to Flysted, who's still on his Bluetooth. On my phone I download the internet data about his Android. On the way home, I stop at Safeway and buy a ham steak.

When I get home, it's still midafternoon but Blake is fast asleep. I take the Android manual to the workshop, and studying its design, over the next three hours I produce a credible papier-mâché replica of Flysted's Android. I fetch Mekiimos and build an altar in the workshop. I place the phone clone, the cigarette butt, and a couple of pieces of the ham steak on the altar, and I sing a war song.

> *Mekiimos, look and see that your bone child is in pain.*
> *Mekiimos, your bone child has been wounded by his enemy.*
> *Mekiimos, his enemy seeks to destroy your bone child;*
> > *To break the bow string of your blood;*
> > *To break the spear of your bones;*
> > *To break the shield of your face.*
> *Mekiimos, speak to the great spirits of the mountain and the*
> > *river.*
> *Mekiimos, speak to the small spirits,*
> *Mekiimos, speak to the human souls.*
> *Tell them your bone child is in pain.*
>
> *Mekiimos, you shall know the enemy by his name;*
> *His name is Bjørn Flysted.*
> *Mekiimos, you shall know the enemy by his cell phone*
> > *number;*
> *His cell phone number is five-five-one-six, six, oh, oh, one,*
> > *three one nine.*
> *Mekiimos, you shall know the enemy by his voice;*
> *His voice is here in this cell phone.*
> *Mekiimos, you shall know the enemy by his breath and saliva;*
> *His breath and saliva are here in this cigarette butt.*
>
> *Tell them to break the tools of the enemy.*
> *Tell them to break the spirit of the enemy and make him*
> > *fearful.*

Tell them to break the face shield of the enemy and make
*   him ashamed,*
*   so that he will stand silent in the face of his judges.*
Tell them the enemy's tools are sweet for them to eat.
Tell them the enemy's soul is sweet for them to eat.
Tell them the enemy's power is sweet for them to eat.

Tell them your bone child will be grateful if they eat the
*   enemy's tools,*
He will increase their pleasure with sacrifices.
Tell them your bone child will be grateful if they eat the
*   enemy's soul,*
He will increase their pleasure with songs.
Tell them your bone child will be grateful if they eat the
*   enemy's power,*
He will increase their pleasure with dances.

I set fire to the phone replica and cigarette butt, and sprinkle bits of the ham over them as they burn, to produce the aroma the spirits love. I transfer the power of the objects to the spirits, so that their will shall become stronger than ever among men. Flysted himself, whose breath and saliva lie here on the altar within the cigarette butt, should find his mind and speech confused and his limbs weakened so that he feels fear whenever he approaches Randy's Trail. His cell phone should not work, and if he gets a new one, that should not work either, even if he gets a new number.

This is only a first step. I'll take further measures on Flysted, as well as on Harmon. Once the magic takes effect, I'll get word to them that the Randy's Trail project is the cause of their troubles. I make a mental note to relieve the curse on both of them if the work on Randy's Trail stops soon. I'll have to monitor the work.

Blake and I take Friday off as well. I figure he's going to see Lisa this weekend, and I tell him to take good care of her. I need to put my full energy into the battle at hand; the battle for Lisa is still somewhere over the horizon. I feel sure I'll win it when the time comes. My credit card still works, so I drive to the LifeLift Spa where Harmon works out, and buy the introductory offer, noting that I can get a partial refund on unused days if I'm not fully satisfied after a week. As the sales clerk inspects my skinny tanned limbs, long hair, and bare feet, the expression on his face is priceless. He could get in trouble for making this sale. He clearly hates his job, though, so he shrugs and signs me up.

The question of course is, when will Harmon show up? I can't hang out here all week. Since he's self-employed, his hours will be flexible, and he'll be coming in when the place isn't too crowded. I find the service guy and ask when that would be, and he says midafternoon, from about two to four. As I leave the gym, I realize that I don't have any workout clothes, so I locate the nearest Goodwill and buy a set of sweats for four dollars. Maybe this'll be an opportunity for me to grow some muscles.

I'm back at the gym by one thirty, and spend more than two hours there, fooling with the equipment, doing a little treadmill jogging and a little rowing. I have a printout of the photo of Harmon folded up in my sweatpants pocket, and the place is almost empty, but I start getting tense, wondering if I missed him somehow. Finally about four o'clock, a lot of people start coming in, and I figure I might as well go, but then I see a big, athletic-looking middle-aged guy with an expensive watch and Armani sunglasses walk in from the back parking lot. It looks like it could be him. I take a peek at my photo. If his hair has grayed, he's lost weight, and he's wearing contacts, it could be — but is it? One way is to check the license plates of the cars in back — but we're only a few blocks from his office, so he could have walked. I remember it's a black SUV with vanity plates that have something to do with his name, and when I step out into the lot, there it is. By their cars ye shall know them.

I don't need to get next to him, I only need stuff that has his personal essence on it, stuff that will guide the spirits from the ritual song to his person. He goes into the men's locker room to change, but I decide not to follow him. When he emerges, he spends a half hour on the stair thing, then a five-minute rest, then another half hour with various weights. I'm eyeing the towel he keeps using to wipe off the sweat. Finally he heads for the lockers, and I follow. Before he goes in to shower, he gets a clean towel and throws the sweaty one in the laundry bin. There's a couple of other guys in there, but they don't seem to notice when I scoop Harmon's towel up from the bin. While I change into my street clothes, I fold the towel up carefully and stick it in the leg of my sweatpants, then walk across the gym and out the door.

Blake isn't there when I get home. I'm sure he's with Lisa and that he won't be back until . . . when? Tomorrow? Sunday? I won't indulge in that distraction.

I haven't had supper, but I don't feel hungry, so I put Mekiimos and my ritual materials in my backpack, climb in the pickup, drive to the old railroad station at the foot of Randy's Trail, and walk up to the construction site. Under the light of a three-quarter moon, I see that the bulldozer is gone, replaced by a tractor fitted with a backhoe and skip loader. A night wind stirring in the tall surrounding trees gives me the impression of a drawn-out wailing by a chorus of weary souls. On the ground, ruler-straight black shadows mark ditches lined with forms for pouring the foundation. A gray utility trailer and stacks of lumber, concrete block, and rebar stand in the stark moonlight.

I collect small pieces of the lumber. I break off chunks of the concrete block. Reaching inside the tractor's motor compartment, I find a piece of wire and manage to tear it loose. In the center of the site I set up my altar and repeat last night's singing ritual, this time for Harmon. I add to the fire the pieces of building material and the wire from the tractor, and throw the remains of the ham steak on top of it — noting with some disgust that Blake has been gnawing on it. I ask the spirits to disable the machinery and ruin the materials. I add Harmon's towel along with my photo of him. To the spirits of this place, I sing, "Forest spirits, I hear your cries. Your enemy is my enemy. Give me your strength and your knowledge. Help me to take back this place." I take some of the ashes and unburnt pieces of the sacrifice and smear them on the controls of the tractor and on the building materials, and I bury the ragged remains there at the center of the site.

Before I go, fog begins to blow up from the beach, and the moon is completely obscured. I sit there in the total darkness, listening to the wind and feeling the wet fog on my face. I try to keep my mind calm and think about Mekiimos and the spirits, but I'm wracked with wild emotions and images. A few hundred yards away, Lisa may be lying with Blake while I struggle to free her from this evil. With cunning and courage I've accomplished a great deal in the last two days, but my labor has to remain a secret for a long time yet.

I realize that to the world around me I've become, to some extent, a madman and a criminal, but the idea calms me, pleases me, even. This judgment is given by an utterly soulless world. What did Lisa say about the true artist enduring pain in order to bring his vision to the world? I am such an artist, my loneliness and peril the keys to my final triumph.

In the deep darkness I have to feel my way down the path and soon find I've taken a wrong turn and lost my bearings in the brush. At length I look up and see the light of Lisa's kitchen window dimly through the fog, and I turn and run in the direction I now know leads to the beach, branches whipping my face, rocks and potholes skinning my feet, until at last I find the railroad tracks and Blake's pickup truck. Back at the apartment I turn off the lights and lie on my futon bed, but I can't sleep.

The simple thing that I wanted — to be uncomplicated, full of unformed energy, thrown forward like a spear whose target is the arc of flight itself, has somehow turned into the opposite: complex, calculating, heavy as the great *te moka tula* itself. I want to put it down, to be free of its demands, even to trade all my knowledge and power for a hammock in the shade of some unknown palm grove. Even Lisa seems elusive: now a radiance that gives me a lion's heart, now a receding hallucination that leaves me tired and confused. Searching my brain for a remedy and release, I come again to the vague shame of my old life's emptiness, and I know I can't go back. There is no other path: I have to push on.

I want a strong drink, but there's nothing but beer in the house. I've brought betel nut and lime with me from the jungle for such emergencies, and I drink two beers while I chew it. But I forget about spitting out the red juice, and ten minutes later I'm throwing up mucus (as there's nothing else in my stomach), and finally I fall asleep and dream that I am bodiless, my head a thin glass balloon that's juggled relentlessly on the waves of a betel-spit red sea.

CHAPTER SEVENTEEN

PIG MAGIC

S even A.M. Blake's here, and he's still asleep. The acrid taste of betel in my mouth, I stumble into the bathroom to brush my teeth, noticing some pain where I bruised my right foot on Randy's Trail last night, and I notice in the mirror there are also a couple of long scratches on my neck and forehead from my flight through the dark forest. I recall the geometric scars that mark the backs of the Raapa Uu men.

Now the waiting begins. I want to know how Lisa's legal fight is going, but I don't want to call her when she's just been with Blake. I decide to wait until Monday. I need something to occupy me, so I eat a bowl of instant oatmeal and a banana and go into the workshop. The papier-mâché has pretty well dried on the copulation piñata, so I take up the Dremel tool and begin to cut it from the form. As I work, I begin to think about Flysted. He's waking up in his marriage bed right now — does he still make love to his wife? Does he love her? Perhaps the smell of Luna Estrada is still on him. Does he love her, too, as at one time, long, long ago, I loved two women — my wife, Ursula, and my paramour, Delfin? Whatever preoccupies him now, all that will change; the spirits have been notified of his offense. I let my imagination play on his fate, and on Harmon's. First there will be puzzling technical difficulties of all kinds. Equipment won't work; the workers will make appalling mistakes. Phones will go suddenly and permanently dead in the middle of conversations. They will begin to get tense, maybe sensing the curse. Their minds will become clouded, their conversation unfocused, their decisions erratic. They may injure themselves. Finally, the project will go bankrupt, and they will leave, shocked and confounded. The spirits might have a few witty embarrassments for them along the way, just for their own amusement.

The weekend passes with maddening slowness. I try to occupy my mind by working on the piñatas, but even that has now become routine. I simply follow Blake's instructions for things I've already learned how to do; I need the income, so I do it without comment. All the time, I'm thinking about Flysted and Harmon and the trail. But this war magic is only the first stage of my battle. Once the enemy has been defeated, I face the greater task of freeing Lisa's soul.

I call her on Monday, and she tells me that the court hearing is still eleven days away.

"What will the procedure be?"

"I've asked for an injunction to stop construction. The judge will have read our statements and will have questions for both sides. I've also filed a lawsuit for the costs of repairing the damage to the site, but that could take a year or more."

"I want to be there in the courtroom." I want to watch Harmon's defenses crumble; see the confusion on his face when he realizes he's lost.

"That's extremely kind of you, Morse, but you can't. It's a closed hearing. Still, it's great to know that I have friends behind me."

"We're going to win, you know."

"I wish I did know that, but thanks."

"No, I mean we can't lose. Really."

There's a little silence, and then she says, "If you know something I don't, please tell me. Or is this is more of your . . . ahh, mysticism?"

"You'll see. Will you call me afterward?"

Another pause. A sigh. "Yes, I'll call you."

The late date of the hearing irritates me. Every evening I go to the building site, and I'm disappointed to see that the work seems to be going as planned. The foundation is poured; the rough framing has begun to take shape; prefab gables, plywood, girders, and shingles now stand ready next to the rising structure. At work I'm distracted; I seal up one of the piñatas before the electronics are in place, and we have to open it up and repeat the whole finishing process. Maybe the spirits need something a little bigger — a real animal sacrifice, for example: a live pig.

I go online and locate a farm with piglets for sale, in Escondido, a rural area of the county a half hour away. Yes, they can sell me a fifteen-pound piglet. This has to be planned. I can't keep the pig at Blake's apartment; I'll have to sacrifice it the day I get it; and I'll have to find a place that's both spiritually powerful and secluded. That evening after work I drive over to the foot of the trail as usual, but this time, I wander through the trees until I find a dense stand of eucalyptus, well off the path itself. I clear a space on the ground and build a small altar with rocks and wildflowers, where I offer a song, consecrating the space. As I leave, I mark the direction to the site from the path with small branches.

That evening I tell Blake I'm going to get up early to start working, and take the afternoon off. At two P.M. I check the contents of my backpack — Mekiimos, candles, matches, gallon water jug, flashlight. I add a ball of orange nylon twine from the workshop and a butcher knife from the kitchen. As I handle the knife, I go over in my mind the steps of the sacrifice that Sosi taught me.

I take the pickup and drive to Escondido. The so-called farm is really just a small house and single, evil-smelling metal shed about a hundred feet long, by the side of a country road. A couple of mud-spattered stake trucks are parked next to the shed, one of them with a sign that says McRae Livestock, Inc. I knock on the door of the ranch-style stucco house. A chubby teenage girl with her hair in curlers appears, and I tell her that I priced their piglets on the internet, and I want a fifteen pounder. She looks at my bare feet. "You got boots?"

"No, sorry."

She looks at my truck. "You want me to butcher it?"

"No thanks, I'll take it live."

"Okay. Where's your cage?"

"I thought I could just tether him in the back of the pickup."

"That's illegal, you know."

"I didn't know that. Can you sell me a cage?"

"For just one pig? It'll cost you fifty-nine ninety-five."

Damn! The Raapa Uu never use cages. I don't have time to go to a pet store and buy one. They take credit cards. I'll take the cage. She goes to the back of the shed, fires up a garden-sized tractor hitched to a utility cart, and drives it inside. I hear some furious squealing, and for a moment I'm worried that she's misunderstood and is actually butchering the pig; but in a few minutes she's back with it on the cart. Pinkish white and the size of a strapping six-month-old child, it's still squealing, chewing the metal wires of its cage. It throws itself around in the cage as we lift it into the pickup, and it stands there panting, its nose twitching, its little head down, eyeing me quizzically. It stops squealing and makes a kind of groaning, whimpering sound more like a child begging for something. I shut the tailgate, pay the girl, get in the cab, and we're on our way.

Do pigs have imaginations? Do they think about the future at all? "Listen," I say to the piglet, "You were born a pig. This is your karma, okay? You have nothing to complain about. Cooperate, and we can do this in a dignified way."

It might calm him down if he had something to eat, I guess. They say pigs will eat anything, but what about small ones like this? Is he weaned? I should have asked the girl. When we get back to Encinitas, the sun is going down. I stop at the 7-Eleven and buy a quart of milk and a loaf of white bread, and one of those disposable foil roasting pans to put the food in. While I'm at it, I think this might go easier if I have a drink — I buy a pint of rum too. When I come out of the store, four boys — they look like fourth graders — are standing on their skateboards, looking at my pig, who is looking back at them with intense curiosity, grunting softly. Seeing me, three of them back away, but the smallest boy is absorbed looking at the pig.

"And it ain't even Halloween," says one boy, staring at me boldly. They snicker.

"Can we pet your pig?" the smallest boy says.

"Sorry, men," I say, "I've got to be somewhere."

"Yeah, to put him on the barbecue," the oldest boy says.

I throw my groceries in the cab and turn to them. "No, this is not a barbecue pig. This pig is going to save the wilderness for all of us. He's going to please the spirits of the wilderness. Do you know what that means? This is a *sacrifice* pig."

"You're not going to hurt him, are you?" says the smallest boy.

"Sacrifice! That means, like, cut off his head!" the oldest boy says.

The smallest boy watches my face, fidgeting. "Will . . . will . . ." I wait. "Will you sell him to us? I'll give you five dollars for him."

Their eyes are fixed on me. For a second I'm tempted to give them the pig, and then I remember: The spirits are playing with me, testing me, searching for my weak spots. I smile. "Maybe your Mom will buy you a pig, little spirit man." I get in the truck and drive off.

It's almost dark when I reach the bottom of Randy's Trail. It would be too awkward to carry the cage up the trail; I'll have to take out the pig, who's still bouncing around, grunting anxiously. I pour some milk in the foil pan, then break up a few pieces of bread and throw them in. I open the cage and slip the pan in. He immediately lunges forward, stepping on the edge of the pan and spilling its contents in the truck bed. Now he smells it, and begins licking the empty pan. I guess I'll have to hold him while I feed him, but I have an idea. I uncork the rum and take a few swallows; then I take the pan from the cage, half fill it with milk and bread, and pour about a half cup of rum in too. I set it on the truck bed and take the pig from the cage. He's squealing and squirming like anything, but I manage to get his face into the pan, and he eagerly gobbles most of the mixture before knocking it over again with his snout. I put him back in the cage, fetch the orange twine from the cab and tie a length of it around his neck. He's stopped squealing and seems to have calmed down, so I fill the pan again and repeat the process. This time he eats the whole thing.

I slip the pack on my back, secure the other end of the twine to my belt, then wrap him in my jacket and, using the flashlight, start up the trail. I find my ritual site, set the pig on the ground, and tie his tether to the branch of a coyote brush, giving him room to wander around a bit. He stands there swaying to and fro for a minute, then takes a few staggering steps, falls on his nose, stands up, and in trying to shake himself the way a dog would, he falls over again. Obviously, he's very drunk. As I'm setting up my altar, he staggers over to me and tries to climb in my lap. I set him back on the ground, but he immediately comes back, grunting pitifully, so I move him to the side of the ritual circle and tie him there, shortening his tether. It would be best to start my ritual with the pig sacrifice. I make a small fire, get the knife out of my pack, and offer a short song of praise to the spirits. When I'm finished, the dim flickering light from the fire throws ghostly shadows on the trunks of the surrounding rocks and trees. Finally I make out the pig, lying on his side, his eyes shut, his nose and feet twitching slightly from time to time, apparently fast asleep. I decide to put off slitting his throat until I've sung my war song, essentially the same song I've sung against Flysted and Harmon before.

Finished with the song, I close my eyes for a while, concentrating on feeling the presence of the spirits, the power and mystery of the magic. Then I take up the knife again and look for the pig, but I can't see him in the flickering shadows. I take the flashlight and get up to look for him, and what I find is the chewed end of the tether. The pig is gone.

Where the hell would a goddamn drunk pig go in the middle of the goddamn night? Why didn't I butcher the little bastard a half hour ago?

Over the next couple of hours, I search the woods in a radius of a hundred feet, crisscrossing and circling, getting down on my elbows to peer under bushes, sifting through piles of leaf litter. I find a wood rat nest and almost get sprayed by a skunk, but no pig. I try luring him back by pouring milk around the altar site. There's nothing I can do except hope that he comes back before daylight, so I make myself comfortable on the ground, my head resting on my backpack, and soon I'm asleep.

I wake to birdsong. The stars have faded in a clear sky over the tree canopy. No sign of the pig. It wouldn't be safe to perform the sacrifice here in the daylight anyway, but I want my pig back. Think, think. I finish off the rest of the bread and milk. He'll be easier to find now that it's getting light, and I had better get started before the workers show up at the construction site. I dismantle the altar and cover the ashes, placing Mekiimos and other objects in my pack, spreading a few leaves around to cover the marks of my night's work. For an hour or so I again crisscross the area near the altar, but there's no sign of him. Think, think. Did a coyote get him? The thought makes me chuckle — if so, he was sacrificed after all, not to the spirits, but to the forest itself. Think. Pigs have a keen sense of smell. There's a lot of freshly turned earth at the construction site; he might have been attracted to it by the smell of roots and bugs.

As I approach, I'm surprised to see someone already moving around the site. Peering through the brush, at first I make out a single human figure, a slightly paunchy man wearing a windbreaker and baseball hat, a roll of large papers under one arm. Then I see the tan pickup truck with Flysted's logo on it and realize the man is him; he's come to set up the day's work. I creep closer, staying hidden in the brush, and out of the corner of my eye I see something else move. There's a piece of orange nylon twine twitching and jerking. It leads to something behind a tool box. The other end of the twine is tied to the foot of an aluminum ladder that reaches to the top of the two-story frame. As I watch, the pig appears, nosing his way through the dirt and sawdust. Suddenly he raises his nose and sniffs vigorously in my direction, then lets out a squeal and dashes toward me. Alerted, Flysted runs toward him, peering in my direction. I try to duck back into the bushes, but he sees me.

"Hey, you!" he shouts. "This is private prop—"

Pig makes a mighty lunge toward me, yanking the ladder sideways. As Flysted and I watch, dumbfounded, it comes crashing down on the power line fixed to the utility shed and, in a blaze of crackling white sparks, lands on a pile of construction debris, which bursts into flame. The pig, now free, joyfully throws himself on me, while Flysted runs for his truck and emerges with a small red extinguisher, cursing furiously.

I'm frozen in my tracks. My impulse is to take the pig and run like hell, but if I do that, I'll have to leave town, as Flysted will surely come looking for me. If I stay to help him, I'll have to explain what my pig and I are doing here — a fearful prospect, especially if he remembers my face from Ruby Blue's. Besides, I don't want the fire out, at least not until it's destroyed the construction site. Meanwhile Flysted is yelling, "Help me, help me, for Chrissake!" His extinguisher is having little effect on the fire, which has already reached the house frame. He throws it on the ground and grabs his cell phone from his belt.

"I'll go for help!" I yell, and grabbing Pig I turn and run down Randy's Trail. As I throw him and my backpack into the cab of Blake's pickup and jump in, I can see a thick column of black smoke rising above the trees. A few minutes later, as I drive through town, a couple of wailing fire engines pass me. I seriously need to disappear, and I need to get rid of this pig as well; but how? I can't just abandon him somewhere. I wish I could find the kid who offered to buy him yesterday. I don't want to involve Blake in this, either, but I can't just take off without collecting a few things, so I drive in the direction of our apartment.

The story about the wild man and the pig who started the fire is surely going to circulate. Flysted will tell the authorities; the newspapers might even pick it up. When Lisa hears it, she'll have no trouble connecting the dots. In other words, running and hiding is the worst thing I could do; it would almost certainly destroy my relationship with her, which is to say, destroy me.

Plus, what just happened is, of course, the direct result of my songs.

Like the calling of the cassowaries in Sangrapa, the strength of my magic is something I can't fully control. I have recruited the spirits to my side all right, but I haven't clearly communicated with them. As I turn this over in my mind, it becomes clear to me: A shaman makes his power visible by taunting death; his power kindles admiration in his allies and fear in his enemies. YES!! THAT'S IT!! What an idiot I was to suppose that I could use the power of the spirits *in secret*, that I could escape the danger that necessarily comes with it. A man who handles wild beasts constantly risks being eaten alive.

I turn the truck around and head back to Seacrest Road, at the top of Randy's Trail, and take the construction access road toward the fire. The road is blocked by the fire crew, so I get out and ask to see the officer in charge. Eyeing me the way that I've gotten used to since I came back from New Guinea, the fireman wants to know my business here. "I witnessed the start of the fire," I say.

"Were you the one who called it in?"

"No." I want to tell him that I am the mastermind of this incident, that it proves my ability as a shaman. I want to see the awe in his face when I tell him this, but I can't think of a way to put it that won't be misunderstood.

He speaks into his walkie-talkie, using some sort of verbal shorthand I don't understand. Then he motions to me to follow him, and we walk down toward the action. There's still a lot of smoke in the area, but it doesn't look like the fire has spread past the building site. When we get there, I can see that the crew has contained the fire, but the site is pretty thoroughly destroyed. Blackened sections of the house frame are still standing, and firefighters still douse piles of reeking debris everywhere; tools and equipment, now soaking wet, are blackened and twisted by the heat.

The fire captain takes my contact information. "How did you happen to be here when it started?"

I feel elated. This is my moment. "I am a shaman. I was here in the forest, asking the spirits of this place to protect it against destruction. The spirits responded in the form of my pig. I saw it happen. Flysted saw me. I told him I would go for help."

He eyes me for a moment. "Okay, okay. We know, the pig started the fire. That's one reason not many people keep pigs. They're hard to control. They can do a lot of damage."

"The pig was commanded by the spirits of this forest."

He looks annoyed. "Whatever. At least you did the right thing by contacting us. We'll need you to come in and file a formal report. There's a significant loss here. You're not planning on leaving the area, are you?" He hands me a card with the information numbers of the police and fire departments, and then, scowling and shaking his head, he turns and walks off.

I can't believe it. Did he even hear me? I almost run after him, grab him, shake him, but I control myself. After all, he's just a bit player, an extra in this scene. Already he's talking to someone, shouting orders, making notes. On reflection, it makes perfect sense. The people of the Upper Sepik are attuned to the supernatural; they fear it, but they know it intimately. No spirit work escapes their study, their analysis. Human beings are judged more for the parts they play in spirit dramas than for the way they live their ordinary lives. Here, ordinary men have only the fear, none of the knowledge. It's no wonder that the mere mention of the spirits throws them off; the only response in their repertoire is to deny it.

Getting back in the pickup, I notice with a start that the pig has gotten up on the seat where my backpack is and eaten half the left ear off Mekiimos! I'm going to strangle the little bastard!

No.

This is another trick of the spirits. Sosi was certainly right about them. This latest trick must have some potent significance, but what the hell does it actually mean?

CHAPTER EIGHTEEN

To feel enormously powerful, and at the same time to feel invisible, is strange indeed. My study with Sosi certainly didn't prepare me for this. As I look around me, I can't avoid the perception that the slick, civilized world I live in has shrunk drastically. If that world was a bit pretentious to begin with, now it's positively contemptible. I need to act on these feelings, and I don't have to grope around for ideas: I need excitement, dramatic action. I need a woman, with an intensity that's almost frightening. The mythic White Man with Hard Prick has come to life.

Going to Lisa's and simply dragging her to bed is out. Although she certainly enjoyed our loving in the past, this could be a disaster. I need to overcome someone by using spiritual power, not physical. Looking for a hooker is also out. Although I've never been with a whore and don't know what to expect, it seems to me the chance of finding one who's impressed by anything but money is too remote. Going to a singles bar is out, too. Even when I didn't look as eccentric as I do now, even when I was young and buff, I was never the type of guy who could make a smooth impression on a strange woman. What, then? Who, then?

Flysted's girlfriend, Luna Estrada?

At first, the idea seems preposterous. If she remembers me at all, it will be as the idiot who showered her lunch table with wheat flakes. Besides, she is, as they say, "in a relationship." But let's look at the other side. I instantly knew from her face that she's a kind and sensitive person, the kind of person who doesn't judge others harshly. She said she would definitely remember me, after my performance. She thought that I was coming on to her, but her reaction was one of amusement, not hostility. And then there's the matter of power. I'm reminded of the first time I took Lisa by storm with my newfound strength. Yes, now we get down to it: I've just beaten Luna's lover badly in a serious game. The more I think about bedding her, the more exciting, and the more likely, it feels. I visualize telling her how I stalked Flysted and turned him over to the spirits, and how they unleashed their fury on him through my magic. She's Latina; such knowledge runs deep in her people's consciousness. Although she might pretend to scoff at me, she won't be able to dismiss what I say. I can see the play of emotions on her face, and I find that I'm almost busting out of my pants.

Blake is out when I get to the studio. I put Pig's cage in a corner of the garage and give him a pile of wilted salad ingredients and carrots I find in the fridge. I shower and change into clean jeans and a sport shirt borrowed from Blake's closet. Should I get a haircut? Should I use some of Blake's styling gel? No. It'll be a wild shaman who conquers Luna Estrada. It's a little after lunchtime; she's sure to be at Ruby Blue's. If Flysted is there too, that might even make it more exciting. I'll play with the cards I'm dealt. As I drive up the Coast Highway, I feel the same strength and energy surging through my body that I felt when I first kissed Lisa.

Luna is waiting tables. I nod to her, but she doesn't seem to notice. Rather than take a table, I wait for her by the service counter, and when she comes up I step forward and say, "Hi, Luna."

She looks at me and smiles a bit mischievously. "Oh yeah, my old buddy, uhh, Mike, isn't it?"

"My name isn't really Mike, it's Ashton. I've got something important I want to talk to you about."

"I'll bet you do," she laughs.

"It's about your boyfriend, Bjørn Flysted."

A troubled look. "He's not my boyfriend, he's just a friend."

"Good, then he won't mind if you talk to me."

She looks me in the eye. "You can see I'm really busy. Why would I want to talk to you?"

"I'm sorry. If you're not interested, I guess you're not. I know something about his mishap with the fire today." I start to go.

"That fire in Del Mar?! Just a sec." She takes a small notebook and pen from the pocket of her apron, scribbles down a phone number, tears it out, and hands it to me. "I get off at five. Now please go sit down." She rushes off. I walk out of the restaurant and drive to Torrey Pines Park, where I set up Mekiimos and thank the spirits for my victory. I take out Luna's notebook page and memorize the number. Then I lay the page on the altar fire and offer a song asking for her love.

At seven I call her. "Luna, this is Ashton, the guy you gave your number to today."

"Yeah, you said you knew something about that fire. Listen, I know who you are. I told Bjørn you were in Ruby's; I described you. He told me about the fire. He said it was your pig that started it. I don't want to see you."

"That's up to you. It wasn't my pig that started the fire; it was the spirits of the forest; they're angry about what Bjørn is doing to their land. I'm a shaman, a *brujo*; I speak the language of the spirits. I'm the one who called them."

She's silent for a few seconds. "You're crazy."

"You talk like a *gringa*. Come on. You know witchcraft is anything but crazy."

"What do you want?"

"That bar up the street from Ruby's, the Carousel. I'll be there at eight. Bye." I know she won't show up, but the hunt is on. She's unsure about how much to believe, doesn't know what to do. She wants to see what happens if she ignores me, but she won't be able to ignore me; like a lover, she won't be able to get me out of her mind. I don't bother going to the Carousel.

CHAPTER NINETEEN

THE SHAMAN PREPARES

For the next several days it rains on and off, the kind of light, swirling rain that gets onto and into everything. I go to the police station and give my statement on the fire. There appears to be no activity at the building site, now that someone — presumably Flysted — has salvaged what he can of the tools. On Thursday, another stroke of magic. A reporter from the *San Diego Journal* calls and says she heard about me and my pig, and she's on her way up to talk to us. Here's the chance for Harmon and Flysted, and those who would support them, to learn about their shaman adversary.

"What's his name?" she asks brightly, squatting next to Pig. He sneezes violently, probably reacting to her perfume.

"Pig."

"Yes, the pig, what's his name?"

"That's his name. Pig. The Raapa Uu don't give their pigs names."

"The who?"

"The Raapa Uu. They taught me shamanism."

"Okay . . . Pig. Can I get a picture of the two of you?" She snaps off a few shots. "How do you happen to own him, Mr. Caldo?" She's moving around the workshop, popping her flash.

"I'm a shaman. I bought him as a sacrifice to the forest spirits, but the spirits released him and sent him to the building site."

She lowers her camera and looks over the rims of her glasses. "Sacrifice him?"

"Yes. Mr. Harmon is illegally destroying a beautiful wild area. I enlisted the power of the forest spirits to stop him. As you can see, I . . . or rather the spirits and Pig and I . . . succeeded, at least for now."

She stares at me for a moment, and I can almost read her mind.

"You commanded Pig to set the fire, then?"

"Absolutely not. The spirits commanded him. I asked them for help saving the forest, and this was their response."

"You amaze me, Mr. Caldo. You want me to print this?"

"I haven't done anything illegal. Unlike Mr. Harmon."

"I noticed on your police statement that you listed your occupation as . . ." she flips through the pages of her notebook, ". . . oh yes, 'shaman and piñata artisan.'"

"Yes, as you can see, this is where we make the piñatas."

"Are they works of shamanism too?"

"No, they're simple art objects."

"Tell me about being a shaman."

Without mentioning Lisa or Randy's Trail, I give her a synopsis of my journey: that I learned the rituals and songs of the Raapa Uu, and that when I came back and saw what Mr. Harmon was doing to the forest, I felt compelled to use my skills.

"People cut down trees to build houses every day. What made you think you had a right to do that in this case?"

"Like I said, the construction was illegal."

"How did you know that?"

"These things get around."

She stands and picks up her camera bag. "Will you stand by what you've told me, Mr. Caldo?"

"Yes."

"Is there anything you want to add?"

"Yes. Most so-called civilized people don't believe in the power of the primitive. They point to the fact that our science and technology can easily destroy — has destroyed, over and over — people like the Raapa Uu. You and your readers have no idea of the kind of power such people command. I'm only a neophyte, yet I can direct the anger of the spirits."

"Do you do this without warning?"

"I understood that these people had been asked to desist, that they had applied for a permit and been refused."

"And what is your next, ahh, project?"

I shrug. "That's up to the spirits."

On Saturday, the *Journal* prints an item on the second page of the Local News section, alongside a photo of me holding Pig:

Pig Is Suspect in Local Fire

The fire on Seacliff Avenue in Del Mar last Tuesday was much like the six other construction fires this year in San Diego County, except for two things: One, the builder was not in possession of a construction permit; and two, the fire is said to have been started by a pig. A hearing is scheduled for next Wednesday in the county court to determine whether in fact the owner of the property, Mr. Prentiss Harmon of La Jolla, is entitled to a building permit. A neighbor of the damaged building site, Ms. Lisa Berman, has challenged his right, on the grounds that there is no public access to the property, and Harmon has been crossing her land to develop it.

Mr. Harmon told the Journal that an estimated $300,000 in fire damage began when a stray pig upset a metal ladder onto a power line. The pig, he said, was running loose on the construction site, when the building contractor, Mr. Bjørn Flysted of Encinitas, captured it and tied it to the ladder. Asked whether he intended to bring suit against the pig's owner, Mr. Harmon had no comment.

The Journal learned that the pig, named Pig, belongs to Mr. Ashton Caldo (photo), who works at the studio of artist Blake Orkowski in Del Mar. Mr. Caldo has studied primitive magic in New Guinea and describes himself as a shaman — a type of sorcerer common among the tribal people of the world. He said that he believes he has befriended

*spirits of the forest near the construction site, and that Pig was
directed by these spirits to start the fire. No charges have been
filed against Pig or his owner.*

By that afternoon my voice mail is overflowing. Reporters from Los
Angeles to Boston have found the story on social media and want to interview
"the urban shaman with the miraculous pig," as one message put it. My
email is also full, and scrolling through the messages I find one from Lisa.

*Ashton: I tried to call you but your voicemail is down. Do you
realize you are making a joke of my case? This might seriously
undermine me at the hearing. After I begged you to stay away
from it. You need professional help. I've called the County
Mental Health Services, and they will see you without charge.
Will you please contact them at (719) 502-0010? Ask for
Dr. Benabhai. And will you PLEASE not speak about your
shamanism, or my property, to anyone? Thank you. Lisa*

This is the reaction I expected. Her missionary persona is speaking
from its very essence: not only closed off from the world of magic, but
actively hostile to it, and completely unaware of the paradox that she's
seeking to protect the magic place of her childhood by suppressing magic
itself.

The time has come for the fearful task, the task of freeing the magic
child from the missionary, the ritual cleansing of Lisa.

I sit down at the computer and type:

*Dear Lisa. I'm sorry my shaman performance has upset you. I
fully realize that my behavior has seemed crazy, but you will
soon see that it has been completely rational. The construction
has been stopped for now. The attention of your adversaries
has shifted to me. My work as a shaman is done, and I'm glad
to get back to my normal life, as you will see in the coming
days. I can't expect you to forget all this, but I do hope we'll
be friends again before too long. Of course I tell you all this
in confidence. Affectionately, Ashton*

I delete all the messages from my voice mail and email inbox. That afternoon I shower and wash my hair, cut off my beard, and shave. The pale skin of my jaw next to my brown face looks a bit comical, but it'll blend in soon enough. I open my storage boxes and put on a clean T-shirt, jeans, and shoes, the clothes hanging a bit loosely and the shoes feeling too tight. I drive downtown, walk into the barbershop, and say, "Make me look as normal as possible." Deception is a key element of Raapa Uu magic. I need a peace offering, but not something romantic. I know she's especially fond of scotch, so I buy a bottle of Laphroaig.

"Hey, Prof! You're back!" laughs Blake, surveying my new look. "What happened?"

"The wild man has served his purpose."

"You stun me, man. You really do. I thought you had lost it. Or are you going to take up some other crazy kick? You going to raise pigs or something?"

"Pig goes up for adoption; you want him? Blake, I really appreciate your putting up with all this stuff. I know Lisa hated it, and I know that put you in kind of an awkward position. I'll make it up to both of you."

"I still don't get what you're up to, Prof."

"I'm not entirely sure myself, but anyway I'm finished with it. Let's say it was an experiment."

"Man, are you ever weird."

"Was I ever not?"

"So, seriously, what's your plan now?"

"No plan. Got to keep searching for the way, you know? A life that feels genuine for me, that brings my real values into play."

He shakes his head. "And all those years I thought you had it made . . . had it figured out."

"I think maybe *you* have it figured out, if anybody does. Anyway, I've learned a lot with this experiment. You have to try different things, right? If you have the luxury, I mean."

The next day is the hearing on the property. We try to work in the studio, but things don't go well. I mess up cutting one of the piñata casts, and we have to repair it and set it to dry. Now I'm half watching a stupid quiz show on TV, and half watching Blake, who's sitting on a resin drum, trying to teach Pig to shake hands by rewarding him with apple slices. Pig looks like he's doing pretty well, until he mistakes Blake's thumb for a piece of apple. Blake yells, Pig squeals, they hug. Exactly the same as the people on the TV show. At five thirty the phone rings and Blake picks it up. I can tell the news isn't good.

"They gave them the permit," he says, hanging up. "They only have to pay her market value for the right-of-way."

"I'm not surprised. How's she doing?" He scowls, picks up Pig and scratches him on the belly. "Maybe you better go over there," I say. "Was there any talk at the hearing about the fire?"

"She didn't say."

I fetch the bottle of Laphroaig and hand it to him. "Tell her I'm sorry."

I drive to the foot of Randy's Trail again. The weather's overcast and gloomy, with smells of wet earth. As I walk, condensation from the trees drops on me, some of it running down through my short hair and into my shirt, making me shiver. I see deer tracks crossing the path; I hear a distant hawk screech. I can feel the presence of the spirits, watching. They've decided that the fire was enough punishment for Harmon and Flysted, for now at least.

I go over in my mind, for the hundredth time, the stages of the ritual cleansing of Lisa: assembling materials; picking an isolation site; getting her there; the ritual itself; the return of the new Lisa; her reintegration into life. Thinking of the beauty of it, my eyes fill with tears. This will be the consummation of my struggle and the defeat of my suffering. The new Lisa will be the person she herself longs to be — joyful, playful, creative, overflowing with self-confidence and warmth. The barrier she spoke of that night with Nat King Cole in the background, the barrier she broke when she opened her heart to a stranger and told him of her childhood dreams — that barrier is the possession of her spirit by another, the chain

I will dissolve with my magic. Everyone will love the new Lisa, but she'll be mine.

As for me, I've plunged into the fire of rebirth, and I already carry the scars. Professor Ashton Caldo has become a museum piece, a curiosity like the dial telephone. The new Ashton is not yet fully a shaman and an artist, but he has mastered the courage and is mastering the craft. In the end she and I will both be the Zogons of her dreams. Our limbs will move to the simple, unerring rhythms of nature. Ordinary people won't be able to return our gaze, and the wisest of them will look at the work of our lives and nod their heads, a little reverently, a little enviously.

But nature is cunning and deceptive as well. This vision will have to wait, while the weeks ahead will be the time of preparation — time for the disciplined and unseen work that precedes the crisis of battle. I breathe in the dank musk of Randy's Trail, feel the soft wet earth on the soles of my feet. I hear the hawk cry again, and I answer him with a shrill sound of my own.

Before I have Lisa's confidence, I've got to have her interest. To get her interest, I must seem to lose interest in her. The first step will be to go back to Ruby Blue's.

CHAPTER TWENTY

LUNA

When Luna comes out of Ruby Blue's after work, she sees me looking at her. I'm leaning against the fender of Blake's pickup. She's used to guys looking at her, and of course she doesn't recognize me, and she hurries off.

"Luna."

She looks again.

"It's me, Mike, also known as Ashton, also known as the shaman."

"The wild man?"

"Yep."

"How come you changed your outfit? Maybe now no one will believe you're a witch. You won't be able to scare people."

I fall in step with her. "Did I scare you?"

"Everybody's scared of a crazy person."

"They said Saint Francis was crazy. Let me buy you dinner."

"Saint Francis? You? Hah! That's a good one! Anyway, I have a boyfriend, remember?"

"He's not your boyfriend, remember? Listen. You have your own life and all that. But it doesn't hurt to have another friend, one who doesn't scare you. A drink?"

"I don't drink."

"Well, then I'll cast a spell on you, which will be the same as two margaritas."

She smiles. I softly touch her elbow and steer her in the direction of the Carousel Bar. She hesitates at the door, then shrugs, and we go in.

It's a good bar, bright and noisy, a lot of young people, even a few families with kids, the smell of good food. We find a table near the back. She waits for me to talk. I say, "Reading faces is a skill of shamans. I can tell you're troubled, and I can tell you've been thinking about me."

"You don't know anything. What do you really want from me?"

"You're pretty, and you're used to guys lying to you. It's true I want you, but that's not the main thing."

"Go on."

"I was interested in Bjørn, because I'm a defender of the forest spirits, and his project, the thing he's building in Del Mar, was destroying the forest. Did you know that?"

"He told me they were clearing trees, but how did you know he was my boyfriend?"

"Clearing trees! Is that what he said? Well, never mind how I knew about you; I'm a shaman, remember? I don't want to criticize your boyfriend, but I think he sometimes isn't completely truthful. Anyway, when I met you, I realized . . ."

"Wait a minute. Are you saying you deliberately set the fire?"

"Not me, the forest spirits. Don't you read the newspapers?" She scowls. "I'm sorry," I say. "Let's not talk about that. I have a sense about people's souls; I can read them. When I met you, I was looking for Bjørn, but I felt you deserved a friend, and you needed a friend."

The bar hostess comes. We order margaritas.

"Why did you cut off your hair?" she says.

"You know those superheroes in the comics, like Spiderman and Superman? They hide behind their normal appearance until something needs to be done. Well, that idea doesn't come out of thin air, it actually comes from a knowledge of shamanism. My job as a shaman is done for the time being. Now I'm just an ordinary person again."

"You're such a liar!"

"Yes, I am. Is Bjørn a liar, too?"

"All men are."

"Do you love him?"

She gives me a hard look and doesn't answer, but I keep still and pretty soon she says. "I don't know. I do, but lots of times I feel bad when I'm with him. Are you married?"

"No. I was, many years ago. I had a girlfriend until recently, but she didn't like me being a shaman, so right now I don't have anybody."

"Did you love her?"

"Yes."

"Why didn't she like it? You being a shaman, I mean."

"That's a very complicated question. I think the short answer is this: She's unhappy, because she's lost her connection with her own spirit, her own nature. But like many people, she's afraid to change. She thought that if she stayed with me, she would have to change, and that scared her. So, she started thinking I was, like you said, crazy."

She laughs. "And are you?" Now she has the look that I was longing to see — not exactly wonderment, but that beautiful confusion they show when they're unexpectedly aroused.

"Are *you?*" I ask. She meets my eyes for a second, then looks away. I lean forward to kiss her, and she turns her head and presents me with her cheek, but her breathing is excited.

"What time is it?" she says.

"Do you know how to tell if canary is male or female?" She shakes her head. "Put some seeds in the cage, *y si se pone contento, es canario, pero si se pone contanta, es canaria.*" She laughs a little. I go on. "There was once a *canaria* who lived in a cage. Even though she had plenty to eat, and her owner would tell her how beautiful she was every day, she was not *contenta* because every day she heard the wild birds singing in the trees. Then one day, her owner left the cage open. Did she fly out? . . . Did she? . . . Did she?" Luna looks stunned. I stand up, smiling, and toss a twenty on the table. She follows me out.

"I have to go," she says.

"I'll give you a ride."

"My daughter and I live right over there." She points up the block. I take her arm and walk with her to a nondescript stucco apartment building. In the doorway I say, I'll phone you. You gave me your number, remember?"

"Bjørn pays for our phone. I know he has the remote code to my answering machine, and that he listens to my messages." She hesitates a moment. "Can you wait here a few minutes?" She lets herself in and runs up the steps.

While I'm standing in the doorway, I hear the sound of a diesel motor. Bjørn's truck stops right in front of me. Bjørn has his Bluetooth in his ear, and I think I hear the faint ringing of a phone in the building. He sees me, but doesn't acknowledge me. He's talking rapidly on the phone; I can hear his angry voice but can't make out what he's saying. He gets out and comes quickly toward me, his shoulders hunched forward, his face contorted in a scowl. Should I run? Catch him by surprise with a blow to the face? He has a key in his hand, attached to a silver smiley-face ring ornament. Without looking at me or saying a word, he pushes past me and starts to unlock the front door. I make a one-second prayer to the spirits and then say, "Flysted."

The door is already ajar. He lets go of it and slowly turns toward me, the veins standing out on his neck. As he approaches, I duck and jump to one side. Thump! Jesus! I feel a sharp pain just at the outer corner of my right eye. I see blood running all over everything. My head is spinning, and I almost fall, but Flysted catches me, holds me up. Luna appears in the doorway.

"My God!" she screams. My vision is blurred, but it looks like she's just standing there, gaping open-mouthed at the two of us. Flysted pulls a handkerchief out of his hip pocket and holds it over my wound.

"Do you know this guy?" he says.

She nods. "You hurt him!"

"Hurt him? He hit his head on the mailbox there. How come he knows my name? Who the hell is he?" He lets go of me, and I stagger but keep my balance. I can't see out of my right eye now.

Luna looks at me. "Did he hit you?"

"I . . . I don't know."

"You goddam men!" she yells. "Well I'm not part of this. I got my own life!" Turning to go inside, she sees Flysted's key in the lock and yanks it out, taking it with her as she goes in and slams the door. We can hear her footsteps hurrying up the stairs.

"Okay," says Flysted. "What the hell is this? Who are you? How the hell did you know my name, anyway?"

"I'm . . . the shaman."

"The shaman, the shaman . . . Oh, yeah! The guy with the pig! The loony magician!" He starts to laugh wildly. "I see! No wonder you ducked!

So now you want to do some magic on Luna, eh?" My head is still spinning. I can't concentrate on what he's saying. I hear, "You've got balls . . . magician . . . better stay away from me . . . stay away from Luna . . . get your ass out of here."

I can't think. To my surprise, I say, "I think this is a public street."

He ignores me, his attention now on his phone. He punches her number, waits, scowls, punches some more buttons, then begins to curse through his teeth. He rings the intercom for apartment 14. No answer.

I start to laugh. "I put a curse on your phone. Go ahead, try calling her again." I sit down on the front step.

"You better be gone when I get back," he says, and off he goes. I wait.

An elderly couple enter the building, pretending not to notice me. A bit later, a teenage boy bounds out and goes off down the street. My face has stopped bleeding, but it really hurts now. My head clears a little. In a while, the door opens again and Luna comes out, carrying a plastic bucket and a scrub brush.

She scowls at me. "Still here, eh?"

"You asked me to wait for you, remember?"

"Well, I excuse you. Go see a doctor." She throws soapy water from the bucket on the porch and begins to scrub it with the brush. "It's bad luck to have this blood on my doorstep," she says.

"Leave it," I say. "If it's a shaman's blood, it's *good* luck. It's the same as a sacrifice to the spirits. No, leave the blood, Luna. Now go get a candle and put it here, then make a wish." She stops and looks at me, trying to read my face. Gravely, I say, "Nothing happens by accident. The spirits brought us together, they blessed your doorstep with a shaman's blood. Now you *have* to make a wish, or the spirits will be unhappy."

"With that beat-up face you must be a shaman. You look like a *duende* — a goblin. Come up and let me clean it for you."

Her teenage daughter, whose name is Manuela, says hello to me from the studio couch, without getting up from her TV show. In the kitchenette, Luna gently daubs my face, then pulls me to the bathroom where she shows me my face in the mirror and takes out bandage materials. My swollen right eye sits in the center of a deep purple circle the size of a softball, but I won't let her bandage me.

"Bjørn was mad because I broke a date with him tonight. If you want to fight somebody, use witchcraft, not your fists," she says as she works. "Sure, a woman likes to be fought over, but not with blood!"

I want to ask her what she plans to do about Flysted, but something tells me she isn't ready. "I'll phone you," I say again. "I'll hang up after two rings, then call you back. I won't leave messages." She writes her number on a piece of bandage tape and sticks it to my wrist. "Be careful," I say. "If you need help, here's my number," and I take the pen and do as she did, sticking the number on her wrist.

"I can handle Bjørn," she says. I say goodnight and start down the stairs, and when I reach the bottom I see that she's behind me, carrying a lit candle.

"What will you wish for?" I ask.

She only smiles, but then she reaches up and kisses me softly on my purple eye.

Back at our place, Blake looks at my face. "You're smiling, Prof," he says. "You must have won that fight."

"I won."

"Are you going to tell me about it?"

"The spirits have strange ways. Fantastic and wonderful ways. I fought like a bull, without having to fight at all. The boyfriend is beaten by his own lies."

"Whose boyfriend? Wait a minute. One, I thought you were totally in love with Lisa, and two, I thought you gave up the spirit shit."

"So did I, on both counts. But it looks like the spirits haven't given up on me, and maybe I was wrong about Lisa, too."

"Well, you're smiling, I guess that's the main thing. So who's this woman?" He's obviously pleased about that part.

"Hah! If I introduce you, next thing I know you'll be after her yourself."

"If you disappear into that jungle for another three months, maybe she'll come after me."

Laughing, punching and wrestling, we exhaust ourselves, then lie there on the floor. "Let's go surfing tomorrow," says Blake. "Your fuckin' spirits can get us some waves, right?" I smack him another good one.

CHAPTER TWENTY-ONE

FACING THE TEST

The first time Luna and I make love, if you can call it that, is a few days after my encounter with Flysted. We have dinner at the Carousel, then we go to her apartment so that she can minister to my face, which looks like it might be getting infected, she says. Manuela is staying with friends. As Luna works on my face, it isn't long before we begin to kiss. She's being playful. She gets this look in her eyes like a mischievous child, a look as though she has some startling secret and can hardly wait for me to discover it. She leads me to her bed and starts matter-of-factly undressing, saying nothing but with this look still on her face. I'm a little mystified by this, and when we're both naked, I'm still only half hard. She pushes me down on my back and straddles me. If I try to move, she stops me. I think if she was either crazy with passion or yielding and compliant, I could get into this, but I can't seem to deal with this teasing-dominating thing; my body just won't respond, and I tell her, ask her, to lie down next to me, and after I hold her for a while I start getting turned on — somewhat. I wish she would suck me or something, but I want her to be the one who asks, or who figures it out herself, but she doesn't, so I sit up, turn her over on her stomach, and give her a back rub.

While I work the muscles of her back, I can feel her soften and relax. I'm in command. She tries to turn over, and I push her back down. Now I'm pretty aroused, and I pull her to her knees and with some difficulty manage to get it into her from behind, but then, pow, I come just like that. I want to go down on her now, but she won't let me, and I lie there aching with frustration and shame.

A week goes by. Luna and I are at a party at Sid's house, along with Lisa and Blake and a lot of other people. To my surprise, Lisa joins us. While Blake and I discuss the art trends we see in Sid's living room, Lisa and Luna are talking. I watch them out of the corner of my eye. Lisa smiles. Luna makes emphatic gestures with her hands. I strain to hear them. Something about computer courses, women's careers, and now about places — Mexico, Hollywood. At length Lisa turns to me and says, "When did you develop such good taste in women, Ashton?"

"It's her taste, not mine."

"Are you saying you'll take anything you can get, Prof?" says Blake.

"There isn't a man in this room that deserves a good woman," I say, looking at Luna, who gives me a lovely smile.

Hot from flirting, Luna and I leave early and go back to my place. This time we're a little drunk, and I feel ready for a good screw, but when we get in bed, Luna wants to know all about Lisa. "She's jealous of you. You had a relationship with her, didn't you?"

"What if I did?"

"What happened? Are you in love with her?"

"She's the one I told you about — the one who didn't like me being a shaman and all that. It's over."

"I won't be her substitute."

"Why did we come here, Lunita? To fight about my loyalty?" She tries to talk, but I put my hand gently over her mouth and climb on top of her, pressing her into the bed, kissing her neck and breasts until we're panting. But when I try to enter her, I find again I'm not ready. As before, I turn her over and give her a massage, but this time she simply falls asleep, and I'm left with my own sour thoughts.

When I wake up, Luna is in one of my T-shirts, drinking tea at the kitchen counter. There's no sign of Blake. She comes over and sits on the bed. "I'm sorry I fell asleep, honey," she says. That's the first time she's called me honey. "But I'm awake now," and she peels off the shirt and crawls under the covers with me. This time she pleasures me with her hands and mouth until I'm ready, and when we really do make love, she keeps saying, "I'm yours, honey, I'm yours." I feel so grateful to her, for the moment I almost mean it when I say I'm hers, too.

She has to go to work, and after I drop her off, I begin to realize that my plan is threatening to spin out of control. Women know how to do this so much better than men do. But I can't fall in love with Luna. I need her for the project with Lisa, and I have to focus on that. As long as the Zogon still lives in Lisa's dream, I must bring him — bring that dream — back to life. In the process, Lisa's life and mine will be transformed too, the power and emotion of our deep selves will rise to fill the reality of our everyday lives.

My project, it seems, has become more urgent than ever. The guy who just made love with Luna was not the Zogon, the warrior-body full of ease, the taut bowstring of will, the keen shaman mind. He was, if anything, Professor Caldo, the haughty wordsmith brought low by his own desires. I have to get on top of this.

As the weeks go by, I'm studying her. She doesn't seem complicated like Lisa. For her, dreams come from somewhere else, faint signs of danger from a mysterious spirit world, omens of things to be avoided or forces to be placated. The idea of life as a mystic journey, as a heroic project, makes no sense to her. One lives life as it is given, trying to make the best of scraps and shreds, rejoicing in the little sweets that come one's way among the strenuous days. She offers me love as she knows it — her gentle touch and her body, her good humor, a homemade tamale, an oddity picked up at a garage sale, a glimpse now and then into her private thoughts, her jealousy of other women. For my part, I enjoy pleasing her in little ways as well. I buy her a cell phone and start calling her on her lunch break; I give her rides to class; I write her the occasional poem.

And all is not lost. When I'm with Luna, I can't talk to Lisa much on account of the jealousy factor, but when it's just Lisa and Blake and me, it's quite easy.

One night she and Blake and I are having beers at La Cantina in Del Mar. She's in a loose gauzy black thing with a deep V-neck, and she's idly playing with this completely stunning necklace, a series of large iridescent sea shells, strung together with gold and red cords. "Once you said the stuff in Sid's gallery was vulgar, Ashton," she says. "What do you think about the stuff you and Blake are making?"

"It isn't art," I say, "but it isn't my vocation. It's like when I was in graduate school, I paid the rent by writing ads for a radio station. It beats flipping burgers."

"What *is* your vocation, Ashton?"

"To discover my vocation."

"Hmm. You once said that I had everything to do with this need of yours, with your leaving your profession."

"*You* did. Have everything to do with it, I mean."

"And now?"

She's found the most slippery ground. If I admit she's still part of the plan, I'm sure to engage her defenses. If I say otherwise, she either won't believe me or take it as evidence of my shallowness. "I'm not guided by a clear vision or a plan, but rather by certain deep feelings," I say. "Meeting you set these feelings in motion. It was like the opening of a door. It seems to me that you have certain characteristics, certain instincts maybe, that provide a kind of light to me in my search. Now I think that your path and mine sometimes run together, and sometimes diverge. What do you think?"

"I find this path of yours confusing," she says. "Sometimes frightening. It's always seemed strange to me that you think I put you on this path, and even more so that you think I'm guiding you somehow."

"Is that all you feel about our relationship?" The question just comes out before I can suppress it. She thinks for a minute. Looking at her pensive face, I feel a great surge of emotion. I want to tear my heart out and lay it in front of the child who dreamt of Zogons. I want to assault the missionary, to drive her from our lives. Will the time ever come?

"Oh, Ashton, I think I've hurt you. But believe me, you've changed me, too. You're extremely intelligent, for all your . . ." she breaks off.

"My adolescent rebelliousness."

"Adolescent or not, you've made me think about my own values, what really matters to me. I'll always appreciate that." The missionary thanks the depraved savage for reaffirming her faith, but . . .

"But where are you going now?" she asks. "Disturbing as your shaman act was, at least I felt I could sort of track it."

"If I get any brilliant ideas about where I'm going, I promise you'll be the first to know." In a way this is literally true. She will be the first to know.

"What if you and Blake grow your workshop into a real business?"

I look at Blake. "You guys have been talking about that, it seems."

He looks a little uncomfortable. "You know . . . more marketing, more space, more equipment, maybe a couple more guys."

"I know," she says looking at me, "that sounds to your partner like a sellout, a cave-in to bourgeois values, right, Ashton?"

"I thought this would come up sooner or later," I say. "This is a big, important discussion. Blake and I will have to spend some time on it." As I look at the two of them, a knot of dread starts to form in my stomach. They're forcing me to choose between their world and what I really believe. I want to be free of Blake and his pseudo-art, but I can see that Lisa doesn't. The more respectable he gets, the more he engages her missionary persona. Shit, she might even marry the guy.

The liberation ritual will have to be very soon.

I've already sketched in the overall plan. I know Baja California pretty well from my surfing days. There are stretches of coast that are absolutely deserted and wild, where no one will disturb us for several days. Lisa won't consent to the ritual the way she thinks now, so I'll have to use magic, aided by the Raapa Uu medicine, *wegura,* to bring about an initial change in her consciousness. I'll also need to take some of her things — clothes, personal stuff, to use in the ritual. There will be three phases. The first two will take five days — first, and hardest, the destruction of the possessing spirit, two days; the second, the healing solitude, three days, including the trip back to Del Mar. The third phase will be her gradual reentry into life as the new Lisa, and that may last weeks or months.

Now it's time to lay out the many difficult details. How to get Lisa to take the *wegura.* How to deal with Blake, and with Luna, so that they'll accept our brief disappearance. Then the logistic preparations for the trip itself. Water, food, shelter, fuel, emergency precautions.

I buy a used pickup with a camper shell on the back. I begin to load it with supplies, keeping it locked so that Blake can't nose around. Dried or canned camp food, rice and beans; a patio-sized sun awning from army surplus; eight seven-gallon plastic water cans; a hand winch in case we get stuck in the sand; two kerosene lamps and a camp stove; two sleeping bags; an ice chest that will hold eggs, bacon, milk, chicken fillets, butter, salad greens, fruit, fresh vegetables, and bread.

Lisa will need new clothes and jewelry after the ritual — things that proclaim her new identity as the restored wise child. I've never shopped for women's clothes before, and I try to imagine her in a range of fashions. Feminine but not flashy, a little old-fashioned — retro? Peasant blouses, dirndl skirts, patent leather shoes? No, too timid for her. I wander the shopping streets of San Diego, and when I reach North Park I find it: full hippie — bangles, crystals, headbands, crazy hats, long India print skirts and bare feet, dazzling colors. I don't know what fragrance she uses now, but I buy patchouli oil and sandalwood as well. I buy her a one-piece yellow bathing suit with diagonal blue stripes, to swim in the Baja surf.

I wonder if I should buy a gun for protection against bandits, but decide that might actually make us less safe. If we get robbed, we get robbed, and I'll defend Lisa's person with my magic, and with my life. I search the internet for details on roads and beaches, and to my satisfaction, except for Google Earth, there's practically nothing about where we're going. As for local obligations, I have only one: Blake will take care of Pig.

At times I feel the old familiar wave of anxiety, the physical sensation of vertigo, thinking about my secret plan. In the evenings, when Blake is often at Lisa's, I take Mekiimos (with his battered ear) and my ritual things down to Randy's Trail, build an altar, and sing for the success of the cleansing of Lisa. I dedicate my life to the ritual. I ask that the *wegura* work its magic. I have no specific vision of how to use it, but I'm confident Mekiimos will help me when the time comes. Above all, I ask that Lisa herself should be easily awakened from her ignorance and returned to the power of her dream self.

I pick up Luna from work one evening, and we go out for drinks and tapas. She's talking briskly, about her work, about her classes. I'm nodding, thinking I'll have to tell her I'm going to be gone for a while. The rest can wait until Lisa and I get back. Somewhere into the evening she grows quiet, and I can see that something is bothering her, too. We go to her house, we undress, and I can feel this distance between us. In bed I try to communicate tenderness — I really do love her in a way — but she's tense, and she stops me when I try to make her come.

I'm giving her a back rub, and I say, "Mi amor, I'm going to take a few days off. I want to be by myself. I'm stressed out from work."

She's silent for a while as I massage her. Then she turns around and meets my eyes. "You're going to see Lisa, aren't you?"

"What makes you say that?"

"You men are so stupid. At first you tried to fool her into thinking that you love me — or at least that you don't love her. Now, you're trying to fool me. Aren't I right? Of course I am." I wait. I know there's more. "Stressed out from work? You quit your real job. You can quit this one any time you want. You're stressed out all right, but not from work. You've dug yourself a hole, with two women in it. What could be more stressful than that?" She sits up and turns on the light. "Look at me, *Señor Ashton*. Look at me and tell me you love me."

I can't hold her eyes. "Right now I don't know what I want, or who I love. I want to go away. To think. To clear my mind."

"Go, then." She starts to cry. I put my hand on her shoulder, but she shakes it off.

I get up and start to dress. "I have something big to do with my life. I do love you, but I can't stay here and fight with you now. I'm too . . ." I'm about to say "too confused," but I don't want to leave with a lie on my lips.

"You're too what? What is it that you're afraid to say to me? What is this big thing in your life? You shit!"

She's crying as I walk out the door. I feel sick. I sit in my pickup and try to reconstruct the path that led me to this point, but it's all a tangle in my mind. I resolve that once Lisa has been restored to herself, I'll make it up to Luna. I'll bring her into our circle. I'll teach her to be a shaman. Right now I've never felt more lonely in my life, and my own eyes fill with tears.

It's late. Blake's asleep, but I lie tossing in bed. Everything is ready; it's a matter of going to Lisa's house and getting started. I get up and go over the ritual in my mind, fixing the details, arranging and rearranging the materials. I try to meditate, with no luck. I turn on the TV, but its banality depresses me as usual. It occurs to me that I haven't talked to Ysabel in weeks. I don't want to talk to her, and it's too late to phone her anyway, so I go to my email, which I haven't looked at in a week. As I scan the messages, one catches my eye: it's from Thelma.

hi, daddy. sorry I'm terrible about writing you. mom showed me something in the newspaper about you, it said you're a SHAMAN! is it true? mom laughed about it, but I looked up shaman, and I think it's awesome. anyway, I was thinking about you because my therapist says he thinks it would be a good idea for you and me to talk.

i have a boyfriend named rick who's a fabulous in line skater (really he wins prizes) and a cat named sneezeweed that my girl friend wendy gave me from her cat's kittens. he has a moustache like hitler. do you remember that fat cat soloman we had when i was little? i thought all cats were girls, and so soloman was a girl's name; and you couldn't convince me otherwise, especially when "he" had kittens. rick loves sneezeweed, but she is scared of his skates so she runs under the nearest car when she sees him. she thinks i'm a bad mother. i still hate school. i know you want me to go to college and everything but i feel like i need some time to just think. don't worry I won't do anything stupid like get pregnant or join the marines, i just want to work for a while and take a rest from academics. where do you live now? it would be nice to see you, if you're not too busy casting spells on people (kidding). love, thelma. sneezeweed says hi.

How did it happen that I hardly know this person, this *personality,* who calls me Daddy, and who touches my sorest old wounds with memories of shared foolishness? That was another life: a life whose sweetness now hurts me worse than anything ugly about it. I'll never go back, but now I vow I'll bring Thelma with me when I've reached my goal, which will be soon.

Dear Thelly, I'm the one who's a bad correspondent; I've neglected you terribly. A lot of things are changing in my life, and I want to share them with you soon, when I've settled down and have time and energy. Of course I remember Soloman. We named her Soloman Grundy, because she was born on Monday, and because who knew she should really be Salome? I'm so glad I have your e-mail now. I live in Del Mar, where I grew up.

About school: I know you're very smart, and I'm so sorry you're unhappy in school. I won't ply you with Wise Advice about that, you don't need it. There are many ways to get to the future, and the only thing you have to keep in mind is that you are an extremely, extremely precious and valuable person who's not to be wasted (in all senses of the word). If school seems absolutely unbearable to you now, find something that's more bearable, and that lets you feel like you're growing in a direction you like.

I'm glad you're interested in shamanism. I've been to New Guinea and studied it with the natives. It's nothing spooky or weird like people think. Let's stay in touch, and I want you to come visit in a couple of months. I love you very much. Dad.

Tell Sneezeweed hi, and tell her that you're a very good mother. Don't say that to Rick, though, he might get you wrong.

Suddenly overcome with fatigue, I log out and climb back in bed.

CHAPTER TWENTY-TWO

THE HOUR ARRIVES

It's Friday morning, a cool, sunny spring day. There's nothing left to prepare, no excuse to put it off. I phone Lisa and ask her what she's doing tomorrow. "It depends on how much I get done today," she says. "I'm not feeling too well, think I might have a touch of the flu or something. What's up?"

"I've been thinking about our conversation a couple of weeks ago, about where I'm headed in my life. Could we spend some time talking about it? I'd find it helpful."

"Actually, I've been wanting to talk with you about my own future." It's fixed. I tell her I'll come over around ten.

Blake is in the studio, covered as usual with plastic dust and flecks of fiberglass. I tell him about seeing Lisa. "Great," he says. "I'm glad you guys are friends again, actually." Putting down his paint roller, he examines his work for a second, then leans back on the workbench and peels off his rubber gloves. "She's been kind of weird lately," he says. "I think she's unhappy about something, I don't know what."

"What's your guess?"

He scowls. "I'm not good at guessing. I think if you leave those things alone, a lot of times they work themselves out, know what I mean?"

"And what about you?"

He looks thoughtful for a minute, then pulls a new pair of gloves out and puts them on. "I always get by," he says, and picks up the roller again, signaling that the conversation is over. I say to myself, Blake's a good enough guy, but he's not of the same species as Lisa. I doubt he'll even miss her once she's restored to her self. "We're pretty well caught up with work," I say as I put on my gloves and pick up my tools. "Tomorrow I'm going up into the backcountry for a few days. Don't look for me until midweek, okay?" He nods. We know each other's boundaries well by now, and we can work together without much conversation.

In the afternoon I drive over to Sid's gallery with a finished piece, a huge and very lifelike ratite bird much like a cassowary: its grotesque head is fitted with ear phones, and one uplifted claw holds an iPod. Once we've got it situated in the shop, Sid reaches into his desk and hands me a small, slightly battered white envelope. "There's a letter for you," he says. "Looks like it's from Russell." Thinking it might concern Sid, I open it on the spot.

The letter is written with a large neat hand in pencil, on a piece of lined notebook paper. It is indeed from Russell.

> *My Dear Morse, I hope you are well, as I am. I have not been back to the Sepik since I saw you last, but I heard by email from the chaps in Wewak that you stayed up there for several months, and have recently returned to America. I assumed you would be going back to Del Mar. I hope this letter reaches you, as there is something that I need to clear from my conscience. You yourself might have reasoned this out by now, but in case you did not, here it is: I did not tell you that the Raapa Uu have a rather mean sense of humor, especially when it comes to foreigners. In other words, the business about the deaf girl was a joke. The men in Komoko put the girl up to it. Kamawi tried to talk them out of it, but once it was decided there wasn't much he could do. Betting on your reputation as a bounder, they picked the prettiest one, and I'm sorry to say it seemed to have worked. I want you to know I was not in on it, and I really hope no harm came to you as a result. At any rate, if you ever go back to Komoko, you owe them one.*

> *I have enjoyed our association, and I truly hope to see you again at one end of the Pacific or the other.*

With sincere good wishes, Russell

When I've read it three times, Sid can no longer contain himself. "Well?"

"It's nothing to do with you, Sid. It's about New Guinea. About the Raapa Uu. Nothing important."

"On, come on now. He didn't write to say 'hello.'"

"Sorry, I'll tell you about it another time. I've got a lot to do right now," and I walk out of the shop.

As the initial shock of the letter begins to wear off, it dawns on me that its message is a bald impossibility. Surely Matthew couldn't have been taken in by such a joke, and surely he wasn't a party to it. Surely Sosi wasn't. No, either Russell is teasing me, or he's deluded himself. Actually, it may be *he* who's the butt of this joke. Somehow Kamawi found out what had happened to me and decided to have some fun with Russell.

But wait! There's an even better explanation. It was the spirits, playing with all of us. They bewitched me, and they bewitched the men of Komoko, making them think that they had done it themselves — a clever plot to keep my human allies from recognizing my illness and treating it. That's it. Is there no end to the mischievous power of the spirits? Matthew was not fooled by the bewitching of the Raapa Uu men, because he's a Christian. That cross he was wearing actually did protect him. The spirits must have known this, too. Their ultimate plan was to deliver me, by way of Matthew, into the hands of Sosi, so that I would learn the magic I sought. Everything is explained. The spirits are my true allies; my success with Lisa's healing is certain.

In my song to the spirits this evening, I thank them for Russell's letter, which may have also been part of their plan. Gradually, they allow me deeper and deeper into their confidence; and as an offering, I burn Russell's letter.

I arrive at Lisa's right at ten o'clock; it's a bright, cool, windless day. I bring my backpack in, and we sit in the kitchen. As she makes tea, I study her expression and movements. She looks a bit tired, a bit serious, and I remind myself that the healing, the exorcism of her banal spirit, will restore her to radiant energy. A wave of intense love comes over me, love for the child Lisa that lies sleeping within her, the Lisa that I will bring back liberated. I feel relaxed — happy, even — and when she looks at me, she seems to catch my mood and brighten a bit herself. She's wearing a tight gray knit top with long sleeves, and tight jeans made of shiny silver-blue spandex. Around her neck she has the same stunning necklace of shells on gold and red cords that she wore a couple of weeks ago.

"You seem full of energy this morning," she says. "What are these plans you have for your life?"

"I am full of energy. My energy, my well-being, comes from not having plans — at least not long-term ones."

"And in the short term?"

"Today, my plan is to be here, now."

"Is this what you came here to tell me?"

"Are you happy, Lisa?"

She pauses, shrugs. "I'm okay."

"And what are your plans?"

"It's been so long since we were . . . close, Morse. I feel funny. I don't want to talk about trivial things, but I don't feel ready to get really personal, either."

"You're struggling with something."

"Everybody struggles. That's life. Struggle, relax, struggle . . ." She's sitting on a high stool, her hands in her armpits, her torso tight.

"What would happen if you just stopped struggling?"

She rolls her eyes and makes the "throat cutting" gesture.

"Maybe you should try it."

"Starting right now?" The absurdity of it amuses her.

I'm feeling the same power I felt the day I first kissed her on Randy's Trail. "Look at me," I say. We stare into each other's eyes for a moment, and before she looks away, I can see that she's wavering. I hold out my hand, palm up. She looks at it for a moment, then slowly takes it by the wrist, turns it over, and lays her own on top of it. I wait. In the silence we can barely hear the chuffing sound of the surf at the foot of Randy's Trail. She seems lost in thought.

"I have something for you," I say it softly. I pull the little bottle of *wegura* flavored with honey from my pocket and pour it into her half-empty tea mug. "There's a touch of herbal medicine in there. I've taken it with good results, and I want you to try it."

"No, thanks."

"Suit yourself. Might help, though."

"It won't turn me into a toad, or a sorcerer, will it?"

"It might, but I doubt it," I laugh. She picks up the cup and takes a sip, makes a face, then drains it.

"There's a healing song that goes with it," and I begin to sing to Mekiimos.

"Oh oh," she says almost at once. "Morse, I don't feel well. What did you do this for? Oh, shit."

"It's okay. Come over here and lie down."

"No, really. Call a, call somebody, or something . . ."

"You're okay, don't be afraid." I put my arm around her and steer her to the couch. "Lie still, you'll be fine." I keep up the singing, take from my backpack the palm leaves I have smoked in my herbal fire and sweep her body with them. She's holding tightly on to my arm, with her eyes closed, now fully under. I continue to sing, so that she can hear my presence near her. I go to her bedroom closet and select an armload of clothes, which I take to the kitchen and put in a green plastic garbage bag. I find her purse and keys in her office and put them in the bag as well. I take the bag and put it in the cab of my pickup. I open the door of the camper and put the stepstool in front of it, then go back in the house. I take Lisa's shell necklace off and place it on the kitchen counter, then pick her up and carry her to the camper bed. I take her cell phone from her jeans pocket, go to "Settings," and select "Voice Message." I delete her message and record this one in a cheery voice: "Hello. This is Bruce, Lisa Calgari's new temporary assistant. Lisa is on a vacation, and will return your call when she returns in two weeks."

I replace the stool, and close and lock the camper door. I phone Blake.

"Hi, Blake. Listen, I forgot to tell you, I was talking with Lisa this morning. She was in a big rush — asked me to tell you, she just found out she has to go to this meeting in LA for a few days."

"What kind of meeting? Did she say when she'll be back?"

"I don't know, man, some work thing. She'll call you when she gets back."

I turn off the lights, pull the drapes, make sure the doors are locked. I climb in the cab of the camper, open the back window so that she can hear me, and continue to sing my healing song as I pull out of the driveway and head south toward Baja.

The true desert wilderness starts at Ensenada, and we're there by early afternoon. Warm wind brings the smell of the ocean over the dunes to the narrow highway. There are few cars — an occasional RV bristling with fishing tackle, a smoky bus bound for Santa Rosilía and La Paz, a Coca-Cola van. It's been about twenty-five years since I was here, but it hasn't changed noticeably, and I think I still know roughly where to turn off to look for isolated shore. The trick is to avoid getting stuck in the sand. There's a cleanliness here that no civilized place can match. The sky hums with blue; the air is barren even of dust; the sparse brush has a mineral hardness. As I drive, I pray out loud to the spirits of this place, telling them what beauty they possess, asking them to accept my rain forest ways and guide me to my goal. Now and then I look at Lisa over my shoulder. When I see her toss and turn, I sing my healing song, and it seems to quiet her.

A couple of hours south of Ensenada I know we're in the right area, and I pull off onto a faint dirt track that weaves along a dry wash through cactus and coyote brush to the west. When the highway is out of sight, we're suddenly in the very midst of nowhere: not a sign of life other than the dry brush, not a sound other than our own. My pulse quickens and I feel a physical thrill. Months of struggle, of decisive action, are about to bloom. The Zogon is in full power.

A little ways farther on, the wash gets narrow and rocky, and the track disappears; I have to pull up onto the dunes where the sand is softer. No problem, west of us is all ocean, but I stop and let some of the air out of my tires to improve my traction on the sand. Then I walk in a wide circle around the truck, picking up dead manzanita branches for firewood, which I tie on the front of the truck with bungee cords. I climb in the camper, find a water bottle with a drinking nipple on it, lift Lisa's head up, and drip the water slowly into her mouth, wait until she swallows, then drip a bit more.

"We're on a journey," I say. "A journey back to your dream. When you wake, your suffering will be gone; every place you are will be Randy's Trail. You'll be healed, and you'll have the power to heal others. This spirit that crushes your wild heart will never come to haunt you again. The water that you're drinking is the water of life. It nourishes and cleans your soul. There. Feel the peace. I've been where you are, Lisa. I have been healed like this. You are being healed as I was. The strange spirit that you had over you has gone away. You have forgotten what that spirit put in your mind. You are starting to remember your real self. Your real mind is starting to come back."

I climb back in the cab and drive on, slowly, bouncing and weaving over the dunes. After about an hour we crest a hill, and I see the ocean below us and zigzag down to a wide, empty beach. A stiff wind is making the breakers roar and blowing the fine gray sand around my ankles as I get out. Looking around, I see that there's a fair amount of small driftwood after all. Leaving the door of the camper latched open, I set up the awning on the lee side, gather a bit more wood, lay a fire but don't light it, eat some crackers and cheese, and wait eagerly for Lisa's gradual return to the world, remembering how glad I was to see Sosi when the *wegura* began to wear off.

Night falls, and the wind dies down a little. I light one of the kerosene lanterns and hang it from the awning, then take Mekiimos from my backpack and hang him on the side of the camper; I light the wood fire and offer Mekiimos the medicine smoke. I go into trance, and ask him to guide her back to her original self. My mind is completely calm, my body alive with power, and now I hear her stirring. I take down the lantern and climb into the camper.

She's sitting up, her eyes open, pupils dilated, looking around.

"Welcome back, Lisa."

She doesn't answer at first, but keeps looking around, confused.

I smile. "It's me, Ashton. The Zogon."

"Get me out of here! Take me home! Oh, shit, here it comes again!" She covers her face with her hands and rolls into a ball on the bed, panting. I begin to sing the healing song again, and she starts to yowl, long, drawn-out sobs wracking her as she slips back into the *wegura* state. I didn't anticipate this. Maybe the possession is much stronger than mine was. She continues to wail for a while, then gradually relaxes as her mind begins to clear again.

This time she sits up and looks directly at me. "You!" she screams and, frenzied, comes at me with her fingernails. I put my hands up to protect myself.

"Lisa, Lisa!" I speak in a whisper, so as not to frighten her. "It's okay! You're okay! We've healed you! Your spirit is free now!" She grabs the lantern off its hook and swings it at me. The glass breaks and the lamp goes out, leaving only the faint light of the campfire through the window and the strong smell of spilled kerosene. She lunges out the door, and in the dark falls heavily on the sand, scrambles to her feet and begins to run. I follow and in a few steps I'm next to her, running alongside. She trips on kelp and falls again, gets up and keeps running. Maybe this is best; if she tires herself out, she'll be calm and we can continue.

We run and run along the beach under a slit of a moon, not talking, not touching. I fix my attention on the idea of Mekiimos, asking him to guide her mind, back to her childhood memories. After maybe half an hour we see ahead of us in the dim light a steep cliff that runs out into the water. I expect her to stop, but instead she heads for the water, and I have to catch her by the arm. She struggles. She kicks. I lose my grip and she takes off again, running back the way we came.

It begins to dawn on me that although I didn't anticipate any of this, I should have — in fact, I should have been worried if she *didn't* react this way. She's returning to her child mind. Her behavior is perfectly normal and healthy. My job, it would seem, is to prevent her from hurting herself until she begins to adjust to her cured state. We continue past the camper and far up the beach the other way until, exhausted, she slows to a walk, then sits down on the sand. In a little while she nods and lies down, then falls asleep. I pick her up the way you would a tired child, with her head on my shoulder, my hands locked under her bottom, and carry her the two or three miles back to bed in the camper. With a bungie cord I secure the door from the outside, then lie down next to the long-dead campfire and sleep too.

She's awake when I open the door in the morning, tense but not hysterical.

"Hi, Lisa. How do you feel?"

"Where are we?"

"We're in Baja."

"What are we doing here?"

"We're performing a healing ritual, to restore you to your true self. You're perfectly right to be angry with me. I'm really sorry I had to do it this way, but I'll explain the whole thing to you now." She listens quietly while I talk. I speak calmly, but with all the intensity of my purpose, the way Sosi would.

"When I first met you, you told me about your childhood, your dreams, your love for Randy's Trail. In just a few minutes, you showed me the incredible beauty and vitality of your real personality. Those few minutes changed my life. I realized that I had lost that same beauty and vitality myself, only I didn't even realize what I'd lost. At first, I was obsessed with saving myself, with getting back the power that I once had, and that you sensed when you met me, met the Zogon, on the trail. But as I got to know you, I realized that to complete my healing, I had to bring you with me, to heal you as well. You had become a critical, conventional person — intelligent, successful by vulgar standards, but without spontaneity and joy. The last year or so of my life has been guided by the goal of freeing you from this dead, moralistic spirit that has dominated and imprisoned your true self, your child self.

"When I saw the artwork of the New Guinea people, I knew instinctively that I had to go there, to learn their ways in the spirit world. While I was there, I too was possessed by an evil spirit, and underwent ritual healing. I studied with a powerful shaman for seven months, until I could see that I had learned his methods, that I could speak to the spirits and produce results."

Expressionless, she studies my face.

"The rest of the healing is easy. Stay with me here for three days. Learn the spirit song that will protect you from these things forever. In this ritual, you cast off the thoughts and habits that the possessing spirit imposed on you, and embrace your true self again — the vital, joyful, creative self that you have always been. When we go back to Del Mar, we'll have a big ceremony to introduce the reborn Lisa."

"What if I ask you to take me back now?"

"Right now you're in a vulnerable state. You've been freed from the possessing spirit, but you haven't yet returned to your self, or learned to protect yourself. To go back now would be a huge mistake."

"You won't take me?"

"Not right now. Give this three days, then do whatever you want. By the way, I left a message with Blake, and one on your answering machine, so no one would worry about you."

"You've been planning this for months, haven't you? You deceived me. You're committing a crime, you know. Kidnapping is a crime."

"Of course it is. It's true I deceived you. It's also true that your whole life was a deception. You were taken over by a spirit with false ideas; the idea, for example, that people's opinions are worth more than the voice of your own heart."

"You seem to know a great deal about my heart."

"When I discovered my own heart, I understood yours, too. Give me until Tuesday, then I'll take you back and you can do whatever you want."

She sighs. "Well for now, what I want is bacon and eggs."

In English, the words to Mekiimos's song are unimpressive, even grotesque. I have written out the Raapa Uu words, phonetically, and I give her a copy. "This song calls your protective ancestor, Mekiimos. Try to cultivate a feeling of respect for him. Sing this song to him with a sincere heart whenever you feel threatened or upset, and he will help you. After a while it'll become natural, and you'll gain confidence doing it. This works for me, and it can work for you, too." As I sing, she follows the words on the paper silently. "Try singing it with me now." This time she moves her lips, smiling self-consciously.

"Can I go for a walk?" she asks in the afternoon.

"It's very important for you to be still, to explore your thoughts and feelings in a quiet place. You've been freed from possession, you need to remember your true self, to feel your true personality."

"For three days? Can't I even listen to the radio?"

"No. We have some other things to do, though. I brought some of your things — clothes and things from your house. These represent your possessed self. Tonight we'll make a fire, and you will burn them. When the three days are over, you'll put on new things and become your restored self. I'm going to go get some driftwood for the fire."

Driftwood is not as plentiful as I thought. Some of what looked like small pieces are just branches sticking up from buried logs, and I didn't think to bring an axe. The wind is blowing like yesterday, and I keep getting sand in my eyes. I'm tugging at a branch about half a mile from the camper, trying to break it off, when out of the corner of my eye I see movement in the direction of camp. The pickup is moving, turning east toward the dunes. I take off sprinting, but I know I'm too late; by the time I reach the site she's disappearing over the dunes, dragging the awning alongside. She's gone.

The spirits are teasing me again. The cleansing is a success. Either she'll come back, or she'll be waiting for me when I get home. Still, what will I do in the meantime? She took everything. I look around and see that she's left one of the large water cans. In the middle of the fire pit, she's planted a driftwood stick with a piece of brown paper stuck on the end.

You need psychiatric help BADLY. I said this months ago. Don't try to contact me or come near me. DO NOT! Kidnapping is a serious crime, and you have no defense.

I can only shake my head. I was so sure of my magic, of Mekiimos, that it didn't even occur to me she would do this. This is the toughest test yet. I've got to get to civilization somehow, but where will I go? I need time to think. I hope she won't tell the Mexican authorities, and I'll be safe if I don't try to cross the border. I sit by the fire pit and begin to sing to Mekiimos for help; then I remember that he is still hanging, chewed ear and all, on the outside of the camper, and I find the image too distracting to continue my song.

The seven-gallon can is too heavy to carry full, so I pour about three quarters of the water out, then pick it up and strike out to the east, over the miles of dunes between me and the highway. She took my wallet with my credit cards in it, and my cell phone, but I have a few dollars in my pocket, and I should be able to get a few more for my watch.

CHAPTER TWENTY-THREE

FUGITIVE

It takes me an entire day to get to Ensenada. Two guys in a broken-down farm truck finally stop on the highway just before daylight, and I ride, comfortably enough, with a pair of warm burros in the back. Without credit or ID, I'm screwed. I've got to get that stuff back somehow. I can't go to the US consulate, obviously. I can call my credit card company and ask for a new one, but I'll need some kind of ID to receive it. On the other hand, bribery generally works in Mexico. Complicated, but not impossible.

Downtown Ensenada has become charming with its gringo money, and as the sun climbs over the horizon, the streets are already busy with delivery vans, vendors setting up their stalls, and the occasional tanned blonde jogger. The warm sea breeze carries smells of fresh-baked *pan dulce* and coffee, but I dare not spend my cash. My bad Spanish is not much of a handicap, but by the same token things are expensive here. At the Hotel Medialuna it costs me a hundred and twelve pesos, one quarter of my cash, to put in a call to Blake.

"Ashton, Jesus Christ, where are you?"

"In Ensenada. I guess you've talked to Lisa."

"Yeah. What're you going to do?"

"I don't know. She said she'd have me arrested, so I guess I can't come back."

"Don't come back, man. You're fucked this time, know what I mean?"

"Listen, I'm not crazy, okay?"

"What you did was crazy, dude. I can't fix that for you."

"I don't want you to fix it. But listen, Lisa took my credit cards and my ID. Can you overnight them to me at the Medialuna Hotel here in Ensenada?"

There's a pause. "I don't think I can do that."

"For Chrissake! Why not?"

"Lisa's blind pissed, man. If I ask her for them, she'll want to know where you are. She'll call the Mexican cops on you, she's that honked. Besides, for all I know she's torn them up by now."

"Has she told Luna?"

"She said she was going to tell everybody."

"Okay, okay. You won't tell her where I am, right?"

"No, I won't tell her. But stay in Mexico, okay? She's reported you as a nut case."

"A nut case?" That would be a fifty-one fifty. In California they can hold you in a psycho ward for seventy-two hours to find out if you're crazy. "I'm not crazy enough to risk a fifty-one fifty."

"Glad to hear that. Oh, one other thing. Your daughter called here, ahh, when was it? Saturday, I guess."

"Thelma? What did she want?"

"She was coming to see you. I thought you'd be back Wednesday, so that's what I told her."

"Oh, shit. What'd she say?"

"Just asked when you'd be here and said she was coming. She sounded pretty unhappy."

"You have her phone number, right?"

"Let me see... Oh, shit, I erased all my recents."

"What will you do when she gets there?"

"What do you want me to do? Take care of her?"

"I don't know. I don't know. Gotta think. Blake, will you please call Ysabel and tell her the situation? She'll help. You must have her number. Will you do that?"

"Yeah, I'll do it."

"Thanks, Blake. I know a lot of people would just tell me to piss off. You're really a good guy."

I call the credit card company and arrange to have a new card sent to the local Banco Pacifico. It'll take twenty-four hours. I don't have enough cash for a room, and the fucking hotel tells me neither they nor anybody else will give me a room without a card and a picture ID. "The US Consul has an office in Tijuana," they say. "They'll give you a temporary ID." It occurs to me that there are probably quite a few Americans hiding out from the law in these parts.

I make my way down to the beach, where at least I can sit for free, although the mariachi music blaring from the boardwalk irritates me. The tourists around me, especially the young ones with their bland faces, make me feel like a space alien. How could any of them even begin to grasp who I am, what I am? And who, after all, am I? A primitive Zogon, who can barely survive for a day without a credit card? A powerful magician with no friends, no job, no credibility, no home? A single-minded lover who has thrown his life away in pursuit of a woman who has absolutely and permanently rejected him? I'm in physical pain from this. It's simply impossible that I can be this powerless. How can I go on living?

Don't think too much, Blake once said.

Wandering along the sand, I feel mocked by the music and the vapid vacationers around me. I want to go back to the desolate beach where Lisa left me; that was the true end of my odyssey; this is only a false reprieve. Clinging to life now just pollutes the purity of my journey and fills me with self-disgust. Why didn't I see it? To hell with the credit card and all that shit. I'll walk south until I'm again in the middle of nowhere, in the clean, hard desert where I can die with my dream. Die, not like an animal in flight, but like a primitive man forsaken by fate. The thought even makes me smile. I square my shoulders and increase my pace.

The crowd thins out, the music fades in the distance behind me. Soon there is only an occasional fisherman folding his nets, a few ragged children from a rural village, the chuff of the surf. And in the growing solitude I begin to realize there's something else, some oppressive presence growing inside me, gradually forming itself. What is it?

Weed.

Sneezeweed.

Sneezeweed says hi.

He has a moustache like Hitler. I thought all cats were girls.

Thelly. I stop in my tracks. I have to go back to Del Mar. I have to draw on whatever power remains to me. I kneel on the sand, instinctively drawing an altar, a sacred space. Can I even sing to Mekiimos for help, when I have nothing to offer him, when even his image mask is lost or destroyed? Is it possible that Mekiimos is angry with me, that he's abandoned me? I know of no songs to remove my own offenses against the ancestors and the spirits. I have no choice but to sing to Mekiimos. But what will I sing for? What I need is protection from my enemies — enemies who would prevent me from being with my child. I wrack my brain, but I can think of nothing that Sosi taught me that applies to this situation. If I had a specific enemy, if I could name him and offer his icons to the spirits . . . but I know of no magic to protect me from the police, from a whole society that would humiliate me and keep me from Thelly. I can't even go into trance without the smoke, but in desperation I close my eyes and sing:

Mekiimos, rest in the company of the spirits of thunder and yams.
Mekiimos, rest in the company of the small spirits.
Mekiimos, rest in the company of the human souls.
Mekiimos, don't forget that I have offered you many pigs.
Mekiimos, forgive me, I have no pig to please you today.
Mekiimos, don't forget that I have offered you much sweet smoke.
Mekiimos, forgive me, I have no fire to please you today.
Mekiimos, eat and enjoy my song.

Mekiimos, speak to the spirits of thunder and yams.
Mekiimos, speak to the small spirits.
Mekiimos, speak to the souls of the Big Men.
Mekiimos, ask them to remember the pigs I have given them.
Mekiimos, ask them to forgive me that I have no pig.
Mekiimos, ask them to remember the smoke I have given them.
Mekiimos, ask them to forgive me that I have no fire.
Mekiimos, tell them to eat and enjoy my song.

Spirits of thunder and yams, there are unknown men who
would humiliate me before my child.

Spirits of thunder and yams, in your wisdom you can see them.
Spirits of thunder and yams, close their eyes when I pass them.
Small spirits, there are unknown men who would humiliate
me before my child.
Small spirits, in your wisdom you can see them.
Small spirits, close their eyes when I pass them.
Souls of Big Men, there are unknown men who would
humiliate me before my child.
Souls of Big Men, in your wisdom you can see them.
Souls of Big Men, close their eyes when I pass them.

Spirits of thunder and yams, small spirits, souls of Big Men,
I will offer you many pigs, I will offer you sweet smoke.
I will offer you many songs.

Far from lifting my spirits, this makeshift song seems to me ugly and worthless. If I were one of the spirits, I would brush it aside as trash. I haven't eaten since breakfast but I'm not hungry. I'll sleep on the beach, collect my credit card tomorrow, and buy a bus ticket for Tijuana. What I'll do when I get to the border, I don't yet know.

If I remember correctly from my youth, you can buy anything here in Tijuana, and you're a fool if you pay more than fifty dollars. Okay, so these days it's probably two hundred. I still have more than that left on my credit card, and what I need is a current US driver's license with a picture and a phony name. But it's already Tuesday afternoon, and I have to get back to Del Mar by tomorrow. The question is where to look. The notorious Tijuana police themselves could probably tell me, but their fee would be exorbitant. Taxi drivers know everything, but what they know best is how to fleece a gringo. Forgers must have to pay substantial bribes to stay in business, so the small shops on the back streets are probably honest businesses.

I pick a large, modern-looking shop right on Avenida Revolución, and I'm right on, except that it costs me $350. My name is now Jim Littlefield, and I live in Homewood, Illinois. They even apply a bit of editing to the digital photo so that I have a different haircut and clothes. Even I can hardly believe the result isn't genuine. I buy a shopping bag full of souvenirs and a cheap sombrero, toss back a couple of margaritas, and take the bus to the border.

"May I see your ID please, Sir?" I show the INS officer my new purchase. He stares at it for a minute, and then he says, "May I see your credit card please?"

"It was stolen the other day."

He sighs, and turns his attention back to the license. "Where did you get this, Mister . . . ahh . . . Littlefield?" He's pecking away at his computer.

"From the Illinois DMV."

"I see. Who's the governor of Illinois?"

"I'm not very interested in politics."

"I see. What county is Homewood in, Sir?"

"I've been away for quite a long time."

"Okay. Just how long would that be?"

"Couple of years."

"Couple of years. That's odd, your license says . . ."

Before he finishes his sentence a very large officer with the name badge THORPE appears in front of me with a handheld metal detector. He has the dead fish look of someone extremely bored with his job. "Arms out, feet spread." He scans me, pats me down, takes my credit card, searches through my shopping bag, takes the telltale license from the guard, and escorts me to a concrete bunker of a building off to the side of the gates.

I realize that now there's no way around telling them who I really am, and why I'm carrying a fake ID. Anything other than the truth — or something approximating it — will just feed their suspicions that I'm guilty of far worse things. But why would they even believe the truth? I'll have to bring Blake, and maybe even Lisa, into this, and Lisa might charge me with kidnapping if she knows what I've just done. There must be a better way. How about a little amnesia? I got drunk in Tijuana, I passed out, and here I am.

The screening center has no amenities of any kind, not even chairs. My escort hands my fake ID to a uniformed inspector and leads me to a service window where I'm photographed and fingerprinted ("Just a formality, Mr. Littlefield"). I try to remember when else I've been fingerprinted — for my driver's license and passport, I guess. With computer match technology, I guess it won't be long before they have my name and background on their computer. The fingerprint clerk tells me to wait with the dozen or so other miscreants and criminals. With time to think I realize that yesterday's song to Mekiimos has had less than no effect, just as I guessed at the time. Have I lost my shamanic power for good?

It seems like hours before someone finally calls, "Littlefield." The man across the desk from me wants know whether this is my real name.

"No."

"What is your real name?"

"Ashton Caldo."

"And how did you get this?"

"I can't remember." He gives me a steely look. "That's right. Last I remember was a couple of days ago. I guess I got really drunk. Then I wake up, all my stuff is gone, including the girl I was with, and my car."

"And who was this girl?"

"I don't remember her name."

"It wouldn't be Lisa Berman by any chance, would it?"

(Holy shit.) "Uhh, maybe, I don't know."

"You don't remember starting a fire on Ms. Berman's property recently?"

"No."

"Do you have magical powers, Mr. Caldo?"

"That's ridiculous."

"Is that a 'No?'"

I nod.

"Are you taking any medication?"

"I don't think so."

"Have you been seen by a doctor lately?"

"I don't know."

He stares at a sheaf of papers in front of him on the desk, tapping his pencil and pursing his lips. "Have you had thoughts about killing yourself?"

"No."

"Are you sure? Almost everyone has those thoughts occasionally, you know."

I shrug.

"Do you own a gun?"

"No, I'm sure I wouldn't own a gun."

"Do you want to enter California?"

"Yes."

He picks up his phone, punches in a number, and puts it down. In a moment, THORPE appears from somewhere, smiling now — leering, actually. Color has returned to his beefy face. His huge hand takes a firm grip on my belt at the back and gives it just enough of a tug that I have to take a step backward to keep my balance.

"Am I under arrest?"

"A complaint has been filed, asking that you be restrained from certain areas. The complaint indicates a legal violation. This, plus your apparent mental condition, gives us the authority to examine you psychologically, if you want to enter California."

My heart stops. "What legal violation?"

"Arson."

"Thank God!" slips out before I can stop myself. The inquisitor is frowning, but I still feel almost gleeful. She didn't file for kidnapping! There's no chance they can keep me. Still, this could get worse. I feel a brief wave of panic and look around for the exits, but something tells me THORPE is dearly hoping I'll try to make a break for it. He keeps clenching his free hamlike fist as, still holding my belt, he half escorts me, half drags me through a gray metal door into a large, bare room with bars on the windows. Before he leaves, he reaches around to the front of my belt, unbuckles it, and yanks it off so violently that I stumble and almost fall. He stands in front of me, produces a white plastic bag from his jacket pocket, dumps my belt in it, then holds out his hand, and I understand I am to deliver the contents of my pockets, which I meekly do. I think I hear him humming as he exits the heavy door and locks it with a convincing click.

There are three other men in the room, sitting on heavy wooden benches that are bolted to the floor. No one makes eye contact or converses, though one guy seems to be talking to himself. His mumbled words, punctuated now and again with a sort of sardonic laugh, echo off the bare walls. After a couple of hours or so, the door to the outside bangs open to reveal THORPE and a sheriff's bus. He's holding a bouquet of plastic zip-tie handcuffs, and as we shuffle out the door and into the bus, he manacles each of us tightly enough that it hurts — just a little, but enough to make his point. The plastic bags of our worldly goods are neatly stacked on the rack above the driver.

After a stop at the county jail, the bus takes me to the locked Psychiatric Ward at UCSD Med Center, where, once inside, they snip my handcuffs off. It's past dinner time before I finally finish my intake interview, physical exam, and paperwork. When I'm allowed to phone out, of course I call Blake's. I get his voice mail, so I say hi to Thelly and tell them where I am.

Everyone around me here — staff and patients alike — seems to be moving with the trance-like slowness of profound depression. They speak in compassionate tones, they call me "Ashton," yet I find it bizarre and unsettling that no one looks me directly in the eye, even while speaking to me. But, look, I mustn't care about those things. I'll be out in three days at the most, won't I?

The ward is patrolled by male orderlies in green surgical scrubs who look like they could give THORPE a lesson or two, but other than that, security is light. I am delivered pizza and lemonade for dinner, and now I have nothing to do but think.

I find it hard to concentrate on anything. If I could perform songs to Mekiimos and the spirits, I could exert some influence over this place, these people (Hah! I almost said "this tribe"), but of course to do anything visible or audible would be foolish, and silent prayer is not the way of my calling. Is Caldo crazy? I laugh. Far more sane, in fact, than he was when he used to give staff lectures in places like this. What a know-nothing he was then! What a confused, ineffectual person — but precisely the kind of person these keepers think of as normal! Look at them, with their soulless eyes. Pale ghosts, *laleo,* indeed. Well, I can play their game. I know their culture inside and out.

Then there's Lisa. What did she mean by arranging this? Is she so lost, so stripped of her soul, that she shares their view — the county psychiatric ward view of normality, of sanity? I can't believe that she does. She's locked in her superficial life just like I'm locked in this ward; there's a key to that lock, and I only have to find that key and turn it . . .

That's it.

Her wish to lock me up is a metaphor! Just as I've devoted myself to freeing her, she — or rather her demon of banality — has devoted itself to imprisoning me, forcing me to share her fate. To see it this way is to know that it is, in fact, a form of love. Lisa loves me, but by a diabolic twist of fate, instead of the free child Lisa, it's the pinched missionary Lisa who loves; the love itself is dark and deformed. But within the missionary Lisa, the child is there, struggling to be free; the very act of imprisoning me is also a message from the child as well: "Free yourself! Free me!"

Why didn't I see this before? The drama of our enslavement continues to unfold, as if it were all a plan, inevitable. Of course, it *is* a plan, every bit of it. So what's the next step of the plan? It seems to me I must not accept, even as a ruse, my keepers' definition of normality. I will free myself as the Zogon, as the shaman . . .

One of the orderlies is approaching me. What does he want? "Ashton, you have a visitor." I follow him out to the day room, and who do I see standing there? Someone I know instantly, even though the child is now a woman: Thelma.

CHAPTER TWENTY-FOUR

THELLY

A sob fills my throat when we hug. Why has it been so long? (I know why.) She's sixteen. She has her mother's long neck and button nose, but she's paler than both of us. Thinner and paler, with short, thick hair bleached almost white, and bluish eye makeup, ragged jeans, and a brown sweater that's way too big. Just like any other teenage flotsam of the world, except that she's not like any other. She's Thelly. We study each other, her looking excited but also a little scared and very tired.

"You always knew I was crazy, right?" I say.

"Dad, are you all right? They didn't hurt you or anything?"

"I'm all right. This is all a mistake; I'll be out of here in a day or two. Did Blake tell you what happened?"

"Yeah. *She's* the one who's crazy, that bitch. And you were just trying to help her! How did you ever get hooked up with someone like that?"

I'm thrown off balance by this. Thelly is speaking from her heart, from her love for her Dad. But she and I both have to live in a world that doesn't think this way at all. How can I explain this to a teenager who's almost a stranger to me, and who desperately wants me to be a hero?

"Thelly, listen. The situation is more complicated than that. Of course I'm not crazy, but it won't help to say that Lisa is, either. What I did was very risky, and I knew that. So I have to take some responsibility for the fact that it didn't work out. Can I tell you what actually happened?"

"I know what happened. You tried to make her well. Mom and I read in the paper about the way you saved the forest, when you made that dog set fire to the bulldozers. That was awesome! When I read it, I decided I had to come and see you. Dad, I've been studying shamanism."

"It was a pig. My pig set fire to their construction site."

"Oh, God! That's so great! I'm the only person in my school whose Dad is a shaman."

"You know, a lot of people who heard about it didn't think it was so great. Which is the same problem we have right now, know what I mean?"

"Your average adult is a real asshole. What can they do about it? Shamanism isn't illegal as far as I know."

"Some of the things shamans do in other cultures actually are illegal here."

Her eyes get big. "Will you teach me, Dad? I could be, like, your assistant!"

"We can talk plenty when I get out of here. You look real tired now . . ."

"I wish I could be here when you do that . . . get out, I mean." Her voice drops to a whisper. "How're you gonna do it, Dad?"

"I won't need to use magic, if that's what you mean." I'm whispering too. "To keep me, they have to convince a judge that I'm nuts."

"Oh." Her face falls. "You know, I always knew you were like, way different from other dads. You used to ask me to tell you stories when I was so little, remember? You used to listen to me talk about the stuff I did with Big Teddy and Cub O'Hare and Red Dog."

"Your stuffed animals. That's right. I'd forgotten."

"The stories I told you were really true, did you know that?"

"Maybe I did."

"I made up fake stories too, but I knew those were fake, because you would ask me all these questions about them, and I only knew the answers to the true ones. I used to try to tell the other kids, but they didn't believe me, or they wouldn't listen. Mom, too. So I would try making up stories that weren't true, to see if I could get people to believe them, and sometimes they would. Then I realized that whether something is true or not isn't a matter of what people believe. But, Daddy, you always believed me, didn't you?"

"I did, yes."

"Why?"

"I don't know. Because I knew you so well, I guess."

"I can tell when people are telling the truth, too," she says. "I knew you were telling the truth about the magic and the dog — pig, I mean."

"That's wonderful, Thelly." We hug again for a long time. "How did you get here?"

"I drove."

"You better go back to Blake's and sleep. I'll call you tomorrow."

We sit in the sun that slants through a barred window and talk for a bit, until I can see she's having trouble keeping her eyes open, and I start to worry about her driving back to Del Mar. I take her hand and gently lead her toward the door. She looks relieved as she kisses me and waves good-bye.

She's the first person I've met since I left New Guinea who understands what's going on. But how could she really understand? Is there something in our genes that has prepared just the two of us to enter the spirit world, or is this just the kind of blind faith that a young girl has in her father? I could take her into my confidence about the real Lisa, who's so much like us, and about my struggle with Lisa's evil possessor spirit, but I know Thelly's not ready. She couldn't know the dangers of shamanism, of dealing with the spirits, as well as the deadly risks of being misunderstood in a human world that has turned against our power. There's so much I have to teach her first.

Teach her? I have no money, no job, no place to live, no friends. Even my car and toothbrush are in enemy hands. All I have, in fact, are Mekiimos and the spirits, and they haven't been so reliable lately. If I weren't in an insane asylum, I'd perform a singing to ask for guidance and help.

Except: How is it that, in my darkest hour, another person comes to join me in my battle? Although she doesn't yet understand the nature of my struggle, she has thrown her life down next to mine. Of course this, too, is part of the plan. But how? What are the spirits trying to say this time? Jeesus, I wish Sosi were here to interpret this! Is it possible that little Thelly has shamanic powers too? She said she had been studying. Of course it's possible. Like the Zogon, like Lisa the child, Thelly hasn't had time to lose her primitive powers. I'm not the teacher here, she is! I'm the student!

Thank you, Mekiimos! Under my breath I sing a song of thanks to all the spirits, and I'm almost asleep before I've finished it.

The psych resident is young, Black, pretty, and tired. I know what she's going to ask: Brief medical history and physical exam, drug history, family and social history, psychiatric history focusing on suicidal and homicidal thoughts, short depression inventory. She manages a professional politeness.

"Well, your amnesia seems to have cleared up. What has been your relationship with Ms. Lisa Berman?"

"We were lovers for a few weeks, about two years ago. We broke up over what she saw as my lack of work ethic."

"How did a former psychology professor come to lose his work ethic?"

"I felt unfulfilled in my job. Thought I'd take a couple of years to just follow my instincts, search for some new meaning."

"And?"

"I'm still searching, you might say."

"Ms. Berman says you believe you have magic powers, and that you were responsible for a fire that destroyed part of her property."

"That was a sort of experiment, a reckless one in hindsight. Lisa was in a legal battle with people who were trying to build on her property without her consent. I wanted to help out, and as a psychologist, I've long been intrigued with shamanism as a way of influencing human behavior. I've even been to New Guinea to observe practices of the Raapa Uu people. In your profession, of course you know plenty about the power of suggestion." I pause, but her face is impassive.

"Go on."

"I decided to see what would happen if I performed a Raapa Uu ritual designed to dissuade Lisa's antagonists from their plan. I thought it might give her a bit of a psychological advantage. The ritual involved letting a pig loose on the building site. By accident, the pig started a fire."

"Why is Lisa convinced that you literally believe in magic, and why is she afraid of you?"

"To reap the psychological gains of the experiment, of course I told everyone who would listen, including Lisa, that I was a shaman and that the fire was not an accident."

"You managed to deceive a woman with whom you had been intimate into thinking that you were mentally disturbed?"

I shrug. "She was . . . she is . . . very angry with me about our relationship and the way it ended."

"But she's the one who ended it."

"These things are complicated." For a brief second I wonder whether this intelligent woman would understand the irony of it all, the shallowness of Certified Sanity, the beauty and fullness of other ways of being. But I know better than to risk finding out.

She leans back in her chair and studies me wearily. "You're a shaman, you're James Littlefield from Chicago, you're an amnesiac — what have you said lately that's actually true? Anything in our conversation, for example?" She leans forward and sorts through the papers on her desk. "Of course I'm not going to recommend custody, but you might like to consider some professional help around getting more truth into your relationships. And if I were you, I'd stay as far away from Lisa Berman as I could reasonably get. You're lucky you're not in jail for arson; but still, I wish you continued luck, Mr. Caldo." She hands me a green sheet of paper. "Take this to the duty nurse and she'll start the discharge process."

As I start for the door, she adds, "And by the way, I've studied a little shamanism too. Honesty is one of its core principles, I believe."

I stop and turn. "Really? You've studied shamanism?" She's already up and making for the other door. "Tell me, Doctor, what's the shamanic concept of respect? Is it, 'Respect what you don't know as much as what you do know?' Or more like, 'Be pissed off when you have to set people free that don't fit your definition of normal?'"

She stops. "Maybe you can tell me, Mr. Caldo. Is it, 'Treat people as though the truth is whatever's good for Number One?' Or is it, 'Challenge people who are hurting themselves and others?'" I don't hear any sarcasm in her voice.

"And how would you know who I'm hurting?" I ask.

"If I don't know, I'm in trouble, and so are a lot of other people. It's exactly what I'm paid to know."

We stare at each other for a minute, and I think I see her face actually soften for a second. Then she turns and leaves the room. I feel a certain vertigo. Thank Mekiimos, I'm leaving this place.

I phone Thelly from the nursing desk (where I know the calls are monitored), and tell her I'll take the bus to Del Mar, but she wants to come pick me up. As soon as an ordeal is over, your adrenalin level drops to zero, your feet feel like lead, and you want a place to lie down for about a week. On the way back I don't feel like talking, but Thelly wants to know about shamanism.

"What turned you on to it, Dad? I mean, was it your research or what?"

"Randy's Trail," I say absently. "It started with Randy's Trail."

"Who's Randy? A healer you met?"

"Randy's Trail is a place, a place in Del Mar, a place I knew well when I was your age. I'll show it to you."

"Masterful! A place in Del Mar. Can we go there right now?"

"Not right now. Later I'll show you where it is, and you can go there by yourself."

"I've got to see it. And you have to come with me. Can't you pleeeze show me now?"

"No. See, Lisa's house is there. She owns Randy's Trail. If she sees me there, she'll have me arrested. That's where my pig started the fire and all. Anyway the place isn't going anywhere, Thelly. How about early in the morning, when nobody's around?"

"Oh, fucking Lisa! Now she's going to ruin *both* our lives. I never get up before noon." Thelly sulks for a minute, then lightens up. "See, I have TSS — Teenage Sleep Syndrome, you know? And I can't see anything when I'm asleep."

"We'll get up at five. Go to bed early. See, I have OFWS — Old Fart Wake-up Syndrome."

Somehow I feel uneasy about showing her the trail, but I'm too tired to think about why. Worst of all, I know I can't expect to keep working *or* living with Blake; even if he's willing to have a designated madman as a partner, his relationship with Lisa and maybe also with Sid would be ruined. When we get to the house, I see my camper truck is parked in his driveway. I find him in the workshop, fiddling with the electronics on a new piñata — a magnificent life-sized rendering of a grotesquely pregnant Barbie doll. He doesn't say anything right away, but he's uncharacteristically silent and edgy, and I know we have to have this talk. I ask Thelly to leave us alone for a bit.

"Blake, I know I can't stay here and work with you. I'd be fucking up your life, maybe ruining your business. And don't worry, I'll stay away from Lisa."

"I think she hates you, man."

"Yeah, I took that chance. I have to live with the result, but you don't. She doesn't come over here, does she?"

"Hardly ever."

"Have you told her that I've been in touch — or that I'm back from Mexico?"

"No." He plugs his contraption into a microprocessor, and when he switches it on, Barbie begins to pulsate with greenish light and make retching sounds. He turns her off. "I've got to train somebody to take over for you," he says at length, "but you're right, I guess, I gotta keep my life."

"I'll start looking for a job tomorrow. I'll be out of here by next week. Don't worry, you'll be okay. You have cred with a lot of people. There must be a hundred surfers around here who know fiberglass better than I do."

He puts his tools down and turns toward me. "You know, you talk like this friendly, sensible person, but I think it's some kind of weird act. What you did was fucking insane. Are you getting psychiatric help, or not?"

"I told you, I'm not crazy. Did they hold me at UC Med? No."

"If you're not crazy, then you're just dicking with everybody, aren't you?" We stare at each other. "Well, aren't you? I thought you needed some help, man, but it looks like you have the whole thing figured out. Fuck everything and everybody, and then bail on old Blake. Well, I don't want your smart-ass here if that's how it is."

"You want me to stay?"

"Stay?! Now that *is* nuts! Not one more day, man. Get your shit and leave, okay?"

I've never seen Blake really angry, and I don't want this to keep up. I start for the door to the apartment, and I see Thelly standing there, clutching to her chest a fluffy white cat, whose black markings and ridiculous black Hitler moustache I immediately remember from her email. It's Sneezeweed. She strides into the workshop and stands in front of Shart.

"You're goddamn lucky my Dad *isn't* crazy," she says, her voice trembling. "If he wasn't this . . . this super kind person, you'd be really big time goddamn sorry you talked to him like that." Sneezeweed puts his ears back and begins lashing his tail.

"Thelly . . ." I give her arm a tug, but she shakes me off.

"Dad's a shaman. You know what 'shaman' means? A shaman is somebody who can't be dissed, if you want to keep your ass in one piece!"

Blake looks at me. "That's beautiful," he says. "You've gone and done your voodoo-mojo on your kid, too. Beautiful. Get the fuck out, both of you." As he says this, the pregnant Barbie piñata begins to glow and retch, drawing a shriek from Sneezeweed, as he leaps from Thelly's arms and flies out the door, a furry streak of terror, with her after him.

"I never told her that," I say, but he turns his back to me and bends over his work with quick, irritable movements. I follow Thelly into the house and find her standing in the kitchenette, holding Sneezeweed, her face stained with tears. I try to comfort her, but again she shakes me off. "Let's get our stuff together," I say, and she nods.

CHAPTER TWENTY-FIVE

A NEW LIFE?

I still have some money left on my credit card, so Thelly and I cart our stuff over to the Seabreeze Motel. It gives me a bit of satisfaction that she brought almost as much stuff with her as I actually own — I've managed to simplify my life down to a single small pickup load, surfboard and all. Of course we have to hide Sneezeweed from the manager, and we have to leave Pig with Blake. I have a brief vision of him and Lisa enjoying a barbecue.

While Thelly goes to town for groceries, I log on to Craigslist and start looking for jobs. There are a few promising leads, but as I'm writing them down, I think: What will my résumé look like if I apply for a white-collar job?

> *Professor of psychology, ten years, Cal State U, quit two years ago to pursue blue-collar employment and self-discovery. In past two years, nine weeks' experience as day laborer, five months as fiberglass artisan. Damaged first boss's car, nearly ruined second boss's career and was fired. Trained in shamanism; patients' names confidential. References: My sister, my daughter, a New Guinea shaman, and a drifter with opals in his teeth (if you can find him).*

Whatever I end up doing, I'll have to work my way up from the bottom — establish relationships, do good work, outlive some of these Fs I've gotten on my life's report card. I go back to Craigslist and click on

"General Labor." This is more like it. Warehouse helper, yardwork, shuttle driver, building maintenance . . . I spread my email address around.

In the evening we walk down to the ocean cliff and sit looking out over the surf. I tell her the basic story of my odyssey; how I felt there was more to life than what I was doing, and decided to take the leap and follow my instincts. I tell her about seeing the Raapa Uu art, and going there to study magic, again about how Pig started the fire on Randy's Trail, and about working in Blake's workshop. She wants to know if I'm glad I did it, and I realize this is a really loaded question, coming from her.

"Yes, I'm glad I'm not still teaching at UC Riverside. I've learned about a whole other world I would never have known if I'd stayed there."

"The world of shamanism."

"That, but more than that. I always wondered about people who were intelligent, but refused to fit in: people like artists and nomadic adventurers who were considered oddballs and pretty much avoided by the average person. There were a few of them around when I was a kid on the beach, and I was deeply intrigued by them, but I never really got to know them. They scared me. Now I see that if you step outside the box — or you might call it the bubble of normality, of niceness — you see a lot of things that the average person doesn't see. Some of these things you would just as soon not see, but others are pretty exciting; you sense how narrow your education has been, how valuable so many things are that you were taught to ignore, or to disrespect."

"That is *so true*! *That's* why I want to leave school. It's such a waste of time. I can find out on my own, if you'll help me Dad, what's important to know. Starting *right now*!"

"I didn't say school is useless. I said there's more to the world than they tell you."

"I don't understand. You went to school all those years to be a psychologist, and then you quit when you were fifty-something. Don't you wish you'd had somebody to teach you this stuff when you were young?"

"You can't quit school, okay? You can stay and visit with me for a couple of weeks, but then you have to go back to Denver and get on with your education."

"I'm not going back. If you won't teach me shamanism, I'll find somebody who will. I'll support myself."

The way she says it, I can see there's no point in arguing with her right now. Trying to dictate might have disastrous results. I'll have to get her confidence first, ease her into a more receptive frame of mind. "Okay, let's think about alternatives. Maybe you could go to school around here for a bit, while I teach you a few things, if your mom will let you."

"She'll never let me, but I don't care. I'm not going back to Denver. I can take care of myself. You could teach me the school stuff too."

"Thelly, I have to work. Listen: Here's your first lesson in shamanism."

"Why do I have a feeling I'm not going to like this?"

"Because you're smart, and you know what I'm going to tell you: Shamanism takes a lot of self-discipline — more than ordinary school, for sure. A lot of it seems pointless at first. You have to show me that you have that kind of discipline, that you can endure the hard stuff to get to the good stuff. Know what I mean?"

"I guess so." She gets up and ambles along the cliff, kicking the small pebbles into the darkening void below. So this is the hand that the spirits have dealt me now: Turn an impulsive, ignorant child into a sage, or lose the love of the one person who believes in you.

The alarm goes off at four thirty. By five, Thelly and I are walking up Randy's Trail from the railroad tracks in the semi-dark. The fog drips from the trees as usual; the wet earth gives off a slightly fermented herbal smell, like mulled wine. I know the way well enough that we don't need light as we climb through the rusted chain-link fence, follow a pale sandy path into the dense eucalyptus trees, pick our way among the broom and coyote brush, shivering a little from the cold. At this hour there's no sound but the distant surf, and we both feel the silence as a message, something like the quiet of an empty church that you don't care to break with your voice. Suddenly a covey of quail flushes from the path in front of us. Thelly gasps and grabs my arm and then, embarrassed, laughs a bit.

Soon we find ourselves standing at the edge of the construction clearing. The sky has begun to lighten. The tools and materials and debris are gone, leaving only the charred foundation, now invaded by new brush growth. We keep silent, and she smiles and nods when I show her with my hands where the house frame was, then how the flames and smoke consumed it. The old path passes up to our left, where I show her the dark outline of Lisa's house among the trees, and she makes a snarling face. Then I take her back through the trees, looking for the place where I built my altar that night, and sure enough I find it — a scattered ring of stones, a circle of black ashes. We stand there and look up, into the high branches, as if to meet the eyes of the spirits whose presence we can feel as keenly as we feel each other in the dim light. When finally our eyes meet, I see a wild excitement in her face, and I'm thrilled by it.

The sky has gotten light when we finally leave the trail and go down to the beach. "Will you start teaching me magic now, Dad? I mean, today?"

"Shamanism isn't a game, sweetheart. It took me nine months of constant work to learn the basics, nine months of living alone and doing nothing else. Since you have to go to school, it'll take you much longer. Tell me why you want to learn it. Do you have a goal, a project?"

"You saved that awesome wild place, didn't you? D'you know how incredible that is? I've read that shamans can, like, cure people and stuff. Can you do that, too?"

"I didn't actually save Randy's Trail. The court gave the builder a permit to start over, and if I tried again I certainly would end up in jail." We sit on a dew-damp log while she absorbs this. "Now, about what I can or can't do: I learned three basic kinds of magic from the Raapa Uu — war, hunting, and cleansing. War magic is very complicated; I used it trying to protect Randy's Trail. In hunting you use the ancestors and spirits to speak to animals. Cleansing is a kind of healing, but it only works to remove evil spirits. It's the hardest and the most dangerous."

"War, hunting, and cleansing. War, hunting, and cleansing," she chants with her eyes closed, then looks at me. "Yeah. With cleansing, you're dealing with evil spirits. Can you tell when somebody's, you know, possessed?"

"Sosi — my teacher — told me the signs, but to tell you the truth, I never tried it on anyone but Lisa. I've never even thought about trying to treat other people. Is that what you want to learn?"

"I wanna learn everything. All of it. Tell me about war magic. Can you, like, kill people?"

I turn to face her. "Thelly, why would I want to kill somebody? You're treating this as if it were a video game or something. I'm not going to teach you anything if you're not going to take it seriously. It's an ancient and powerful thing, an adult thing. It really is. I had to risk my own life to learn it."

Her face turns somber. "Of course, Dad. I'm sorry. I'll do just what you say. But you will teach me, won't you?"

"We'll see."

Thelly is the one good thing in my life right now. It's nearly impossible for a middle-aged man without references to get any kind of job. The fast-food joints and chain stores want kids; the cleaning services and corner cafés want Latinos; everybody else wants a work history and references. After a week on the pavement I'm physically exhausted and realize I'm starting to get that haunted look that scares people into locking their doors, but finally I get a job as a stock boy in a Dollar store. It doesn't pay enough to keep us at the Seabreeze Motel. The best I can do is a cramped upstairs room in an old dump of a house next to the train tracks in Solano Beach. It has a phonebooth-sized bathroom, a hot plate, a tabletop fridge, and a sofa bed with bad springs. I sleep on the floor on the futon I had in the back of my camper. Thelly finds some old bed sheets at Goodwill and makes curtains by stapling them over the windows. We have to clean the whole house and yard on weekends to get the utilities paid for. We're eating a lot of instant ramen and canned tuna.

Employees don't last long at the Dollar store. I figure if I do extra work and help them solve problems, it won't be long before a manager position is vacant, and I may be in line for it.

When we're not fighting for survival, it seems like the two of us are fighting family on the phone — first Ursula and then Ysabel — about Thelly staying here. I tell them that I'm managing a store and renting a two-bedroom apartment; Thelly tells them she'll run away before she goes back to Denver. She hates school, but she seems to be meeting the minimum and staying out of trouble.

True to her word, she's a serious and energetic student of magic. We start with war songs, the same way Sosi taught me. I have her practice them when she's through with her homework, and on weekend nights when there's no one on the beach, we go down to a lonely spot below the cliffs where we can make altars and burn herbs. I find I can get into trance if I combine local medicinal plants like sage and yerba santa with a little cannabis, as of course I can't find herbs to replace the ones Sosi gave me. The sound of the waves substitutes for the jungle sounds of the Sepik, pulling me out of myself so that I fly freely where I'm called by the spirits. I ask them to help Thelly with her schoolwork and to make her a strong shaman. She has more patience than I did when I was learning, but she tends to slip into a kind of hypnotic state that I'm afraid interferes with her quest for a true shamanic trance.

After a couple of months at the Dollar store I'm starting to have problems with itchy eyes and sneezing. I try to ignore it, but it gets worse, and I realize I'm allergic to something, something in the air at the store. There's often a chemical smell in there. Maybe working with fiberglass sensitized me. I'm starting to get tired halfway through the day, too. Of course I don't have health insurance, and I can't afford to go to the doctor.

"Can't we cure you with, you know, herbs and songs, Dad?"

"I don't think this is a spiritual illness, Thelly."

"You look so miserable, and you're getting skinny. We've gotta do something."

"Don't worry, sweetpea. I'll look for another job."

On Monday I phone in sick and spend the next few days on the streets looking for work, without luck. When I get back to the store, the manager hands me a check for a week's pay and a separation notice.

"Those fuckers! Let's sic Mekiimos on them!"

"That wouldn't help us any, would it? What we need is *game*. It's time for some serious hunting magic, Thelly."

I print out a list of low-skill jobs from Craigslist, and throw in a couple of white-collar ones for good measure. That night we go to the Safeway and buy a ham, which we take down to the beach. We make a large fire, and using the ham I show Thelly how to kill a pig.

"Can we eat it later?"

"Whatever doesn't get burnt up. Maybe I should have bought a bigger one."

I sing to Mekiimos and to the spirits, over and over, a new song and a new slab of ham for each job on my list. I'm vaguely aware of Thelly sitting next to me, joining in the songs, but when I've sung the last song and come down from my trance, I see that the fire has burned to embers and she's sound asleep. I cover her with my sweater, lie down on the sand, and drift off.

I wake up shivering in the damp dawn and see that Thelly is still asleep, sand sticking to her spiky hair, which is growing back in its natural chestnut color. Usually I sleep quietly without visions after I've been with the spirits, but now I remember this dream:

> *I'm walking in a city full of ancient buildings; I don't recognize anything specific, but I have a feeling that I've been here before. I hear someone singing, not the chanting song of a spirit ritual, but a plaintive ballad in a foreign language, possibly Portuguese, a language hauntingly familiar but opaque to me. As I walk, I have an image in my mind of an interior space, where a single lamp hangs by a long chain from a high ceiling. I am to meet someone there. I don't know the person, or what we are supposed to discuss; but somehow I will recognize him when I see him. I find what I think is the building, but when I go in, I see men in coveralls busily constructing a gaudy new interior of painted plaster and cloth, and I realize the place of my vision has already been altered beyond recognition. I can't find the person I'm supposed to meet. Instead, a group of tough-looking teenage boys appear, and I watch them through an interior window as they swagger around in a hallway, shouting and gesturing about nothing but their own energetic unhappiness. They want others to be afraid, but instead I find them amusing, even charming. I think, "This explains everything." Then a tall figure wearing a long black gown like a priest's cassock and a medieval-looking hat appears. He discharges something like a foam fire extinguisher at the boys, which turns them*

*into battered papier-mâché figurines, and suddenly I'm
outside in the city again, only it has gotten dark and cold,
and I'm lost.*

A week passes, then two. I sell my truck on the internet for $950, and a few days later I take the bus down to the state office building in San Diego and apply for unemployment and Medicaid. Every day I drop Thelly off at school in the morning, then come home and make calls and send out emails for jobs. But as the days go by, larger and larger chunks of time just seem to disappear unaccounted for. I spend hours going back over in my mind what happened in Mexico, and before that, to the whole history of my relationship with Lisa.

Even teaching the spirit songs to Thelly begins to wear on me, and she seems less interested too; I find that days go by without doing it. Now she spends a couple of hours at the school library every afternoon doing her homework, then takes the after-sports bus home. She says it's because the computers there are better than mine, but I think it's more because of the surroundings. I think she also spends a good deal of time online just emailing or chatting, or whatever they do. She tells me from time to time what's going on with her friends back in Denver. I tell myself I'm lucky she doesn't have boyfriends here. She seems amazingly well adjusted, actually, and for that I thank Mekiimos and the spirits.

Every evening she lights a candle and offers herbs and a little song for my health. I'm starting to feel a lot better, too. The itchy eyes, the headaches, have disappeared, and while Thelly's in school, I'm going for a jog on the beach or even surfing now and then.

One morning I open my email and find this message:

> *Dear Mr. Caldo, We at Gold Cross Weekly received your
> application for a job as a proofreader. We would like to
> interview you. Can you please come to our office at 1102
> ½ Fourth Street, Oceanside, at your earliest convenience?
> You may reply by phone to Mr. Red Kunslaver, 556-0349,
> ext. 22.*

I remember. I sit down at the computer and search for the *Gold Cross Weekly*. A Christian fundamentalist newsletter with offices in Oceanside (about an hour away by bus), their website features the face of the Reverend Robert "Blaze" Long, his glowing eyes cast up toward the image of a golden cross, from which lightning bolts continuously flash, while a rock version of Bach's *Saint Matthew Passion* blares in the background. I look up the local barbershop online. He can take me in fifteen minutes. I turn on the shower, call the *Gold Cross Weekly* back, and tell the receptionist I'll be there in an hour and a half. The spirits are at it again! On the way to the interview I try to imagine what a good (but nonchurchgoing) Christian sounds like. I settle for respectful, conservative, and humorless.

I take the bus to Oceanside and find the tiny office in back of the Nine Bells Mortuary. A plump lady named Emma, with one of those aging but ageless soft faces and a bluish perm, ushers me into the tiny office of Red Kunslaver, himself a perfectly round ball of a man with no hair of any color except a single eyebrow that crosses his forehead from temple to temple like a gigantic black hedge. Hardly glancing at me over his black-rimmed glasses, he motions me to sit down next to his desk, then brings up a word document on his computer, spins the screen around to face me, and hands me his keyboard. I start proofing the document — an article by one Firsty LaSkuhl about a Christian dog training center in Tennessee called The Good Shep.

> Since it is very definitely true that all dogs go to heaven, it looks to us like the folks at *The Good Shep* are here to make sure that you'll be happy to see Towser when you also get there yourself . . .

Ms. LaSkuhl has made few typo or spelling errors, it turns out, but her sentence structure is awkward and hard to follow. "Would you like me to correct the syntax?"

Forty minutes later I'm filling out my employment form, having been asked only one question by Mr. Kunslaver, "Do you own an up-to-date computer?," and one by Emma, "Would you like a jelly donut?" Yes to both questions. I'm on, starting tomorrow, for twenty hours a week (more or less), at two cents a word. I figure I proof and edit seven hundred words an hour minimum, even if the stuff is bad. A sit-down job. No caustic chemicals. Work from home most days. As soon as I get home, I walk down to the beach, where I make a small fire and offer a song to Mekiimos and the spirits, sacrificing half the giant bacon cheeseburger I bought in Oceanside. I even ask them to watch over Mr. Kunslaver and Emma, and to overlook their sins against the spirit world.

CHAPTER TWENTY-SIX

THELLY'S PERIL

I can't wait to tell Thelly, so I walk over to her school. Classes are over, but I figure she'll be in the library as usual, so I find my way there. As I walk in, the room has that long-forgotten high school library smell of floor wax and old paper. I see three or four kids sitting at computers, but not Thelly. A chunky blonde chewing a pencil looks up and takes her pencil out of her mouth. She looks friendly.

"Excuse me, do you know Thelly . . . uh . . . Thelma? Thelma Caldo?"

"Yeah, are you her dad?"

"Yeah. Is she here?"

"She was a second ago. But, hey, you're, like, the witch doctor, right?"

"Huh?"

"Right? I mean, you're the Personal Shaman guy, right? The guy on Shaman Central?"

"Shaman Central?"

"Yeah! Everybody's got it. Look here." She taps a few keys, and up on her screen comes this website. It's quite pretty, actually — a deep orange background, with the pale green words PERSONAL SHAMAN in letters that mimic East Indian script, bracketed with images of eagles, animal skulls, and African masks, and under that in smaller script, SHAMAN CENTRAL. The menu bar is a native drum, bearing the selections:

WHAT ARE WE?

HEALTH!

LOVE!

JUSTICE!

MEET THE SHAMANS!

CONTACT US

It's amusing, but I'm not sure I like this. Thelly promised me she wouldn't make a game out of it. I make a note of the web address.

"Oh, yeah," I say. "Shaman Central. Well, if you see Thelma, tell her I'm looking for her, okay?"

I sit down at one of the computers and log on to the website. I click on WHAT ARE WE?

We are shamans Spirit Rider and Dark Friend. We are here to bring the powerful magic of the New Guinea tribesmen to you who are in need. In the jungle, we learned the secrets of the spirit world — how to call the Unseen Powers, and how to speak to Them so that They will be our friends — and your friends too. It took us two years to learn, but we did it so that we could help people like you; good people who need help to get health, love, and justice in your life.

How do we do it? Our methods are secrets that have been handed down from generation to generation for hundreds of years — secrets we were only allowed to learn because we went to New Guinea and made friends with the Raapa Uu people, the most powerful magicians in the world. Others have tried it, but only we succeeded. Each of our magic services takes at least a whole day; some of them take many days. And if our magic doesn't work, you don't have to pay us anything — we believe that is the way of a true shaman.

How are we different? Today there are many shamans on the internet who promise similar results. Some of them might be helpful, and some probably are not. How can you tell the

*difference? (1) Ask them where they learned how to do it, (2)
Ask them how long they studied, (3) Ask them how long it
takes them to perform a service.*

If you want to learn more, contact us!

What does she do if people contact her, I wonder. I click on HEALTH!

*It is well known that certain illnesses can be caused by "bad
luck," or by the bad intentions of other people. If you have one
of these illnesses, spirits are probably involved. Tell us your
story, and we will be able to tell if this is your case or not . . .*

"Oh, hi, Dad, what're you doin' here?" Then she looks at the computer
screen, and irritation clouds her voice. "Oh. I was gonna show it to you."

"Honey, why didn't you discuss this with me?"

"Shh! Dad! People can hear you."

I lower my voice. "Well?"

She meets my eyes, her jaw set. "I said I was going to. I wanted to, like,
get it looking really awesome first."

"Let me guess. You're Spirit Rider, and I'm Dark Friend, right?"

"The other way around."

"You promised me you wouldn't treat this as a game."

"I'm not! Why shouldn't we really help people?"

"Because 'we' — or at least one of us — doesn't know enough about
it, for one thing. Are you actually collecting clients here?"

"A few people have emailed me." She looks around the room. "Dad,
can we discuss this at home?"

It turns out the site has attracted dozens of emails, some from kids she
knows, some from total strangers. This is beginning to worry me, but I've
got to be calm, try to preserve the sense of partnership. Maybe this isn't so
bad after all, if she can just hold off until she's learned more.

As she shows me the emails, she skips around, selecting here and there
from her saved message box. The first few look pretty innocuous: Skyla

(who is almost illiterate, I see) wants the love of Roland. Thelly writes back, asking for details and photos of them both. Rajif is afraid he's been cursed by his former girlfriend Boona, because now he can't get an erection. She asks him, too, for the details of his plight, plus a description and photo of her. Theresa has a disfigured ear from birth, certainly because a cousin put the evil eye on her. Thelly writes her that we're sorry, but our Raapa Uu teachers don't have knowledge of the evil eye.

"Have you actually done spirit songs for any of these?" I ask.

"Yeah, a couple of people sent me their info, and I did it. I'm waiting to hear from them, you know, what happened."

"Can I pick one?" I ask.

"No! You'll hate some of them."

"Why? Why will I?"

"Oh, fuck. Go ahead."

I pick one she had skipped:

Dear Spirit Rider and Dark Friend,

I never would have looked up anything to do with Shamanism, but I was looking for something else on the web, and I got your site. At first I thought it was sort of ridiculous, the comic-hero names and all. But I did think about it, because, let's face it, I could really use some magic right now. Then you came up again in a totally other search, and I showed it to my boyfriend. He's a hard-nosed engineer, but he went, "Twice? By accident? Wow, either these guys know some secrets about cyber tech, or there actually is more to this than we thought — something we don't know about out there.

Either way, here I am giving you a try. Nothing else I can think of has worked, and I'm going nuts. Here it is: I collect and sell antiques, more as a hobby than a business, but at least it pays for itself. Long story short, for once I got a tremendous deal on some Mayan artifacts, and gave them to this very rich old guy, who promised me a six figure sum, but then he up and died before he paid me. Maybe they had a curse on them. His wife is this crafty old woman who doesn't like me, and refuses either to pay me or give the stuff back. I think she plans to sell it herself. Her daughter sounds sympathetic, but says she can't do anything. If I try to sue I could be screwed even worse, because I don't have receipts, either from the guy who sold it to me, or the guy I sold it to.

You say you can help people get justice. If you can get my goods out of this old woman's hands before she sells them, I'll give you ten percent of the value. I look forward to hearing from you.

Benjason LaMonte

Below this is Thelly's reply:

Dear Mr. LaMonte,

You are indeed wise to contact us. Our teachers, as you know, are the world's greatest shamans, the Raapa Uu of the Upper Sepik River, New Guinea. Over centuries, they have developed a mighty sense of justice, and powerful ways of making it happen through conversation with ancestors and spirits. They gave Spirit Rider and I one of the strongest ancestors in the Raapa Uu pantheon (his name is a secret). What you need is a War Song, done correctly by us. Our spirits will weaken your enemy, so that she becomes scared and confused, and you will easily win. They will also protect you against any counter magic she might try to use against you, and will make her daughter into your ally.

Send us everything you can find out about this woman — what she does all the time, who she knows, where she goes, what she likes and doesn't like. Send us a picture of her if possible, and one of yourself. If you can get some little object she has handled a lot also, that would be excellent. We also

need to know where you live, so the spirits can protect you.
Once we have this information, we can begin the war songs.

Go in Power,

Dark Friend

There's more. In a message dated a week later, LaMonte describes the life of his adversary, Mrs. Joan Braithwyte, in considerable detail. No picture is attached, but he asks for an address to send a bottle of her nasal spray and a couple of soiled Q-tips, which he retrieved from her trash.

"Have you made a singing for this?" I ask.

"Well, yeah."

"What did you ask the spirits for?"

"Oh, Dad, it was brilliant! I figured if she gets really confused, then her daughter will take over, right? So I'm having the spirits really mix up her mind, and at the same time make the daughter fall in love with Mr. LaMonte! So what if he's gay? That just makes it more interesting."

"Thelly, please don't pursue this anymore. It's too dangerous. Remember what happened when I made war magic against Lisa's enemies?"

"Well, yeah! It totally worked!"

"You don't understand. Even a very seasoned shaman doesn't totally control these things. What you're doing is really dangerous."

She gets up and stands looking out the window at the train tracks. "How am I supposed to become a shaman if I don't practice?"

"You're not far enough along to do it alone. You haven't mastered the trance. Have you done singings for anybody else?"

"A couple." She sees the expression on my face. "Really, just a couple. Four. Minor things, like love charms. You told me that I'll know when I'm ready to do it. Well, I know I'm ready. Dad, I can see the spirits, I can talk with them. I know the songs perfectly."

"Please, Thelly."

"Well, shit! *You* do it then!"

"This is all wrong. A shaman doesn't work with people he's never even seen, whose lives he doesn't know personally."

"Dad, there are hundreds — okay dozens — of shaman sites on the internet. You mean they all go around and hang out with the people they treat?"

"I don't think most of them know much about shamanism."

"Well, Dad, I do! You taught me yourself, and now you want to *un*-teach me? What are you worried about?"

"The spirits can turn on you. They're very powerful."

"You told me yourself that's the chance you have to take if you want to be a shaman. So, like, *you* can make that decision but I *can't?*"

"I'm your teacher. I'm your father."

"Well, you should have thought about this a long time ago."

"Maybe so." I figure it's time to put this conversation to rest.

I thought the trouble with Lisa was the hardest test the spirits could put me through, but now it seems here's another one, maybe even harder. I'm beginning to see it clearly. The Raapa Uu teach the songs to their young boys, but the result is completely different than teaching Thelly. In the closely contained world where they live, everyone's life is open to everyone. The boys can only do as they're told or suffer heavy consequences. Magic is something understood as part of life, something feared but at the same time expected as normal. Introducing Thelly and the spirits to one another is like introducing gasoline and matches; they couldn't resist each other if they wanted to, and they certainly don't want to. It's time for me to sing for guidance.

As darkness falls, the fog rolls in. Putting my herb packet and candles in my backpack, I leave Thelly sitting at the computer and walk down to the beach. I make an altar and sing, asking Mekiimos and the spirits to guide me. It seems like hours before I feel them close by and know they can hear me. Clarify Thelly's mind, I ask. Let her see the spirit world clearly; teach her the true way of knowledge; let her wake up from this adolescent dream, this playacting. Play with me any way you like, but not at the expense of Thelly; let her be free your mischief.

The song is over, and gradually the presence of the spirits fades. My little fire has gone out. I feel empty, without thoughts or emotions. Then, as I collect my things to go, this clear sentence forms itself in my mind: *The spirits will not help her. You must cure her yourself.* As I climb the cliff and pick my way slowly through the fog, I turn this over and over in my thoughts. Of course. It is the spirits who have tamed her, not the other way around. In fact, she is possessed, but by whom, by what? I've got to cleanse her, but first I've got to know the exact nature of her possession. Tomorrow I'll sing to Mekiimos for the answer.

It's past midnight when I get back, and she's asleep. She's left the window open, and it's cold in the room. As I pull it closed, I notice an odd smell — faint, but a bit acrid, like something burnt. I sniff again. Weed? No, not herbal, more like cloth. It's stronger by the kitchen trash, from which I pull a wad of newspaper. Unfolding it carefully, I see it contains a handful of burnt sea shells with little holes in them that indicate they had been strung together on something. There are a few burnt strands of metallic filament as well. A necklace, then. Yes, I remember now, and my heart stops. A necklace of iridescent shells, strung together with the remains of red and gold cords.

Lisa's necklace.

Thelly has stolen this somehow, and she's making war magic against Lisa. Of course. She said she hated her. Holy shit. This has been the driving force of her enthusiasm. I want to throw these shells back in the trash, but I stop myself, and instead I set them on top of the TV. I sit down on the bed and look at her sleeping child's face. I'm sorry, Thelly. My God, I'm sorry.

CHAPTER TWENTY-SEVEN

A SHAMAN'S CURE?

I'm due at the *Gold Cross Weekly* for orientation by nine in the morning, but of course I can't sleep. This little room can't contain the turmoil I feel, and I go out to roam the empty streets. As I walk, my thoughts come back again and again to the same point: Thelly is possessed in a way that threatens to destroy her. It's my shamanic spirit world itself, not some alien power, that possesses her. I have no idea what to do; this is completely beyond my understanding. I can plead with my familiars to leave her alone, to withdraw their power from her, but this might just make matters worse. Determined as she is to have this power, Thelly will look elsewhere for it, very possibly in more dangerous places. Mekiimos and his spirit allies are the ones who must carry out the cleansing, driving the alien force away; they can't exorcise themselves.

They can't exorcise themselves.

Of course. A cleansing is required, of a spirit alien to my guardians, who is possessing Thelly.

Am I that spirit? Why was she drawn to me, to my shamanic power? Didn't I know she would learn about the war magic I made on Randy's Trail? Didn't I know she would be drawn to it? It wasn't the spirits themselves who called her, it was me. I am her possessor spirit.

Can I exorcise *myself*?

Maybe not, but I have to try; it's the only hope I have.

Ordinarily, the shaman guides the victim through the ritual, but here we have a situation where the shaman is the possessing spirit, and the apprentice is the victim. The victim must guide herself, with the help of the guardian spirits. But what about me, the possessor? What role do I play? What *happens* to me in the process of being exorcised? I have no picture, no idea of that process, or its result.

As I turn this over and over in my mind, bit by bit the horrible shape of it begins to emerge.

I must lose Thelly, I must send her back to the world that she came from.

As an incentive to the guardian spirits, I must offer myself, my spirit, for their pleasure.

The misty air is beginning to pale with the onset of dawn. By the time I get back to the room I have the outlines of the plan. I'll spend the next couple of weeks teaching Thelly the mechanics of the cleansing ritual and then take her through it under *wegura,* as my teacher Sosi did to train me. Of course I can't tell her that I am the one who's being exorcised, with the goal of separating her altogether from the spirit world. We'll perform the ritual on Randy's Trail at nightfall; in the morning, she'll come back here to the room, where everything will be arranged for her three days of isolation. Afterward, she'll have to be reintegrated, but not back into the world she's known here. I'll have to have her mother come from Denver and take her back for a reintegration with her friends and family there. As I realize this, my eyes fill with tears, but this isn't the time for sentimentality.

I wake Thelly and tell her to get dressed. We sit down to cereal and fruit, and I say, "I've decided it's time for you to learn the hardest part of shamanism, to learn cleansing. I've got to start my new job today, but we'll start your lessons tonight. In the meantime, will you promise not to do any more . . . ahh . . . consultations?"

She looks excited. "How long will it take?"

"Promise me, Thelly. No more consultations, and no war magic."

"Oh, okay; but when will we be ready?"

"That's partly up to you. A couple of weeks, I think. Once you've learned the songs, we'll need to take you through a cleansing yourself, as my teacher Sosi did with me. You'll go through the whole process exactly in the role of a possession victim, so that you can understand it from the patient's point of view."

"It sounds scary. What's it like, Dad?"

"It's not something you learn by explanation; you learn it by experience. You'll see."

At the *Gold Cross Weekly*, as Emma and Mr. Kunslaver show me the office routine and the editing policy, I find my mind more focused and alert than usual despite my sleepless night. Having a purpose again, a mission, brings me back to a level of energy I haven't felt since the disaster with Lisa. As I'm leaving for the day, Mr. Kunslaver actually pats me on the shoulder. "You take very well to the Lord's work, Ashton."

Emma chimes in, "Not everyone does, you know. You're blessed."

My energy seems to radiate to Thelly, too; there's a new bond and a new ease between us. Within ten days, she has mastered the cleansing songs, and I believe she has reached a deeper rapport with Mekiimos and the spirits in her trances. She seems to be growing to a new level of maturity, and I begin to wonder about my plan. Is my decision a hasty one, made in a moment of panic? Is it possible that this new lesson will bring her into a more fruitful relationship with the spirits — that she'll be able to make them her real allies? It's possible, but if so, all the more reason that she must do it without me, I realize. And what about the opposite? Will freeing her only bring her down, leave her confused and unhappy? That too is possible; I'll have to do what I can to prevent it.

It's Tuesday, the first of May, a quiet sunny day. School will be over soon. I'm working from home, sending proofed text to Mr. Kunslaver via email. There isn't much to do, and I'm finished by noon. This is the day.

"Hello, Ursula, this is Ashton. How are you?"

"Ashton! My God, you haven't called me in weeks. Where are you?"

"Never mind. Listen, we're fine, Thelly's fine. She's doing well, school and everything. Here's the thing. I'd like to have a real talk with you about her future, but not on the phone. Can you fly out here a week from Friday? We'll meet you at the airport."

"Something *is* wrong. What is it?"

"Nothing is wrong. I know you want her back in Denver with you, and I've made the decision that she should go. We can talk this all through when you get here."

"You're up to something, Ashton. I don't like it."

"Can you come, or not?"

She hesitates. "I guess I don't have a choice, do I?"

"There's another thing. I want her to have a big welcome party as soon as she gets home. A big happy festival. I'll pay for it. Can you call her friends and arrange a party for her on that Sunday — May twelfth?"

"You want *me* to arrange it?"

"Yes, I want it to be a surprise. It's terribly important."

"Well, Jesus, if it's that big a deal . . ."

"Thanks, Ursula. Email me your flight information, and I'll meet you at the San Diego airport."

"I need your phone number, too."

"I don't have a phone. Send me an email, okay? If there are any hitches, call Ysabel."

"Is that it?"

"Thanks a million, Ursula. Really. I appreciate it. We'll talk when you get here. Bye."

As soon as I hang up, I dial Ysabel at work.

"Hi, Ysabel, it's Ashton. How are you?"

"Hi, Morse. I'm fine, but tell me, why do I start to worry when I hear your voice?"

"I don't blame you. How's everything? Work going okay?"

"Is work ever *okay*? Either it's great or it totally sucks. Today it's too early to tell which. Do you have a job? How's Thelly?"

"Got a decent job. Thelly's well. There's nothing to worry about, actually. I was calling, of course, to ask you a wee favor. I'm going up in the mountains for a couple of days next week, and I'm not sure I'll have good communications up there. I've told Thelly to call you to check in, on Wednesday morning, but you know how teenagers are. If she doesn't, I wonder if you'd mind calling while I'm gone, just to make sure she's okay, you know? You have her phone number."

"And if she *isn't* okay?"

"There's no reason she won't be, for Chrissake. I'm just being responsible. Wednesday morning, all right? If she doesn't answer, leave a message for her to call you, okay?"

"Being a parent is changing you, Ashton. Maybe I was wrong about what a rotten idea it was for you two to stick together."

"Thanks, sistah, your confidence means so much to me. I'll call you when I get back from the bush."

The cleansing, then, will be Monday night, the seventh, a good date.

CHAPTER TWENTY-EIGHT

CRISIS

I t's Tuesday evening; the sun is setting. We'll leave for Randy's Trail in an hour. Thelly is showering. I sit down at the computer and write:

Dearest Thelly,

If you get this message, it's because for some reason I'm not able to say this to you in person.

By now, you've been through your cleansing; you've experienced what it is like for the patient who is cleansed of an alien spirit. There is something I wasn't able to tell you about this particular cleansing, for reasons you'll understand.

This is it: (1) We were not just practicing, we actually cleansed a spirit from you. (2) The spirit was me.

I've now had plenty of experience with Mekiimos and the spirit allies, and I realized that it was me who led you into a very dangerous relationship with them. I knew you would hear about my shaman powers. I knew you would be attracted by them. What I didn't understand was that the spirits are attracted to you, too, but not as guardians. They see you as a kind of playmate; someone who can help them work their will in the human world. My command over them is far from total, but it's greater than yours; and by exorcising my spirit from yours, I believe — I hope — I have freed you from them as well. I knew you would not, or could not, do it yourself, and I felt this was the only way.

I want you to keep pursuing your heroic dream of power and wisdom. But I know that you need time to discover just what that dream really is for you, so that you are not too influenced by the dreams of others whom you love. There may come a time when you can learn shamanism properly, or you might find that your true dream lies somewhere else. But you and I must be apart, at least for a while, until the danger of my spirits' influence is over. If I'm able to, I'm going to work very hard for that.

I write this because I really don't know what will happen to me as a result of exorcising myself. As far as I know, it's never been done. I have called your mother and asked her to come here. She arrives in San Diego at 3:20 on Friday afternoon, March 29, Far West Airlines Flight 913. She'll take you back to Denver. I also called Aunt Ysabel and asked her to phone you tomorrow morning (Wednesday), just to make sure you're okay. Her phone number is (510) 922-4383.

I love you with all my heart — more than I ever loved anyone. We'll always be together in some sense, but I know that for now we have to say good-bye in the physical sense, and this makes me terribly, terribly sad. You have a great life in front of you.

Love always,

Dad

I print it out, open a new file, and write,

Dear Lisa,

These are my last words to you, in case such a thing is in order. I don't want to justify, explain, accuse, or apologize, but only to leave you with words that might be useful. Whatever has become of me, I feel you transformed my life, much for the better. You did so by showing me something unique and extremely valuable: the enduring light of a dream saved and nurtured heroically against a world of dream-grinders, hope-crushers, life-sappers. The glimpse you gave me into your spirit gave me the courage to look for my own vital center, gave me this insight: Once the primitive truths of the self, so alive in the dreams of childhood, have finally been bound and starved, life is nothing, a worn-out player piano.

There are no maps or star charts of the path back to the dream, a path armed and rigged with dangers. Did I make it to my goal? I no longer know how to distinguish between the journey and the goal itself. The last couple of years I've been more fully alive than any time since I was a child full of dreams.

You'll draw the conclusions you want from this. I smile when I imagine that you won't completely ignore it.

Admiration and gratitude,

Ashton

I print the two messages out, put each in a separate envelope. On the front of each I write their names and the word *confidential*. I put them in my backpack along with my ritual materials.

Everything is ready. Thelly and I have rehearsed what we will do. I'll give her a very light dose of *wegura*, and she'll be fully alert by sunrise. We'll go back to the apartment, and she'll stay there in isolation until I come for her; then I'll instruct her in the next steps.

In the gathering darkness, we drive to the foot of Randy's Trail and hike up to the remains of my altar in the eucalyptus grove. We make a new altar, light the fire, begin the songs. She drinks the *wegura* and slips into the drug state. I set my backpack next to me and lay the envelope with her name on it on top. I continue to sing, waiting to feel the presence of Mekiimos and the spirits, waiting for the clarity and certainty of my songs' power . . .

> *Mekiimos, rest in the company of the spirits of thunder and yams.*
> *Mekiimos, rest in the company of the small spirits.*
> *Mekiimos, rest in the company of the human souls.*
> *Mekiimos, eat and enjoy the blood of my pig.*
> *Mekiimos, eat and enjoy the smoke of my fire.*
> *Mekiimos, eat and enjoy my song.*
>
> *Mekiimos, speak to the spirits of thunder and yams.*
> *Mekiimos, speak to the small spirits.*
> *Mekiimos, speak to the souls of the Big Men.*
> *Mekiimos, tell them to eat and enjoy the blood of my pig.*
> *Mekiimos, tell them to eat and enjoy the smoke of my fire.*
> *Mekiimos, tell them to eat and enjoy my song.*
>
> *Mekiimos, tell them to eat and enjoy the blood of Thelly's pig.*
> *Mekiimos, tell them to eat and enjoy the smoke of Thelly's fire.*
> *Mekiimos, tell them to eat and enjoy Thelly's song.*
>
> *Spirits of thunder and yams, don't forget you have enjoyed*
>   *Thelly's pig blood.*
> *Spirits of thunder and yams, don't forget you have enjoyed*
>   *Thelly's smoke.*
> *Spirits of thunder and yams, don't forget you have enjoyed*
>   *Thelly's song.*
> *Small spirits, don't forget you have enjoyed Thelly's pig blood.*
> *Small spirits, don't forget you have enjoyed Thelly's smoke.*
> *Small spirits, don't forget you have enjoyed Thelly's song.*
> *Souls of Big Men, don't forget you have enjoyed Thelly's pig blood.*
> *Souls of Big Men, don't forget you have enjoyed Thelly's smoke.*
> *Souls of Big Men, don't forget you have enjoyed Thelly's song.*

Mekiimos, Spirits of thunder and yams, small spirits, souls
of Big Men,
Let this song gladden your hearts until Thelly's descendants
sing this same song to their Mekiimos.

Mekiimos, Spirits of thunder and yams, small spirits, souls
of Big Men,
There is a foreign spirit here, a foreign spirit has taken Thelly's
soul.
A foreign spirit has closed her eyes, has caused her feet to lose
the path.
A foreign spirit has taken her weapons away, has made her
limbs weak.
A foreign spirit has made her afraid, has made her dreams
confused.
Mekiimos, Spirits of thunder and yams, small spirits, souls
of Big Men,
Drive this spirit from her, restore her to her original mind.

. . . but as I sing, something else begins to happen. Instead of the usual
trance state, I start to feel a tightness in my chest. I begin to shiver. In a
few minutes my breath is coming in short gasps, and my body is shaking
violently with chills. The grove seems to be filled with a roaring noise, like
a tremendous wind. I try harder and harder to breathe deeply, to keep
singing . . .

Mekiimos, Spirits of thunder and yams, small spirits, souls
of Big Men,
The foreign spirit is I, Ashton, the one who sings to you now.
The foreign spirit, I, wish to leave Thelly's soul, to be pulled
out, never to return again.
Mekiimos, Spirits of thunder, small spirits, souls of Old Men,
Use your power to weaken . . .

. . . but I can't remember the words. The fire seems to be going out, and
I want to feed it, but I can't move. Everything's getting dim, sight and

sound. I drift, without sensation or time. I find myself standing alone on a completely empty plain, either in twilight or dawn, I can't tell which. There are no landmarks or paths. One direction is the same as another. I feel cold. I begin to walk, hoping to go in a straight line until I find something, but when I look behind me, I can't see my footprints, and without bearings I'm not sure my path is straight. I walk for a long time and begin to realize that the horizon around me is getting narrower. I must be going very gradually down into a valley or crater, but in the featureless landscape I can't tell. Now I think I hear a very faint sound, a deep hum that slowly fades and then comes back. I have the impression that there's some texture to the sound, a roll, a vibrato, but it's so faint I can't be sure. At the same time, it seems to me that the light around me has become textured. Instead of a horizon, with dark earth below and lighter sky above, I begin to see a slight stippling of light and dark all around me. It gives me the impression that I have my eyes closed and am seeing a pattern projected from my brain. I close my eyes, and indeed the view does not change. I find I have stopped walking and am now sitting, with my chin on my knees. Now I sense that the "sound" is not a sound but a wave taking place in all my senses at the same time. I feel a growing terror; each time it subsides, I feel the beginning of its new onrush with increasing dread and alarm.

I want to scream, to run, but I'm completely paralyzed. It goes on and on.

CHAPTER TWENTY-NINE

RELEASED

A sensation of light, of warmth. I open my eyes and see I'm in a hospital bed. There's an IV drip in my arm. "He's waking up!" someone says. I look over and see Mr. Kunslaver's round face with its single eyebrow. His eyes are closed and his lips moving rapidly in prayer.

"Daddy!" says Thelly, bending over me from the other side of the bed. "Can you hear me?"

I nod.

"Jesus be praised!" whispers Mr. Kunslaver.

From somewhere in the room I hear Ysabel: "Great. I'll tell the nursing station."

A door opens. "Mom! Dad's awake!"

I hear Ursula's voice too: "See? It's just like that time with Grandma Spellman. Tell me I don't know anything about comas."

I sit up, and I can see them all now. "What happened? What day is it?"

They all start to talk at once, but it's Thelly who prevails. "It's Friday, Dad. You scared the shit out of us. When I woke up Wednesday morning, you were lying there, like, totally out. I couldn't wake you up, so I called 911. I stayed right there and helped them find, ah, you know, our place. They brought you here to UC Med. You'd given me Mr. Kunslaver's number, so I called him when we got here, and when I told him you were sick, he came right over. He's been great, helped me the whole time. I figured I'd better call Mom and Aunt Ysabel.

"What do you mean, 'helped the medics find your place?'" says Ursula.

"There's something fishy about this whole thing. Thelma won't talk about it. Just what did happen, Ashton?"

"I think he should rest for the time being," says Ysabel. "We can browbeat him when he's feeling better."

A nurse comes in, and they're all whispering while she checks my pulse, blood pressure, pupil reflex, IV drip. Thelly edges toward Ysabel and puts her arm around her. Ursula takes off her sunglasses to rummage in her purse, muttering, "Can't find an aspirin in a damn hospital . . ."

"Can he go?" asks Thelly.

The nurse jots down a few notes, her face inscrutable. "Any nausea, Mr. Caldo?"

"No."

"Blurred vision?"

"No."

"Pain? Numbness?"

"No."

"What day is today?"

"Uh, Friday."

Who's the president of the United States?"

"Bernie Sanders."

"How many fingers am I holding up?"

"Three."

She closes her notebook. "The resident will stop in shortly," she says over her shoulder on the way out the door.

Mr. Kunslaver also stands. "Call me when you're ready to work, Ashton."

"I will, Mr. Kunslaver, I can't tell you how grateful I am for everything. Ysabel, Ursula, I'm really sorry about all this trouble. I do need time to think and rest."

Everyone is silent. I feel the tension and turmoil in the room — a room of people full of feelings, unable to speak to me or to each other. I too search for words.

"I need to tell you all something, but I'm not sure what. It's too early to say, but I believe a phase of my life is over — a difficult phase, an experiment that failed, maybe. I feel as though I've been gone a very long time — I mean, like, years."

"Be that as it may," says Ursula, "Thelma comes home with me now. You know I can't leave her here after this."

Thelly starts to protest, but Ysabel squeezes her, hushing her, and says, "Ursula, let's you and Ashton and Thelly work together on what's best for her, hmm? Let's let him rest now." No one moves.

"Can I be alone with Dad for a minute?" Ursula and Ysabel glance at each other and leave the room.

"Do you remember what happened before you, like, passed out, Dad?"

"I think so."

"I didn't tell them about the cleansing or anything. They know something funny happened, but I think they'd just as soon not know what."

"Thanks, Thelly." I squeeze her hand.

"I found the letter you wrote me," she whispers, smiling. "Nobody else will ever see that either. Do you remember what it says?"

"Sort of. I remember the gist of it."

"There was a letter to Lisa, too, in your backpack. I didn't open that one. I'm going to put it in her mailbox. As for you and me, I don't think we have to split up. I'm okay, and I want to take care of you. Anyway, what did happen, Dad? Do you remember?"

"I do remember, very clearly. But you know something? I can hardly believe it."

"Hardly believe what?"

"The whole thing. Thelly, this is going to be a shock to you, I think. Sit down here, honey. Look at me. I'm your Dad. I love you. This is going to be hard for you."

"Dad, you're scaring me."

"Don't worry." I take her hand again and think for a few moments. "I'm really glad we were shamans together. It brought you back to me. It made us close. But, Thelly, that part, the shamanism part, is over. The business of commanding spirits. It's like I've woken up from a very long dream."

"What?" She keeps her voice low, but she looks stunned. "You don't believe in the spirits, in Mekiimos now?"

"Let's just say, Mekiimos and the spirits have released us. They're finished with us. They've gone somewhere else."

She sits with her eyes shut, holding her head in both hands for a long minute, then starts to cry quietly, with lots of tears. "You know, Dad," she manages to say between soft sobs, "I th-think you're ri-right. When I saw you passed out, a-and then I read your letter and ev-everything, I was so scared. I tried to call the spirits to help you, but I c-couldn't do it. I c-couldn't remember the songs. I couldn't feel anything. It was so awful." Slowly a look of horror comes over her. "Oh my God! Do you think they're angry with us, that they might . . ."

"No, I can't believe they're angry. We did our best. We do have a problem, though. The human world is pretty unhappy with us."

We sit quietly for a while, then I say, "The spirits did help us; they helped us a lot. They taught us something about how little we can know without having lived our whole lives among the spirits, without having drunk deeply from their rivers for centuries. That's really valuable knowledge. What we learned was rare and precious. Don't you think so?"

"Precious for what, Dad?"

"I don't know yet, but I'm sure it is. Together, we'll figure out how to use it; I just know we will."

The door opens and in come Ysabel and Ursula, in the company of a serious young woman wearing green surgical scrubs and carrying a stethoscope.

CHAPTER THIRTY

THE AWFUL TRUTH

Luckily I wasn't physically hurt, and a few days later I was back at work at the *Gold Cross Weekly*. Mr. Kunslaver likes my work so well a couple of weeks ago he asked me to take over much of the editing and nearly doubled my salary. He says I have a gift for making the truth of Jesus seem real. I bought a used Honda Civic that burns oil but makes commuting to Oceanside much easier. Thelly and I have moved into a bigger apartment with a view of the Pacific. We've converted her website to a kind of clearinghouse and blog on the varieties of shamanic healing, stuff we get from the rich literature on it, and from other websites.

It's Friday evening. It's hot, and I'm tired when I get home from work. Thelly's home, studying our website at the kitchen table, while I kick my sandals off and mix myself a margarita. She points to a large white padded envelope on the kitchen counter, addressed to me.

"There's no return address on it. I'm surprised they'd deliver something like that. Careful, maybe it's a bomb!" she grins.

It has an irregular shape, not like a book, and it's rather heavy. I rip it open and reach in. There, wrapped in brown paper, is my mask of Mekiimos — a bit battered and still sporting his chewed ear, thanks to Pig.

"Wow! I guess Lisa sent this. Either that or she had Blake send it." I hold it up and Thelly studies it for a moment, a look of puzzlement growing on her face.

"Dad, what *is* that?"

"It's Mekiimos."

"That's our ancestral spirit?"

"Well, the Raapa Uu vision of him, yes."

'Where did they get this vision?"

"I'm not really sure, I think from a shaman in trance."

She takes it from me, turns its face toward me. "Doesn't it remind you of something familiar?"

"Like what?"

"Like *Mickey Mouse,* for Chrissake! Look! The snout! The ears! This black and white coloring!" She turns it toward her, and a look of confusion grows on her face. "*Mekiimos. Mickey Mouse!* I'll tell you where they got it. They got it from the fucking *missionaries* you told me about!" Her voice drops to a whisper, tears gather in her eyes. "Oh my God! Our all-powerful ancestor is *Mickey Mouse!*"

Now that I look at it again, I begin to see what she means. Except for the usual Raapa Uu mask decorations, it really does look a lot like Mickey Mouse: The big round ears, the pointed snout. Maybe the Raapa Uu were influenced by a Disney cartoon, but there has to be more to it than that.

"Wait a minute, sweetie. Don't get so upset. What's likely is that they already had a spirit named Mekiimos, or something similar, and their vision of this native spirit was simply influenced a bit by missionary cartoons."

She drops the mask on the table, holds her head in her hands. "I had a horrible feeling it might be something like this, that the whole Mekiimos thing might be some naive tribal mistake. Oh, Dad, Dad . . ." She comes over and puts her arms around me, quietly crying.

As I hold her, my mind races back over the past months, searching for evidence that she's wrong. There was the impossible success with the cassowaries in Sangrapa. What else? Dammit! What else! The fire at the building site? That produced nothing in the end, except a trip to the looney bin. My amazing success with Luna? That too came to an ugly end. I don't even want to think about what happened with the cleansing of Lisa. My self-exorcism? That almost ended my life. My head is spinning. I need time to think.

As if she reads my thoughts, Thelly tightens her arms around me. "Don't worry, Daddy, I won't leave or anything." She lets go and takes my hands in hers. "So what if you're not a huge fucking shaman; you risked your life for me back there, didn't you?" She tries to smile, but instead breaks down into convulsive sobbing while I just stand there, numb.

CHAPTER THIRTY-ONE

BACK

Almost a year has passed since then. Thelly has gone back to Denver, but we talk and text weekly. I'm now teaching my seminars in personality studies at San Diego State, thanks to some good letters from former students and colleagues.

For several weeks after the day Mekiimos was unmasked, I was a classic case of depression — constantly exhausted, unable to sleep, absent-minded, tortured with negative thoughts and self-loathing. But as a psychologist, I knew a few things about depression, about self-delusion, and about narcissism. The path into the past, to self-blame, to regret, leads to hell. With great effort I still had enough of the old discipline to force my eyes forward and see that Thelly and I had built something truly valuable, a mutual project that required the strength and maturity of both of us. It was the opposite in a way of the path I had been on, the narcissistic obsession with regaining my youth.

This doesn't mean I'm "cured," of course — like any addict I'll be "in recovery" until my last breath. The main difference between Ashton the would-be Zogon and the present Professor Caldo is not moral superiority; if anything, it's a kind of bemused humility, an acceptance of my balding pate, my shrinking physique, and, yes, my lechery. Of course this is a cure that's subject to frequent relapses. The Zogon still stalks the more primitive regions of my brain, and when my eyes light on a Michelle or a Delfin, I can hear him down there yanking his chains, muttering spells of erotic magic, cursing Professor Caldo for his cowardly failure to mount the hunt. I often have to remind him of his tormented side in order to shut him up. At times I look in the mirror and see in in this wrinkled face the lines of heroism: "Here is a man who exorcised his own demons, and he did it *without* magic spells." But in my saner moments I know it was not I; it was that shaman of shamans, love.

Printed in the United States
By Bookmasters